He wondered how many times she'd stood on tip-toe, her small frame stretching to accommodate his height. He wished suddenly he'd written it all down. Kept a record somewhere. *Today I made love to Jenny...* Each time carefully recorded so those memories could never be lost, never destroyed.

She put her hands on his shoulders. He loved Jenny's hands. They weren't manicured or particularly well cared for, but to Mac they looked exactly as a woman's hands should look. Felt as they should feel. Whether calming an injured horse or moving over his own body in the darkness. And it seemed to Mac he had always known how they would look cradling the rounded, darkly fuzzed head of an infant. His son or daughter.

That was all Jenny had ever asked him for. A baby. And not to get himself killed. And he couldn't guarantee either, it seemed.

No promises, Jenny-wren. I can't make you any promises. Except to love you. Always, I'll still be loving you.

Dear Reader

Welcome to Intrigue™! This month brings you the last in the fabulous **McCullar Brothers** series, *Remember My Touch*. Husband and wife Mac and Jenny McCullar had never doubted they'd be together—until Mac was killed. But five years later, Jenny meets rugged stranger Matt Dawson, and something in her just seems to welcome him home...

Meanwhile, in *Only a Memory Away*, Judd Maxwell's only connection with his past is a recurring nightmare about running from the law. Social worker Karen Thomas is trying to help him uncover the truth, but what if he is guilty of a crime he doesn't even remember?

The heroes of our next two books are equally enigmatic. In *Never Cry Wolf*, Donovan Wilde meets Laurel Newkirk, who claims she is engaged to him. He knows she has the wrong man—but who is impersonating him and why? While in *Priority Male*, Rand Sinclair is the only one who can help Jasmine Ross uncover her family's secrets, and protect her from their attempts to silence her...

Enjoy them all!

The Editors

Remember My Touch

GAYLE WILSON

SILHOUETTE

INTRIGUE

All the characters in this book have no existence outside the imagination of the author, and have no relation whatsoever to anyone bearing the same name or names. They are not even distantly inspired by any individual known or unknown to the author, and all the incidents are pure invention.

First published in Great Britain 1999
Silhouette Books, Eton House, 18-24 Paradise Road,
Richmond, Surrey TW9 1SR

© Mona Gay Thomas 1998

ISBN 0 373 22469 9

46-9906

Printed and bound in Spain
by Litografia Rosés S.A., Barcelona

Dear Reader,

Although we were both born and bred in Alabama, my husband and I were fortunate enough to live for several years in West Texas, very near the Rio Grande. Accustomed to the fertile black soil and virgin forests of the Appalachian foothills, we were both surprised by how quickly and passionately we fell in love with the border and the desert. The truly unique blend of cultures and the unhurried pace of life there enchanted us as much as the magnificence of the country that surrounds the river. We have always vowed to return, and now, in this **McCullar Brothers** trilogy, I have, in some small way fulfilled that vow.

The three heroes in this trilogy—the McCullars—are strong men who love the rugged, desolate land they've inherited with the same passion I felt for the desert. With roots deep in the land they love, they choose to fight the increasing lawlessness that threatens both the ranch and the people they love. I think you'll find that the women who stand beside them are well matched with these lawmen heroes. And I also hope you will see a reflection of your own family in the sense of strength, pride and unity I've tried to instil in these three books.

Thank you for allowing me to show you the McCullars and the border country I still consider a second home. I sincerely hope you enjoy these stories as much as I enjoyed creating them for you!

Much love,

Gayle Wilson

For Huntley Fitzpatrick,
who is both my editor and my friend,
with love and gratitude

Prologue

"What's going on here, Mac?" Jenny McCullar demanded. Her voice was soft, but her dark eyes were flashing. "What kind of game do the two of you think you're playing?"

Mac knew he probably should have been expecting his wife's questions, except Jenny had never been one to fret or nag. And he thought she had learned a long time ago to live with the dangers inherent in his job as county sheriff.

But there had been a lot of pressure on both of them lately, unexpected stresses on a marriage that had been rock solid for the past five years. That was the reason he hadn't told her he'd asked his brother to come home this weekend. At least, he amended, that had been one of the reasons.

"I asked Chase to come down because I wanted his advice. Nothing more than that, Jenny."

"Just a little advice about somebody running drugs?" she questioned. The muscles in the perfect, olive-toned oval of her face were tight, a small furrow forming between the winged brows.

That would have been a reasonable assumption, since Mac's brother had spent the last four years working for the DEA. Chase was someone who could certainly provide answers to what was going on and some advice about what Mac should expect. Jenny would have figured out eventually why his brother was here, except she hadn't had to. Almost as soon as Chase arrived, he had spilled the beans.

His brother's eyes had been full of contrition and apology when they'd met Mac's, a matching set of clear McCullar blue. In Chase's there had also been a trace of surprise. Mac knew his brother couldn't believe he'd been keeping secrets from Jenny.

"*Maybe* running drugs," Mac hedged.

"In this county?" Jenny's voice was full of the same doubts Mac himself had had when he first began to suspect what was going on.

"Better than seventy-five percent of the drugs that enter the States come across this border, and we're sitting right in the middle of it. Why would you believe we're immune?"

"Because...that's never been a problem here," Jenny said.

She was calmer now, but the fear was still in her eyes. She raised her hand, running small fingers distractedly through the gamine cut of her dark brown hair. "Why do you think...?"

The question faded as her intelligence and her knowledge of the way things worked along the border provided the answer to that unfinished question.

"They made you an offer." She spoke that sudden realization aloud. "Oh, dear God, Mac, they've already approached you."

Mac McCullar had never outright lied to Jenny, and he wasn't about to start now. Besides, she had a right to know. If the other hadn't been going on, he would already have told her.

The bribe he'd been offered had been huge and the warning that had accompanied it subtle, containing little overt threat of violence. That was the way it was done, of course, and not many people held out against the promise of that much money. Not given the salaries of law-enforcement officers. Not in a rural Texas county this size.

Sheriff Mac McCullar had been expecting the overture for months. It had probably been delayed only because of the location of his county, far from the Mexican cities where the drugs from South America were flown in. Or because of its distance from the major U.S. highways that led north into the American heartland.

But law-enforcement efforts were increasing on both sides of the border, squeezing the dealers who had been operating at the major crossing points. Mac had known it was only a matter of time until someone realized that this isolated stretch would be perfect for bringing drugs across.

Too many of the people who had been cooperating with the cartels had gone down in the investigations carried out by federal agencies in both the U.S. and Mexico. Some of those had been respected Texas law officers, men who had given in to the lure of the obscene amounts of money the Mexican cartels offered so freely—enormous sums that were paid them to do nothing besides look the other way when drugs were transported across their jurisdictions.

"Why didn't you tell me?" Jenny asked.

"I figured one of us worrying about it was enough."

"Then you *are* worried?"

"I guess I'd be a fool not to be."

"You told them no," Jenny said, holding his eyes.

Mac thought maybe she was hoping that wasn't what he had said, but she knew him better than that. "What do you think?" he asked.

Then he smiled at her, his soft brown mustache lifting to reveal a flash of even, white teeth set in the strong angles of his tanned face. She didn't return his smile and the fear in her eyes hadn't faded.

"I imagine you told them to go to hell," she suggested.

"I wasn't quite *that* polite," Mac admitted truthfully, his smile widening. If he had been hoping for a lessening of the tension in her small, squared shoulders, he was disappointed.

"Why is it your responsibility?" Jenny demanded. "Where the hell is the DEA? Why aren't they doing something?"

"It's my county, Jenny. My job."

"And when your job gets you killed, who's going to look after your precious county? Who do you think cares about any of this besides you?"

"Anybody who lives here *ought* to care. Anybody with kids, a home, a family."

"What about your kids, Mac? Our kids."

"I'm working on that," he reminded her, his lips tilting again, this time in memory. He'd been working on that with real diligence. Only that kind of pleasure—making love to Jenny—had never before had anything, really, to do with what he considered work.

Her chin quivered suddenly and that movement, quickly controlled, almost broke him. Jenny wasn't a woman who cried. She had never used tears to get her own way. But her emotions had been on edge lately, and Mac certainly understood all the reasons why.

Once they had decided it was time to add children to the wonder of their marriage, they had pursued that goal with a willingness that had little—on Mac's part, at least—to do with making babies. Babies were just something he had always believed would happen naturally, given enough opportunities. And those, he had willingly supplied.

Only, it hadn't happened. Not for three long years, and despite the fact that in the past year they had finally sought professional help, it still hadn't happened. Their lovemaking, once spontaneous and filled with joy, had taken on a clinical aspect that Mac was a little uncomfortable with. He hadn't said anything, determinedly holding on to his patience and good humor in the face of his wife's increasing tension.

He'd walk through fire for Jenny, without any hesitation, and he figured he could survive performing on demand if that was what it took to make her happy.

"And when they bring you home in a box, Mac, what am I supposed to do then?" she asked softly. "What happens to me?"

Her question shocked him. A man didn't last long in this

job if he worried about reprisals or reacted to threats. The thought of him dead and Jenny alone wasn't one he'd ever considered with any seriousness. If the thought had occasionally brushed through his consciousness, he'd rejected it. He couldn't do this job constantly looking over his shoulder.

"That's not going to happen," he said dismissively.

"Is that a guarantee, Mac? Are you making me a promise?"

"Jenny," he began, and then his voice faltered. There was nothing he could say that would satisfy her fear or her anger—emotions she had a right to feel, he acknowledged. Whatever he did impacted on them both. He understood that.

"It's my job, Jenny," he said again, stubbornly. It was his only defense and one that even he recognized wouldn't be much comfort to a grieving widow.

Jenny's lips flattened and she shook her head once, the motion sharp and angry. Her eyes were bright with unshed tears.

"I'll never forgive you, Mac. I swear to God I'll hate you through eternity if you let something happen to you."

"Nothing's going to happen to me," he said softly.

He lifted his hand, fitting the callused palm against the softness of her cheek. His thumb brushed across the tight-set line of her lips. When he felt the minute loosening of the muscle at the corner, encouraged by that response, he lowered his head.

His mouth found the smooth expanse of her forehead under the disordered silk of her hair, and he pressed a small kiss there. His other hand moved to her back, between her shoulder blades. With the heel of his hand, he pushed into the tension he found there, kneading gently.

"Want to make a baby?" he whispered.

"It's not the right time." Jenny's voice was as tight as the muscles in her back and shoulders.

His lips skimmed down the slender line of her nose and settled with familiar expertise over her mouth. Despite her anger, she didn't avoid their touch. She automatically tilted her head to allow the accustomed alignment of his mouth over hers.

He wondered how many times he'd kissed her, how many times she'd stood on tiptoe, her small frame stretching to accommodate his height, how often her body had arched to match the uncontrollable thrusts of his. Suddenly he wished he'd written them all down. Kept a record somewhere. *Today I made love to Jenny.* Each time carefully recorded so these memories could never be lost, never destroyed.

She put her hands on his shoulders. He loved Jenny's hands. They weren't manicured or particularly well cared for. They were working hands, a little rough and reddened from washing dishes and grubbing in the yard. Her nails were short and usually unpolished. The small, slender fingers were often scratched or stained with paint or the medicines she used in treating the animals.

But to Mac they looked exactly as a woman's hands should look. Felt as they should feel. Whether gentling an injured horse or moving seductively over his own body in the darkness. And it seemed to Mac he had always known how they would look cradling the rounded, darkly-fuzzed head of an infant. His son or daughter.

That was all Jenny had ever asked him for. A baby. And not to get himself killed. And he couldn't guarantee either, it seemed.

No promises, Jenny-Wren. I can't make you any promises. Except to love you. And even if I end up dead, while you're hating me through eternity for dying and leaving you, I'll still be loving you. To the grave and beyond.

Mac bent slightly, slipping his left arm under Jenny's knees. He gathered up his wife and carried her easily, cradled like a child against the solid strength of his chest, into the dark bedroom they had shared for the past five years.

Usually when he did something like this, Jenny laughingly protested, pounding on his chest or pushing against his shoulder, demanding that he let her down to get back to whatever she had been doing. Tonight she did neither.

He deposited her on the wide bed and stepped back to take off his shirt, not bothering to unbutton it, but simply tugging it out of his uniform pants and stripping it off over his head in one fluid motion, his undershirt along with it. He threw the garments toward the foot the bed. He stood balanced awkwardly on one foot and then on the other to tug off his boots. When he turned around, he realized Jenny hadn't moved. She had simply been watching him, and whatever was in her face made him hesitate, his hand at the waistband of his uniform pants.

Her eyes slid downward, moving over the broad, muscled expanse of his chest and then to the ridged stomach. She looked up finally, her eyes too dark and wide, straining to deny the tears that he knew were still close to the surface. Tears that were silently pleading for a promise he couldn't give. Not with any honesty.

"Don't be mad, Jenny-Wren," he said softly, lowering his big body onto the bed beside her. His lips nuzzled along the skin under her jawline. He could feel the lifeblood pumping steadily beneath its satin surface. He caressed that small, pulsing movement with his tongue, for the first time forced to think about the precious stability of their lives, to think about how lucky they were.

He had never worried about anything happening to either of them. He supposed men didn't think that way, never anticipating, as women apparently did, some terrible thing happening to the ones they loved. He had just accepted that this was their life and that they would go on this way forever, loving each other.

Loving each other. Until finally they would be old and beyond these needs, beyond the endless desire that sometimes woke him, his body hard and achingly lonely for the feel of Jenny's, even if he had made love to her only a few hours before.

Jenny's hand found his chin, and she pushed his head away from hers so she could look into his eyes. "Anything but that, Mac," she whispered, and the truth of it was in her eyes. "I could bear anything but losing you."

He smiled at her, the slow movement of his lips an invitation, and reassurance, he hoped. "Nothing's going to happen to me. I'll ask Chase for advice. I'll call in the feds, I swear. Will that make you happy?"

"It would make me happy if you just got out. We could run cows again. Or sheep. Raise spinach if we have to."

He laughed, but he knew from the quick pain in her eyes that it had been a mistake. She hadn't been joking. Jenny was scared, and he hated himself for making her afraid. This was why he hadn't told her before. She didn't need this to worry about.

"At least it's safe," she argued.

"This isn't the movies, Jenny. Or TV. You know nothing ever happens here. It's not going to now. They're just putting out feelers. Somebody will bite, and they'll pass this county up like they always have before. They're not going to try anything where the law has bowed its back against them. There's no need. There are too many folks more than willing to cooperate with them for the kind of money they're offering. I'll put out the word that the feds are moving in and nothing will happen."

"You swear you'll get some help?" she asked. "You're not just saying that to pacify me?"

"I promise, Jenny. First thing tomorrow. Chase can tell me exactly who to call."

Again she held his eyes, trying to read what was in them, he guessed. He had nothing to hide. He would do what he'd said. He would never break his word to Jenny.

Finally, she nodded. Her hand moved, following the line of his jaw. Her fingers touched the softness of his mustache and then traced up the high cheekbone, thumb brushing across the long, dark lashes, feeling them move as his blue eyes closed in response to her touch.

Her fingers spread, threading into the slightly curling, sun-touched hair at his temple. They cupped the back of his head, pulling his mouth downward to hers, which opened to the caress of his tongue.

His mouth was warm and sweet. So dearly familiar. His tongue teased across her lips and then invaded them, suddenly demanding. Hot and hard. Evoking memories of his body moving above hers in the darkness.

Waking her from sleep. Or coming up behind her to cup his hands under her breasts and trail wet, pulling kisses down her throat as she stood at the kitchen sink, up to her elbows in dirty dishwater. Pushing his arousal into the softness of her bottom. Once Mac had pulled her panties off and simply unzipped his jeans, thrusting into her as she lay where he had placed her on his grandmother's kitchen table.

Making love to her because that was what he wanted to do. Whenever he wanted to do it. Unthinking. Unplanned and unstudied. Sometimes quick and sometimes endlessly, heartbreakingly slow. This was what their lovemaking had once been. And in her demands for a baby, they had lost this gift.

Perhaps sensing her stillness, Mac lifted his head. His blue eyes were luminous in the darkness. Questioning.

''Make love to me,'' she invited softly.

''What the hell do you think I'm doin', Jenny-Wren?'' Mac asked. The soft humor she loved was back in his deep voice.

Please, dear God, she prayed. *Don't let anything happen to Mac. Please, God, keep him safe.*

Her eyes burned again, but she blinked, determined not to let him see her cry. He was right. It was his job, and he wouldn't be the man she had married, the man she loved, if he didn't do it. At least he had promised to let someone know what was happening. And Chase was home. Chase wouldn't let anything happen to his brother.

Mac's big hand found the elastic band of her slacks and

began pushing inside, moving awkwardly because of the restriction.

"I can take them off," she offered without moving. Her face was in the hollow between his shoulder and the strong brown column of his neck, her breath moving against the man-fragranced warmth of his skin.

"*I* can take them off," Mac said. "I've about forgotten what it feels like to undress you."

"It feels slow," she said, suddenly inclined to giggle at the unromantic discomfort of her slacks, their waistband rolled and twisted, canted to one side as he struggled to pull them down.

"Damn it," he breathed, his big hands tangled in the offending garment.

"You used to be better at this," she teased.

"Your butt used to be smaller," he parried.

"I can't believe you said that."

But she pushed her heels into the mattress, obligingly lifting her bottom off the bed, and felt the slacks and her panties slide downward, guided by his hands. Then his hands deserted her for a moment, and she used her bare feet to push her clothing the rest of the way off her legs.

She was just in time. Mac's hips and thighs lowered between hers, spreading them. His hand had found her breast, thumb flicking over the cotton-covered nipple that hardened into an tight, aching bud with the first stroke.

She could feel the cloth of his pants against her bare legs and the roughness of that texture was sensuous. Sensual. Teasing and tantalizing her as were his long fingers, which had caught the pearled nipple and were rolling it between them. Rolling it with hard, demanding pressure. Almost to the edge of pain.

The sound that feeling evoked came from deep within her throat, aching with want. With need. He responded immediately, pushing into her so strongly that it literally took her breath. She was a little surprised to realize how ready she had been for his entrance. Wet. So wet for him.

Her heels pressed again into the mattress, lifting her body upward to meet the hard downward thrusts of his. It hadn't been like this between them in a long time. Almost primitive. Need-driven. No whispered endearments. No laughter or "old married" teasing. Just need. Desire. Hot and hard and aching for each other.

She was so empty. Only Mac could fill her. Only Mac could satisfy the aloneness that she hadn't even been aware of. The awful black aloneness of even thinking about having to try to exist without him.

She blocked the horror of that thought, denying it, and arched upward again. The sound she made this time was guttural, a response to her desperation to enclose him. To hold him to her. To keep him with her forever.

She locked her legs around his waist, her bare ankles twined, and then closed her mind to everything but the sensations that grew and expanded in her body as his strained above her in their familiar darkness. When she felt the beginnings of his release, she thought it was too soon, and she tightened her hold on him, trying subconsciously to slow him, to slow what was happening.

There was no need. Her own response was again a surprise, its force exploding in shivering torrents throughout her lower body, sensations spreading upward through veins and nerves and muscles like warmed honey. She could hear her own gasping breath above the harsh panting of his. Could feel, despite the chill of the December night, the sweat on his face, its masculine roughness tight-pressed against her cheek.

Slowly, slowly, the sensations faded, retreated, his body stilled, and the world shifted back to its familiar focus. The room was dark and slightly chilled. She shivered involuntarily, either from the temperature or from the aftereffects of their lovemaking. Mac rolled onto his back, muscled arms locked around her body to carry her with him. She lay on top of him, half clothed and totally relaxed, and listened to his heart beat just beneath her ear.

"I love you, Jenny-Wren," he said softly.

She heard the words, not in the night air that surrounded them, but the sound of them rumbling through their very skins, slick with commingled sweat and still joined. Always joined.

"I love you, too," she whispered. Her fingers moved across the hair-roughened contours of his chest.

She lay and listened to his breathing, slow and even as his body gradually relaxed under hers. His arms loosened their hold, and she knew finally that he slept.

Still she didn't move away, and it was a long time before she closed her eyes. She stared instead into the darkness, thinking about what he had promised. Thankful the hot tears that seeped onto the broad, dark chest pillowing her cheek didn't wake him.

JENNY DIDN'T HAVE ANY idea what time it was when the phone rang. It wasn't all that unusual for them to get a call in the middle of the night, and Mac's voice when he answered was calm and official, if not yet fully awake.

She lay and listened to his monosyllables and soft questions without really hearing them. He'd tell her what was going on when he hung up. She closed her eyes and snuggled her bare bottom against his hip. She realized Mac was still wearing his pants, and it wasn't until the incongruity of that attire penetrated her sleep-fogged consciousness, that she remembered last night.

She sat up, but Mac was already moving out of bed. He stood and put the phone he had been holding back into the cradle on the nightstand. He reached out and grabbed the shirt he'd discarded last night from the foot of the bed and, turning it inside out, began to pull it on over his head.

"Who was it?" she asked.

"Somebody who's got folks on his property who aren't supposed to be there.'' Mac's deep voice was muffled momentarily by the shirt.

"What does that mean?"

"That's what I'm going to find out."

"Drugs?" she asked, feeling a viselike tightness invade her chest. "Are they—"

"Somebody wants me to check out some trespassers. That's all I know."

"Call Chase," she said.

He had sat down on the edge of the bed and had begun to pull on his boots, but he paused and slanted a look at her over his shoulder.

"What for?" he asked.

"Because...I asked you to," she suggested. That alone should be reason enough, she thought, and he already knew all the others.

The blue eyes studied her face for a moment before he nodded.

SHE DIDN'T HEAR WHAT he told Chase. He had made that call from the kitchen, and she guessed that had been deliberate. At least he had called. This might not have anything to do with what they had talked about last night, but it didn't hurt to be careful.

"Chase is coming over here," Mac said.

She opened her eyes and found him standing in the doorway to the bedroom. His body blocked most of the light that was filtering around him from the distant kitchen.

"I can make coffee," she offered.

"Don't get up," he said. He walked across the floor, his boot heels echoing on the hardwood. "Chase said for you to have breakfast ready when we get back."

"'Chase said,'" she teased.

"I thought you wouldn't let your brother-in-law go hungry."

"But I *would* let my husband," she said.

"I hoped not, but I figure I'll get better if you know we're having company."

She smiled at him, reaching up to catch his fingers in hers. She held them for a moment, still remembering last night.

"Chase sounded strange," Mac said.

She looked up from his hand. "Strange how?"

He shook his head. "Just…strange. I don't know. Different. He didn't want me to go over there and pick him up. Said he'd come here. That's when he said you could fix breakfast."

"Ulterior motive," she suggested, smiling at him.

"I guess."

"Want anything special?"

"Uh-huh, but I don't think I've got time for it before Chase gets here." He put his knee down on the bed and the mattress dipped under his weight. He leaned down and kissed her on the cheek.

"Sanchez ranch," he said, his breath warm against her face. "In case anybody needs me."

She nodded. She wanted to tell him to be careful, but she'd done enough nagging. Mac had promised, and if he told her he'd do something, he would.

"I'm going to wait out in the truck. Go back to sleep."

He pulled the sheet and the quilt over her shoulders, tucking them around her. She listened to his footsteps fade away over the wooden floors and the sound the front door made as he closed it behind him.

She shrugged off the covers he'd tucked in and pulled his pillow into her body, resting her cheek against the soft cotton of its case. It smelled of Mac. He didn't use cologne. This was soap. Shampoo. Always the same no-name-brand brands. Or maybe this was just the familiar, beloved scent of his skin.

She closed her eyes, willing herself not to think about anything but that. About last night. *After* the argument.

It was possible that she had gone back to sleep. She could never say for sure whether she had been awake or asleep when she heard the explosion. But she had known at once what it was. There had never been the least doubt in her mind, not from the first sound, exactly what she was hearing.

Chase would sometimes say that he could close his eyes and see Mac's truck exploding, his brother's burning body thrown out onto the ground. Jenny had no clear memory of any of that. The horror for her always began and ended with that sound.

The rest of it simply blended into the endless black nightmare she had always known living without Mac would be.

Chapter One

Five years later

"You going to the wedding?" Chase McCullar asked his sister-in-law. His blue eyes were directed downward toward the coffee cup he held, rather than at Jenny, and his voice was almost innocent of inflection.

"Of course," Jenny said, glancing at him over her shoulder. "Aren't you?"

"You think I'll get an invitation?"

"I think a better question might be, do you want one?"

"What makes you think I wouldn't want an invitation?"

She laid the dishcloth she'd been using on the counter beside the sink and turned around to face him. Chase was sitting at her kitchen table, a table that had been in his family for three generations. He must have eaten tens of thousands of meals at its scarred wooden surface. Maybe that was why he looked so right sitting there, as if he still belonged here, living in this house instead of the one he had built on his half of the McCullar land.

Or maybe he looked so right, she acknowledged, because he always reminded her of Mac. They even had the same way of sitting, forearms on the table and broad shoulders slightly hunched, both hands wrapped around a mug, as if savoring against their fingers the warmth of the coffee it held.

She banished that memory as she had so many others in the past few weeks. She had even dreamed about Mac last night, dreamed about him making love to her, and that hadn't happened in a very long time.

There had been too much upheaval lately, too many disturbances in her usually placid existence, she supposed. The kidnapping of Chase's daughter and his belated marriage to her mother, Samantha Kincaid. Rio's return from prison. Doc Horn's brutal murder.

Apparently those things, as unlikely as it seemed, had somehow rekindled the memories of those nearly perfect days with Mac. Or maybe seeing Chase and Samantha finally together had made her remember her own marriage. Or perhaps that had been triggered by the way Rio looked at Anne Richardson, the two of them sitting at this very kitchen table, whatever had been in Rio's black eyes so much like the way Mac used to look at her. Or, at least, she amended, the way she always remembered his look.

Most things were better replayed in memory than they had been in actuality. The reality of long-ago events faded, and the remembrance of them had a tendency to become more perfect with the passage of time, she reminded herself, trying to be fair to Trent. Anne Richardson's brother, Trent, was the man she was fortunate enough to have in love with her now. A good man who wanted to marry her. A man who deserved not to have to fight against all those perfect memories.

Not that she *minded* having only good memories of her marriage, of course. However, she now admitted that savoring those had prevented her from moving on, from getting on with the business of living her life, and she was determined to change that. She had loved Mac McCullar with every fiber of her being, but Mac was dead. He had been dead for almost five years, and she knew it was time for her to begin living again.

She remembered that she had once accused Chase of doing that—of trying to crawl down into that grave with Mac. And instead she had discovered that she was the one who had been guilty of that sin. Once she had had the courage to make that admission, to face what her life had become, she had decided it was time to do something about it.

She realized suddenly that Chase was waiting for her answer, his blue eyes—eyes that were just like Mac's—studying her face as she stood, lost in memory and regret.

"You and Rio haven't exactly been..." She hesitated, searching for the right word, thinking about the strange relationship that existed between the half brothers.

"Not exactly bosom buddies," Chase suggested caustically.

"Not exactly brothers," she countered. "At least you haven't *acted* like brothers."

"I thought he killed Mac. At least had a part in Mac's death. How did you want me to treat him?"

"You *thought?*" she asked, emphasizing the past tense, which was, to her, the pertinent part of that statement. "But you don't think that anymore?"

"Hell, Jenny..." Chase began, and then he hesitated. "Sometimes even I don't know what I believe anymore." He shook his head, eyes lowering again to the steaming coffee. "It just doesn't..." He shook his head again.

"Feel right to hate Rio any longer? Or to blame him for Mac's death?" Jenny suggested.

Chase looked up. "You think I was wrong about that."

"Yes," she said simply.

Chase's mouth tightened. It would be hard for him to make that admission, she knew. Almost as hard as it had been for her to make the unwanted one about her own life that she'd recently made.

"If that's true," Chase said, "then *he* probably hates me."

Rio had tried to warn his half brother about what was going to happen to Mac. He had ridden across the river to tell Chase about a snatch of drunken conversation he'd overheard in a Mexican cantina. Only, he had made that ride the same night

Mac's truck had exploded, and the two events had become inextricably linked in Chase's mind.

Chase hadn't believed Rio's claim that his mission that night had been a warning. Instead, he had interpreted his bastard half brother's words as threat and had viewed Rio as the messenger of whoever had killed Mac. In the months following the murder, Chase had poured every ounce of his energy into seeing that Rio Delgado was punished for his part in that crime.

"You cost him five years of his life," Jenny acknowledged. "If *he* is innocent, as he's always claimed…"

"Then the wrong man got punished. And whoever killed Mac got away with murder," Chase added bitterly "I didn't stop looking for them, Jenny. I always thought something would turn up. I never believed Rio was the mastermind. I thought he was just their damn messenger boy."

"But he was the only one of them you could identify."

Jenny understood all Chase's motives in pursuing Rio. She had always understood them. She, too, had wanted somebody punished, but knowing Rio now, she had gradually come to realize that he hadn't had anything to do with what had happened.

"Buck told me nothing else has ever come to light about that night," Chase said. "There was never any indication that anybody was transporting drugs through this county. Or had even been planning to."

Buck Elkins had been Mac's deputy as well as his friend. He had been appointed sheriff after Mac's death and had thoughtfully kept Jenny informed about the county's progress, or in this case, its lack of progress, until she had finally asked him not to make any further reports to her about the investigation. There seemed no point in constantly being told that nothing else had been uncovered about her husband's murder.

"Rio doesn't seem to think too much of Buck's detective skills," Jenny reminded her brother-in-law.

"Couldn't find his ass with both hands," Chase said, repeating his half brother's colorful assessment. Unconsciously, his lips moved, almost into a smile.

"Maybe Rio's right," Jenny said, "but I know Buck tried. Mac was his friend."

"Elkins thinks Mac was wrong."

"About what?"

"About everything. About the drugs."

"Somebody approached Mac," Jenny said, remembering, almost against her will, the argument they had had that night. The night Mac had died. "*Somebody* made him an offer."

"Mac didn't give me any details. Or anyone else, apparently. Not even Buck."

"He didn't have time. He would have told you. That's why he asked you to come down here that weekend. And he had promised to contact the DEA. Officially, I mean. He promised me that night."

"And instead... Hell, Jenny, we're no closer than we were five years ago to knowing what really happened."

The frustration she heard in his voice had played a role, she knew, in Chase's determination to make certain that Rio, at least, paid for his part in his half brother's death.

"And in the meantime," he continued, his tone containing a thread of self-castigation now, "I got my half brother sent to prison for a crime neither of us believes anymore that he had anything to do with."

"Have you told Rio that?" Jenny asked.

Chase pushed his cup away from him, the sudden motion strong enough to cause the coffee it contained to slosh out over the side. "How the hell am I supposed to tell a man that I've just realized my bullheaded stupidity cost him five years of his life? How do I do that, Jenny? How the hell do I ever make up for that?"

"I don't know. I don't know that you *can* make up for it, but I do know that admitting you were wrong would be a good first step."

Chase's laugh was short and harsh. "Somehow that doesn't

seem to be quite enough,'' he said. ''It damn well wouldn't be enough for me.''

''But then you're one of those hardheaded McCullars. Maybe Rio...'' She hesitated, realizing that Rio was a Mc-Cullar also, that unmistakable heritage from his father stamped as indelibly on his beautiful Latino features as it had been on the faces of his two half brothers.

''Maybe Rio's a better man than his brother,'' Chase suggested quietly.

''A more forgiving one,'' Jenny said, finally smiling at him. ''At least I hope so. And you didn't answer my question. Do you *want* an invitation to Rio's wedding?''

The depth of the breath Chase took was visible and audible, but he still didn't respond.

''If it's any help to you in reaching that decision,'' she said, ''I'd really like for you to be there. I think Trent would appreciate your showing up.''

''Trent's not too thrilled about this, I guess. About Anne marrying Rio.''

''I think he's trying to make the best of what he's bound to see as a bad situation.''

''Senator Richardson's beloved little sister marrying an ex-con.''

''Who shouldn't have been an ex-con,'' she reminded him quietly, feeling the need to defend Rio, even from Chase.

''And who wouldn't have been, except for me,'' he acknowledged.

''That sounds like justification enough for you to feel obligated to show up at his wedding.''

''*Obligated,*'' he repeated bitterly. He pushed his chair away from the table and stood.

''They wore hair shirts in the Middle Ages,'' Jenny said, working at keeping her own lips from tilting, although the teasing note was clear in her voice. ''All you'll need to put on is a suit.''

''You don't think Rio will throw me out?''

"If you show up, you can probably even dance with the bride."

"I think I'll settle for dancing with the groom's sister-in-law," he said.

"Samantha will be delighted to hear that, I'm sure." Chase's wife, Samantha, was one of Jenny's best friends and had been long before she married Chase McCullar.

"I wasn't talking about Samantha," Chase said. He crossed the small distance between them and leaned down to press his lips lightly to Jenny's cheek—something she couldn't ever remember him doing before. Then, without another word, he went out the kitchen door.

Jenny turned back to the dishes in the sink, but she was smiling, and as the long afternoon passed, she found herself remembering that unexpected brotherly kiss, and smiling again.

It was good to have Chase home. And Rio, another of Mac's brothers, whom she had really never known until he, too, had come back home. Rio had arrived at her ranch, angry and vengeful, determined to make Chase McCullar pay for what he had done, and instead he had ended up becoming part of Jenny's family.

Two men who were, in spite of all the bitterness and betrayal that lay in their past, finally becoming brothers. She only wished there was some way Mac could know about that. She really believed Mac would have approved.

HE TOOK ANOTHER LOOK into the motel's mirror. Doing that wasn't something that ever gave him pleasure, although he thought he had probably done the best he could with his appearance this afternoon. His thick brown hair, brushed with gray at the temples, had just been trimmed. The suit he wore was new and expensive, and it had been expertly tailored to fit the tall, lean body. The white shirt was also a recent purchase, as was the maroon silk tie, its darkly subdued pattern very appropriate, they had told him, for an afternoon wedding.

These weren't the kinds of clothes he was accustomed to wearing. Not like any he'd ever worn in his life, but then that was really what this was all about, he thought. Disguise and deception. He hated them both, hated the necessity of them, although he couldn't deny that they were necessary. Just as he knew the brown contact lens he wore was necessary.

Before he left the room, he took the clipping he'd been carrying around with him for the last couple of months out of his wallet and laid it on the top of the dresser, carefully smoothing the creases with his left hand until it lay perfectly flat.

Knowing that he would need the courage it would provide, he made himself read it again, slowly, although by now he knew the words by heart. At least he knew the ones that mattered. The ones that had finally brought him to San Antonio today.

The newspaper column he had so carefully preserved contained the announcement of the engagement that had led to the wedding he would attend this afternoon. An engagement between Anne Richardson, Texas State Senator Trent Richardson's sister, and a man named Rio Delgado. That announcement had been the crux of the column, but that hadn't been what had caused him to read and reread this well-worn clipping.

It had been the two-sentence teaser the society writer had included at the bottom that had been branded into his consciousness, that had gnawed at his gut since he'd first seen it. The words he had read over and over concerned the impending nuptials of Senator Richardson himself. To the widow of slain Texas lawman Mac McCullar.

The man's gaze lifted again to the mirror. He didn't recognize the reflection there—the black patch that hid the empty socket of his right eye; the strange, reconstructed features; the deliberately altered color of his remaining eye. A stranger in a stranger's body, and he guessed that was the way it should be. He felt like a stranger.

He picked up the clipping, which was beginning to come apart along the creases from the number of times he had unfolded the paper to reread those words, and he held it for a long time, thinking.

He had given up any rights he'd ever had to interfere in Jenny's life, he acknowledged, given them up by conscious decision. He shouldn't be here. He had no right to be. That had been the guiding principle of his life for the last five years. And then...and then he had seen this, and all the reasons he had known and understood had seemed to fade into insignificance in the face of those two sentences.

Finally, he took a breath and allowed his long, brown fingers to close around the small piece of paper, crumpling it between them. He wadded the clipping into a ball, and on his way out the door, he pitched it accurately so it landed in the metal trash can the motel had thoughtfully provided.

CHASE MCCULLAR WAS leaning against the wall watching the crowd at the wedding reception. The dancers were hugging the postage-stamp-size dance floor, working to avoid the long, lace-and-flower-covered tables that were filled to overflowing with finger foods and punch and wedding cake. The other guests were standing, balancing glass plates and cups, most of them managing to talk and eat at the same time, despite those burdens.

"You thinking they're gonna let an ugly old cowpoke like you kiss the bride?"

Chase glanced up at the soft comment. The man who had asked that sardonic question was standing beside him. He was tall and broad-shouldered, yet whipcord lean, without an ounce of excess fat on his body. And his face was unfamiliar. Eerily unfamiliar.

Chase couldn't prevent the telltale reaction that might have given him away if anyone had been paying the least bit of attention to either of them. Chase's blue eyes had widened, the dark pupils dilating suddenly, and his heart had literally hesitated a few beats before resuming its steady rhythm.

"What the *hell* are you doing here?" he asked softly, his breathing uneven from shock. He pulled his gaze away from the man who had spoken and made himself focus instead on the crowd, automatically picking out the figures of his wife and his sister-in-law, who were engaged in an animated, laughing conversation on the far side of the room.

"I'm crashing a wedding," the stranger said, his tone barely audible under the noise of the crowd, certainly audible only to Chase. "Think somebody's gonna throw me out?" he asked casually.

That wasn't something that he seemed to be concerned about, and he was probably right not to be. Given the size of the crowd and considering the impeccable cut of the charcoal gray suit, and the white shirt and maroon silk tie the gate-crasher was wearing, it was certainly unlikely that would happen.

At any wedding of this size, the bride's friends would assume anyone they didn't know belonged to the groom's party, and vice versa. And at this particular wedding, since Rio knew almost no one in the throng, the groom was unlikely to protest the presence of one more strange face.

The features of the man who was now leaning against the wall beside Chase were, in fact, the slightest bit strange. There was nothing obvious, other than the black patch that hid his right eye, but still the alignment of the underlying bone structure was unusual. The angles were strong, almost harsh, and although he was clean shaven, the texture of the skin that stretched over those strong bones was as subtly different as the bone structure itself.

What *made* them unusual, however, would have been difficult to articulate. It wasn't an unpleasant face, but it was hard, and the black patch gave it an air of danger that was somehow in keeping with the rest.

He looked like a man who had seen a lot, who had *endured*

a lot, Chase found himself thinking, his eyes skimming over the features again as if he had never seen them before. He had, of course, but they were always disconcerting.

"Well?" the stranger asked. The left corner of his mouth moved, twitching with amusement at whatever he saw in Chase's face.

"Well, what?" Chase asked, deliberately forcing his eyes back to the crowd. Samantha and Jenny had moved away from the place where he had spotted them before, and now he couldn't find either of them in the colorful, shifting patterns of the mob.

"You think they'll let *me* kiss the bride?" the stranger asked.

The same amusement that had briefly touched the harsh features was in his voice. It, too, was unusual. Deep and almost hoarse, like someone getting over a bad case of laryngitis.

"That's *not* why you're here," Chase said sarcastically.

"It just seemed as good a time as any," the stranger said laconically, his own gaze drifting over the throng.

"To do what?"

This time the corner of the thin mouth lifted, and the one-sided smile revealed genuine amusement. "Renew old acquaintances," he said softly. The single brown eye continued to move over the crowd, as if searching it. "I heard somewhere that this might be a double wedding."

"You heard wrong," Chase said. He turned at that comment, his gaze focused again on the man beside him. His anger was apparent in the set line of his mouth. "I would have *told* you if that had been the case."

"You tried to tell me. I wasn't listening."

"But you are now?"

"I am now," the stranger agreed calmly.

Chase took the breath he had missed while he'd waited for that reply. "It's about time," he said softly. "What the hell changed your mind?"

"That," the man said. His gaze was now following one of

the couples moving on the crowded floor. A handsome man, tall and blond, his features remarkably well put-together by anyone's standards, was guiding a small brunette in a slow waltz. They moved together flawlessly, despite the difference in their sizes. Her fingers were on his shoulder, the soft rose of her nail polish distinct against his jacket.

Chase nodded, knowing that there was probably nothing else in the world that would have brought this man here today. Nothing but the feelings that were revealed now in his face as he watched the attractive couple circling the small floor.

"Well, it's about time," Chase said again, speaking almost to himself. "It's about damn time."

"DID SOMEONE GIVE YOU birdseed?" Jenny McCullar asked. It was a question she had asked, it seemed, a thousand times. The decorated wicker basket over her right arm, which had once been full of packets of seed enclosed in small squares of tulle and tied tightly at their tops with narrow satin ribbon, was almost empty.

The cake had been cut and eaten, the reception line dismissed, and the bride had gone to change clothes for the honeymoon journey. It was almost time to shower the departing newlyweds with the traditional onslaught of rice. Nowadays, of course, the more ecologically correct birdseed had taken the place of grain.

The man she addressed had been standing in the narrow doorway that led from the reception-room hallway to the front of the country club. He was almost isolated from the excitement of the waiting guests who had gathered on the steps below. He hadn't joined them; instead he stood alone, simply watching the commotion.

From the back, Jenny had been aware of nothing but his height and the width of his shoulders, which almost filled the narrow opening. And when he turned in response to her question, Jenny hoped her shock wasn't too apparent. Mac used to warn her that she should never play poker because every emotion she ever felt was revealed in her features—as she was afraid they had been this time, revealed at least for an instant before she regained control.

She couldn't say now why she had found his face so disconcerting. It was...unusual, she thought. There was a hint of gray in the brown hair and weathered skin stretched over strong bones, with a small fan of white lines around his eyes. Eye, she amended.

Maybe that was what she had found shocking. Jenny realized she had never known anyone who wore an eye patch. Those were for cover models on pirate romances, she thought, almost smiling at that sudden image, superimposed over the six-foot-four hunk of male reality standing before her. He probably would have made a damn fine pirate, she thought.

But of course, the patch hadn't been all she'd reacted to, she realized, her eyes still fastened—fascinated, somehow—on his face. The texture of his skin was different, too. Slightly rough and maybe even...scarred? The light in the hallway was so poor that she couldn't really be sure about that. She found a smile for him, trying to soften her rudeness if he had noticed the effect he had just had.

For some reason it wasn't the forced, automatic smile she had been giving to strangers all afternoon as she tried to help Trent see to it that Anne and Rio's wedding went smoothly. That wasn't her responsibility, or really any of her business, she admitted; but at some time during the hurried preparations for this wedding, she had begun to feel like the mother of the bride. Or maybe the mother of the groom, she thought, her lips tilting upward a little more when she remembered that Rio still called her "ma'am."

"Birdseed?" the man questioned, his gaze reacting to the upward tilt of her mouth. The brown eye was suddenly touched with amusement. As was his voice.

Even that was unusual. Deep, but...strained? Jenny wasn't accustomed to having to search for words, but she was finding it hard to think right now, and she suspected it might have something to do with the intensity of the look this man was directing downward at her. He was taller than Trent. Taller even than Chase, she thought.

"Instead of rice," she offered.

The left corner of his mouth moved, slowly lifting, and Jenny's stomach reacted, tilting just as slowly. She couldn't even decide whether that sensation was pleasant or not.

"No cleanup," she explained. The words were a little breathless, and she broke contact with that disconcerting dark gaze by looking down into her basket.

She picked up one of the ribbon-tied bundles with her left hand and realized that her fingers were trembling. Recognizing that she didn't have another option, she held the packet of seeds out to him, willing her normally competent and cooperative hands to stillness.

"The birds eat the seed, and then no one has to worry about sweeping up."

"Cheap labor," he said.

"Exactly," Jenny agreed, smiling at him again, relieved that he'd grasped the idea from her muddled explanation.

He hadn't reached out to take the little bundle from her fingers, and she realized belatedly that they were still vibrating. Obviously vibrating. She took a breath, striving for control.

What in the world was the matter with her? He wasn't even handsome—not in Trent's league by any stretch of the imagination. Her reaction was childish and ridiculous, she chided herself.

"Of course, throwing rice at the newlyweds is considered to bring good luck." She offered the conversational gambit with the best intentions, just to keep talking until she grew up.

However, her voice was barely above a whisper and she thought he was bound to notice. Despite the crowd, they were almost alone here. Most of the guests had moved down the steps and onto the sidewalk where the car was awaiting Rio and Anne.

"I thought it had something to do with fertility," he said.

"I..." She hesitated. *Fertility?* She didn't think she had ever heard that before, but then she wasn't thinking too straight right now, and she still couldn't imagine why.

"Did they throw rice at your wedding, Mrs....?" His voice rose slightly at the end of the question, waiting for her to fill in the blank he'd deliberately left.

"McCullar," she supplied obediently.

His left hand caught hers, which was still holding out the tulle-covered packet of seed. The smallness of hers was almost lost in the grasp of his long, tanned fingers. He turned her hand over, and they both looked down on the plain gold wedding band she still wore.

She had worn it for almost ten years, since the day Mac had slipped it on her finger. She had never thought about taking it off, not even when she had begun to give serious consideration to accepting Trent's proposal.

"Mrs. McCullar?" he said.

Her eyes moved slowly up to his face. Its features were less strange now. Less off-putting. As a matter of fact, she found herself wondering what she had found so disconcerting before.

His lips moved, only the left corner inching up. "Did they throw rice at your wedding?" he asked again.

Suddenly there was a thickness in her throat, and her eyes stung. Ridiculous, she thought again. She was about to say yes to planning her second wedding, and an offhand question from a stranger had made her want to cry about her first.

"I don't remember," she lied. "That was a very long time ago."

She pulled her fingers from his. At their first movement, he released her. But his hand didn't drop to his side. Instead, it opened in front of her, palm up.

For the birdseed, she realized. She placed the tiny package on his outstretched hand.

"I don't think I'll be able to manage the ribbons," he said. "If you wouldn't mind doing that for me?"

Because his fingers are too big? she wondered. The narrow satin streamers she and Samantha had tied did look absurdly small in comparison to his hand. And absurdly feminine against its hard masculinity. Without comment, she pulled on one end of the bow and slipped the ribbon from around the gathered neck of the tulle, which fell open.

"Unless you think the newlyweds would like to be showered with the net as well as the seed, you might want to remove that, too," he suggested.

She lifted her eyes to his, questioning. Whatever hint of amusement had been in his face and in his voice was gone, wiped out and replaced by an emotion she couldn't read. She shook her head, her eyes still questioning.

"My right hand doesn't work too well. Certainly not well enough to pick up something that small. That demands a kind of coordination my fingers no longer have."

Again she was forced to fight the revelation of her feelings. There was a hollowness in the pit of her stomach when she heard those words, created not by the words themselves, but by whatever had been in his eyes when he'd said them. She fought to keep her gaze on his face, and not to let it drop to his other hand.

He would hate that, she knew instinctively. It was obvious that he wasn't comfortable even talking about whatever was wrong with his hand. Jenny was sensitive enough to realize that that quiet confession hadn't been lightly made.

"Of course," she said. She lifted one corner of the tulle and slid the small pile of seed into his palm.

"Thank you." The tightness in his deep voice had eased, and she took a breath in relief.

"You're very welcome."

She knew that it was time to leave, although, since he was blocking the outside door, she hadn't quite figured out how she was going to accomplish that. She had already begun to turn back toward the interior of the club, deciding that discretion might really be the better part of valor in this case.

"Was that Mr. McCullar?" he asked. "The blond man you were dancing with?"

She hesitated, again schooling her features before she turned to face him.

"My husband's dead," she said. Her voice spoke the words evenly and calmly, words she had learned to say during the past five years without revealing any emotion. It was something that should have gotten easier with time, but it really hadn't. "I'm a widow," she added, finishing the rest of that practiced explanation.

There was a minute movement of his head, almost a nod of agreement. For what seemed to be an eternity their gazes held, and then, again breaking the spell, Jenny turned and retreated. She looked back when she reached the shadowed sanctuary of the door on the other side of the big reception room. The man was still standing in the other doorway, looking out on the milling guests, his left hand closed around the birdseed she had poured into his palm.

But by the time she reached the front of the club once again, the doorway where he had stood was empty, and no matter how often her eyes searched the crowd of guests, she couldn't find any sign of the stranger.

Chapter Two

"This is Matt Dawson, Samantha. He's an old friend of mine. He's going to be staying with us."

As Chase McCullar made the required introduction of the man he had brought home with him from the wedding, his face was almost guileless, but his wife knew him too well to be fooled by that look of innocence.

Samantha and Amanda had stayed behind in San Antonio to help Jenny with the presents that had thoughtlessly been brought to the wedding and to decide what to do with the food left over from the reception. The arrangement had been that Chase would drive back to the ranch alone, and she and Mandy would ride with Jenny.

Which would give her a good excuse to go home, Jenny had explained to Samantha, without having to chance hurting Trent's feelings. Having been in San Antonio for several days before the wedding, Jenny was obviously more than ready to get back to the ranch.

All those arrangements had been understood by everyone involved. Samantha and Chase had certainly discussed them beforehand. What she *didn't* understand was why Chase had brought home a guest without giving her any warning. The small house was big enough for the three of them, but there was no room to spare, and certainly no spare bedroom.

Samantha remembered the condition in which they'd left

the bathroom this morning, all three of them in and out of it, trying to get ready for the wedding. She also remembered that the dirty breakfast dishes were still in the sink. Her green eyes met Chase's with an "I'll-get-you-later" look, before she smiled and held out her hand to the tall man who was standing beside her husband in her suddenly narrowed kitchen.

"Mrs. McCullar," he said, nodding slightly. He didn't return her smile.

When Samantha realized he was ignoring her outstretched hand, her eyes flicked to Chase's face again, just in time to catch the barely discernible sideways motion of his head.

"What Chase is trying to tell you, with his usual lack of subtlety," the stranger explained, "is that I don't shake hands."

Her eyes went back to his face. Samantha had noticed the patch, of course. She would have to be blind not to have noticed. And she wondered what other surprises were in store. *I'm going to kill you for this, Chase McCullar,* she thought, before she smiled at the man again, allowing her own hand to fall—naturally—she hoped, to her side.

"Did Chase offer you something for supper, Mr. Dawson?"

"Matt," he said. "And Chase has already taken care of supper."

Samantha's eyes moved to the sink. More dishes had been piled on top of the ones that she had left there. Matt Dawson was probably feeling sorry for Chase right now, saddled with such a wife.

"I'm surprised you survived that experience," she said with a touch of asperity. Chase could boil water, but just barely. To his father, anything that went on in the kitchen had been women's work. Chase and his brother Mac had worked like dogs on their father's ranch, but none of that work had ever been done in the kitchen.

"I've survived worse things than Chase's cooking," Matt Dawson said, his voice amused. One corner of his thin mouth moved upward, inviting her to relax and stop worrying.

Yes, you certainly have, Samantha thought, trying to keep that conclusion from being reflected in her face. It was good, she supposed, that he could smile about whatever had happened to him. And something obviously had, although it was just as obvious that whatever had occurred had been a long time ago and someone had done some good repair work. Except for his hand, she supposed.

"We had hot dogs," Chase said. "I stopped for the stuff on the way home."

At least she'd been right about the boiling water, Samantha thought—all the cooking skill that had been required for Chase's choice of menu.

"We'll try to do better than that for breakfast, Mr. Dawson. Are you going to be in our area long?" she asked, trying to think about sleeping arrangements. She supposed she could move Mandy into their room on a pallet if this was only for tonight.

"Matt's going to sleep on the couch," Chase explained.

"Which couch?" Samantha asked, her eyes deliberately surveying Matt Dawson's height.

"We don't have but one," Chase said.

"I thought maybe you'd picked up one of those on the way home, too. He's not going to fit on the couch, Chase. *You* couldn't."

"I'll be fine, Mrs. McCullar," Matt Dawson said. His lips were carefully controlled this time, but it was obvious he was amused by their small, politely phrased argument, maybe even amused by her discomfort over having an unexpected guest foisted on her. She hoped she hadn't made him aware of that, despite her genuine annoyance with Chase.

"You won't sleep worth a damn," she said bluntly. "You can have Mandy's bed. She can sleep on the floor in our room."

Chase's eyes widened slightly when he realized the obvious consequences of that. It served him right, Samantha thought.

That was something he should have thought of before he brought home a guest without giving her any prior notice.

"In our room?" Chase repeated softly, as if he couldn't believe she had just said that.

Samantha smiled at him sweetly before she turned to his friend. "And how long will you be staying, Matt?" she asked.

"The couch will be fine, Mrs. McCullar," he said instead of answering her question.

DEA? she wondered, trying to place him, trying to remember every friend that Chase had ever mentioned. *Was this someone Chase knew from back then?* He certainly looked the part. He appeared to be as tough as an old boot, despite the patch and whatever was wrong with his hand.

"If I'm going to call you Matt, I think you might call me Samantha."

"You're Sam Kincaid's daughter."

"Do you know Sam?" Samantha asked, with more genuine warmth in her voice than before, despite her efforts to be hospitable. It was certainly possible that he did. Her father knew almost everyone in south Texas.

"I'm afraid not. Only by reputation."

"Believe only *half* of what you hear about my father, Matt."

"The half about his horses," he suggested, his mouth lifting again at the corner.

"No, you can believe *anything* you hear about Sam's horses," Samantha said. The Kincaid ranch was noted worldwide for the incredible horses they produced, both Thoroughbreds and quarter horses. "Do you ride?" she asked.

She was aware that Chase had moved, some physical reaction to that unthinking question. She had asked it out of habit, never thinking about its possible awkwardness in this situation.

Guests on the Kincaid ranch were always asked if they'd like to ride. People hesitated to make that request themselves, and yet riding one of the magnificent Kincaid animals was often the highlight of a visitor's stay. Once Sam had figured that out, it had become ranch policy to invite them to ride.

Samantha hadn't had many guests at the small house Chase had built, but the breeding stables she had started here with Kincaid stock almost five years ago produced horses of such excellence that even her father had admitted to being impressed, and it took a lot to impress Sam Kincaid.

Matt Dawson's "I'd really like that" fell almost on top of Chase's "Matt doesn't ride." Samantha laughed. She couldn't help it, not given the looks on their faces.

"Well, you two can work out which it is between you. I'm going to fix Mandy a pallet in our room. I'll see you in the morning, Mr. Dawson. Matt," she amended.

"Good night, ma'am," he said.

"'Night, Chase," Samantha said. Then she added, "Be real quiet when you come to bed so you don't take any chance of waking Mandy." The look she gave him with that admonition spoke volumes on its own.

THERE WAS A LONG SILENCE in the kitchen after Samantha left. When Chase was sure she was far enough away that there was no chance that she might overhear, he said, "You aren't serious, are you?"

"About sleeping on the couch?" Matt's question was as full of innocence as Chase's introduction had been.

"About trying to ride."

The single, suddenly cold eye held Chase's. "Are you telling me I'm not welcome to ride one of your fine Kincaid-bred horses?" he asked softly.

"You can damn well *have* any horse out there, and you know it. I'm just telling you that it would be a hell of a note if you broke your neck now."

Matt Dawson laughed. "I'll choose one with short, arthritic legs. Will that make you happy?"

"It'll make me happy if you let me come with you. There's a mare Mandy rides that should be perfect for starters."

"I rode my starter horse about thirty-five years ago. I don't think I need Mandy's," Matt said. A trace of his amusement lingered at the corner of his mouth.

"I think you need your head examined," Chase said, his voice full of frustration.

"Hell, you've thought that for a long time."

"You're damn right, I have, but I'm just now finding out how right I was. Mandy's room is down the hall, second door on the right." Chase started across the kitchen, the length and quickness of his stride clearly denoting his anger.

"Be careful you don't wake Mandy," his houseguest reminded, but he controlled himself until Chase was out of the room, and even then his laughter was soft enough that no one else in the small house heard it.

JENNY TRIED TO THINK how long it had been since she'd saddled her horse and set off by herself for a dawn ride. A month? she wondered, spending a few futile seconds trying to pinpoint the last time she'd done this. Maybe it had been even longer than that. At any rate, she decided, as she rode out of the yard, it had certainly been far too long.

The air was cool, still touched with the chill of the desert night, although the sun was already pushing yellowed streaks upward across the horizon. Almost anywhere else in the world, she thought, a woman might be afraid to be out alone at this time of day.

She couldn't ever remember having been afraid out here, not even as isolated as the ranch had been during the brief period when there had been no one living in the small house Chase had built a couple of miles down the road. And not even lately, when the violence that seemed to be the norm in the outside world had now touched the people of this south Texas county.

She guided her horse toward the river, savoring how wonderful it was to be outdoors, to breathe deeply of clean air. She had been enclosed, surrounded so much lately by people, that only now did she realize how much she had missed the sprawling, empty vastness of the desert.

Yet the ranch house had felt empty last night when she had returned from San Antonio. For the first time in memory, it had seemed to her to be too quiet out here. And she had been lonely.

She had just gotten too accustomed to having company, she supposed. First Anne had come to stay with her. And then Rio, she thought, remembering that time with pleasure. It seemed almost as if she had had a family again during the weeks he'd lived here. Then these past few hectic days had been spent at the Richardsons' big house in San Antonio helping out with the wedding preparations.

Last night, when the wedding was all over and she had returned to the isolation of the ranch, it had seemed like a letdown rather than a homecoming. There had been something unsettling about finding herself suddenly alone. She had once been used to that, she thought, had truly enjoyed the silence that surrounded this place. But last night the house hadn't seemed peaceful. It had just felt empty, way too empty.

And she knew one reason why. She had not been able to get her encounter with the stranger at the wedding out of her head. Even when she thought she was fully concentrating on something else, the image of his face would suddenly appear in her mind's eye, effectively interfering with whatever she was doing.

Determined to escape from the slight depression she seemed to be falling into, Jenny touched Spooner with her heels and the quarter horse obeyed, breaking into a gallop. The resulting rush of air across her cheeks felt invigorating, even though she knew that, despite the chill of late fall in the air, within a few hours, that breeze would become a hot wind. But of course, she wouldn't be out here then.

She was approaching the river, the gleam of its shallow water almost silver in the thin morning light. She would ride downstream toward Chase and Samantha's and then cut cross-country to the dirt road that joined the two houses. The time it would take her to do that would be about as long as the dawn coolness would last.

She had covered more than half the distance to her brother-in-law's spread when she realized there was a horse standing near the river, almost at the ford. The animals Chase and Samantha raised were too valuable to be running loose out here, and she knew it wasn't one of her horses. They were accounted for back at the ranch, even Rio's big black, which she had agreed to keep until he had time to make some other arrangements.

She was still trying to figure out what the horse was doing out here when she realized the animal was saddled—and, more important, that it had a rider, a man who had dismounted and was bending down to examine something on the ground.

She pulled up her mount, trying to recognize either man or beast. The rider apparently sensed that he was no longer alone. Even as she hesitated, watching him from this distance, he straightened and turned toward her, the horse's reins held in his left hand.

Since she had been seen, she realized that her options had narrowed: Confront the rider or turn tail and run. She'd be damned if she'd leave, she thought, damned if she'd be the one to run away. This was McCullar property, and *he* was the trespasser.

She urged Spooner forward. The man made no attempt to remount. Obviously, he didn't intend to leave any more than she did. He simply waited for her as she closed the distance between them. Finally she was near enough to recognize the animal he was holding.

It was one of Samantha's—her beloved Lighthorse Harry, a stallion that she'd brought from the Kincaid ranch when she'd moved out here. *Horse thief?* flitted through Jenny's head, but that was pretty unlikely, given the fact that the man would have had to saddle and ride that valuable animal out, under Chase and Samantha's very noses.

By the time Jenny had come to that reassuring conclusion, she was also close enough to recognize the rider. Her identification was instantaneous, with no doubt in her mind as to who he was. Not a single doubt, not even given the poor quality of the dawn light and the distance. It was the man from the wedding.

And he was watching her, she realized. Although she was not yet near enough to distinguish his features, she felt his gaze focused on her with the same intensity as yesterday. Her own reaction was almost the same as it had been then—a slow, hot, roiling in the lower part of her body.

There was no shock from seeing his face to explain that feeling, as there had been before. But still there was reaction, undoubtedly a reaction to him. She put that realization aside for the time being, promising herself that she would take it out and examine exactly what her reaction was. Later, she thought, taking a breath and pulling her horse up in front of him.

"You're on private property, I'm afraid," she said. "This is McCullar land."

"'Morning, ma'am," he responded. His voice was just as she had remembered it, deep and pleasant, despite the graveled hoarseness. And it was calm. Obviously, he wasn't disturbed by her unwelcoming comment.

She had chided Rio for calling her "ma'am," making her feel like his mother because she was a few years older than he. But that wasn't the case with this man. *You, I'm not older than,* she thought, and that falsely polite butter-wouldn't-melt-in-*my*-mouth "ma'am" had grated. Far more than it probably should have. Despite her teasing comments to Rio, Jenny McCullar hadn't really considered her age in relationship to a man's in a long time.

"Private property," she said again.

"This is your land, Mrs. McCullar?"

He pushed the Stetson he was wearing upward, off his brow, with his gloved left thumb. The thumb of his right hand, the hand he had told her didn't work, was hooked into one of the belt loops at the front of his jeans.

He was wearing a denim shirt that looked as if it had been washed as many times as his faded Levi's, which fitted the long legs like a second skin. The jeans covered the tops of worn boots. Her eyes must have traced down the length of his legs, she realized, to have discovered those. She fought the almost-unbearable urge to allow them to retrace that journey, moving upward this time. Moving upward to...

Out of an instinct for self-protection, she glanced instead toward the road that connected the two McCullar ranches, although she could see nothing of either of them from here. Only arid desert grassland stretched toward the horizon. And of course, technically, she admitted, this part of it *wasn't* hers.

She looked back down and met the impact of that single dark eye. She reacted even to that, breath faltering, gloved fingers trembling against the reins as they had trembled yesterday.

The strengthening light of the morning sun was less kind to his face than the subdued lighting of the reception-room hallway had been. She had been right about the scars. Her throat tightened as she tried not to think about what might have caused that kind of scarring.

"This belongs to my brother-in-law," she managed.

"Then it's okay," he said. "I have Chase's permission to be out here."

"You have...Chase's permission?" she repeated. Was he someone from Chase's days with the DEA? Or someone associated with his security firm? The possibilities about where her brother-in-law might have known this man were almost endless, given the aura of danger and quiet strength that clung to him, that fitted him almost as well as those worn jeans.

Neither Chase nor Samantha had mentioned to her that they were expecting a houseguest. That in itself was surprising, considering their closeness.

"Yes, ma'am," he said.

"You're a friend of Chase's?"

Why did everything she said to this man have to make her sound like a half-wit? First that fascinating dissertation on rice and now the implication that Chase might give a stranger permission to ride on his land.

"Chase and I go back a long way," he acknowledged.

"I thought I knew everyone who went 'back a long way' with Chase."

"And he's never mentioned anyone like me," he suggested.

His voice was amused again, and some of the tension seeped out of her back and shoulders. "No," she agreed.

"Probably ashamed to own up to knowing me."

"If you know Chase McCullar at all, then you know that's not true."

He nodded, and then he smiled at her. That same slow half smile he had given her yesterday. With the growing clarity of the morning light, she realized for the first time why it was one-sided.

The muscles on the right side of his face weren't very mobile. They moved, but not much. That partial paralysis would probably have been much more noticeable if his eye hadn't been hidden by the patch. She wondered suddenly if that was why he wore it, and then rejected the idea. This man wasn't vain. And whatever was wrong with him was really none of her business, she admonished herself.

"You must have made quite an impression on Samantha," she said, groping for something to say and deciding Harry was a safe subject. Then, seeing that one-sided smile suddenly disappear, she could have bitten out her tongue.

He had certainly reacted to that, the dark gaze freezing into ice. Belatedly, she remembered her sister-in-law's vaunted beauty, something Jenny never even thought much about anymore. Dear God, could he possibly think she was making a reference to the way *he* looked?

"I was talking about your horse," she explained. "Samantha doesn't let just anyone ride Harry." Apparently her explanation worked. The tightness in his face eased, and he looked at the big bay standing beside him.

"She asked me if I could ride."

He had been insulted by that question. The memory of that offense was clear in his voice, and Jenny wondered about the impairment that would prompt Samantha, one of the kindest, most sensitive people she knew, to ask it. "And you told her you could," Jenny said.

"Better than I can drive."

He lifted the hand that was hooked into his belt loop slightly, deliberately drawing her attention to it. Reminding her. But given his level of discomfort yesterday when he'd had to ask for her help, that reminder also seemed a little strange.

"I guess she must have believed you could, since she gave you Harry."

He looked almost sheepish, but he answered her.

"I was out and saddled before they woke up."

"Afraid they'd try to stop you?" she teased.

"Something like that," he admitted. Again his mouth twitched, and she realized that really *had* been his reason. He'd been afraid they'd try to convince him not to try to ride the stallion.

"*You're* the one who chose Harry."

"He looked like the best of the lot."

"He looked like the one most likely to throw you off if you weren't up to snuff," she suggested.

She hadn't expected him to laugh in response to her assessment of his motives, and she was caught off guard by the undeniable spontaneity of that shout of laughter. And a little surprised by the pleasure hearing it gave her.

"You seem to be a pretty good judge of character, Mrs. McCullar."

"I am," she said. "But it's funny. You don't *look* like that big a fool."

It *had* been a damn fool thing to do. It was just like a man, she thought. Pick out the most spirited horse in the stable to prove to yourself that, despite whatever had happened to you, you could still ride. She couldn't have explained how she knew that had been his intent, but there was no doubt in her mind about that, either.

"Well," he said, "looks *can* be deceiving. At least that's what they say."

"Can they?" she asked softly. There had been more to that than appeared on the surface. Something else underlay the quiet humor of his comment. "Are they deceiving?" she clarified.

"Most of the time," he said, his voice as low as hers. Again their eyes held until Jenny determinedly pulled hers away to look down at her gloved fingers, the reins threaded loosely between them.

"You should have brought a hat," he said. She glanced up to find his gaze still on her face.

"I didn't intend to be out here long enough that I'd need one."

"Then don't let me keep you, ma'am," he said. "I'd hate for you to get burned."

"My skin's pretty tough."

He examined her skin, his dark eye moving slowly over the smoothly tanned oval of her face and then down the slender column of her throat into the deep V-neck of the shirt she wore. She could almost feel it, trailing hotly over the skin of her throat. She waited for him to make some response to the inadvertent opening she'd given him, some innuendo, some suggestive remark.

Instead, he met her eyes again. There was silence for too long, and she felt the heat of a blush pushing into her neck and cheeks, the rush of blood following the exact sequence his gaze had followed back up to her eyes. She wasn't a blusher, and she couldn't imagine what had prompted that sweep of color, but she knew he had to be aware of it.

"Don't let *me* keep *you*," Jenny suggested.

"You're not keeping me, ma'am," he said politely.

She felt her own mouth twitch at his tone. "Did you find it?" she asked.

"Ma'am?"

"Whatever you were looking for when I rode up."

"I'm not looking for anything, Mrs. McCullar," he said, but his tone said something else, and he had deliberately made her aware of that. If he hadn't intended her to know she had guessed right, then she wouldn't have. He probably was an excellent poker player.

"Okay," she said softly. "Whatever you say, Mr....?"

She did what he had done yesterday—deliberately left the blank for him to fill in. If he wanted to be mysterious about why he was out here, about whatever he had been looking at when she rode up, he could at least provide her with his name so she could check him out with Chase.

"My name's Matt Dawson," he said.

And that, too, is a lie, Jenny thought. Suddenly, it made her angry. She wasn't certain whether she was angrier at Chase for bringing this stranger here and not telling her what he was up to, or angry at this man for doing nothing but lying to her.

"Think you can ride Harry back?" she asked. "I can follow you if you like. Just to make sure you get there safely."

That remark was beyond the pale, she knew, and totally uncharacteristic. But he had goaded her to make it. It didn't have quite the effect she had expected, however. He mounted Harry, swinging up suddenly into the saddle and then turning the horse to face her.

But there had been something undeniably awkward about the motion. She couldn't decide whether whatever was wrong had occurred when he lifted his left foot to find the stirrup or when he swung his right leg across the stallion's broad back.

The remarkable thing was that Lighthorse Harry hadn't reacted. Despite the obvious awkwardness of his rider's movements, Harry apparently had every confidence that the man who was mounting him knew exactly what he was doing.

"Nice to have seen you again, ma'am," Harry's rider said, tugging his hat down a little to shade his face. "Would you like for me to follow you home? Just to make sure you get there safe and sound?"

There was a quiet satisfaction in the question, and she knew then that he hadn't been completely certain he could pull that remount off as well as he had. For his sake, she was glad he had succeeded.

"Oh, I think I'll be able to make it home. Maybe I'll see you later at Chase and Samantha's. Are you making a prolonged visit?" she asked, matching his feigned politeness.

"Looks that way," he said softly. "It certainly looks that way."

He turned Harry toward Chase's house. When they had gone a few feet, he touched his heels to the stallion, and Harry broke into a run, kicking up the dry dirt. Jenny watched until they disappeared over the small rise that led down to the river.

She realized that she was smiling, and she couldn't quite figure out why. She was a little disconcerted that she'd ended up enjoying this encounter. Her second encounter with the intriguing stranger with the unusual face. And again she was conscious, as she had been last night, that she was now alone.

Annoyed with herself, she decided not to head back to the ranch. Instead, she directed Spooner to the area where the man had been looking at the ground when she'd first spotted him. There seemed to be nothing there, nothing but the same hardy grasses that were ubiquitous here. Just to be sure, she dismounted, as close to the spot where she thought he'd been kneeling as she could and began walking in a widening circle.

When she found the duct-tape-covered plastic bag, she realized it was no wonder she hadn't seen it from horseback. The empty sack was half buried, and it was almost the same color as the surrounding desert. That was deliberate, she imagined. The sack itself was certainly innocent enough, the kind of debris that dotted landscapes all over this nation.

Except here. She knew exactly what this had been used for

here. And what the three others she found in the next ten minutes had been used for. No matter what Buck Elkins had told Chase, somebody was bringing drugs across this river. Or had brought them across. Given the half-life of plastic bags, it would be hard to judge how long these had been here. Since yesterday or...five years ago?

Her eyes lifted, scanning the familiar barrenness of the landscape while she fought the burn of tears behind them. *You weren't wrong, Mac,* she thought. *No matter what they say, you damn well weren't wrong about any of it.*

CHASE WAS WAITING for him at the stables when he got back. Mac supposed that Chase's overprotectiveness was natural, but it was an unpleasant reversal of what their roles had been growing up. And an even more unpleasant reminder that he wasn't the man he had once been. During the few minutes he had spent with Jenny this morning, he had almost managed to forget that.

"Where the hell have you been?" Chase asked.

His brother was clearly furious, his big body stiff with rage he was trying hard to control, but his blue eyes were almost glittering with that famous McCullar temper.

"Your horse is fine, little cowpoke," Mac said calmly. It wasn't a comment designed to appease Chase's anger. It was instead a less-than-subtle reminder of exactly who Chase was talking to.

"How many times did he throw you?"

"Me and Harry got along just fine," Mac said, looking down into Chase's tight-set face. "You disappointed?"

"With Doc gone, there's nobody out here to patch you up the next time you decide it might be fun to try to kill yourself." Chase grabbed Harry's bridle, and it was only then that Mac realized his brother's hands were shaking.

Not just anger, Mac realized. Chase had been afraid. A real deep-down fear. His brother had honestly expected him to take a fall.

"If I hadn't thought I could ride the damn horse, Chase, I'd never have taken him. I'm not really a fool, despite what you're thinking."

Chase's lips closed over whatever rejoinder he wanted to make. His eyes held on his brother's scarred face. Finally he swallowed, the movement forceful down the tanned column of his throat. At the same time some of the tension melted out of his body, a visible relaxation of his fury.

"Get down, and I'll unsaddle him for you," Chase ordered gruffly.

"I did the riding. I'll do the unsaddling."

"You don't have to try to be Superman."

Mac laughed, the sound of it remarkably free of bitterness, considering. "Not that I'd have much chance of pulling that off," he agreed.

Mac took a deep breath, dreading making a spectacle of himself after the bravado he'd been spouting. He had been surprised that he'd managed to mount the big bay as easily as he had down by the river. Most of that had been due to adrenaline and sheer determination. And a never-forgotten habit of rising to the bait of Jenny's challenges. He had never failed to do that through the years, and although he had had no right this morning to expect to succeed, somehow he had.

It ought to be easier getting off than it had been getting on, he thought, steeling himself for the attempt. He swung his right leg over the stallion's back, but when he put his weight on it to take the left out of the stirrup, his right knee gave way, and he was thrown against Harry's solid flank as he grabbed at the saddle to get his balance. Luckily, the horse still seemed willing to put up with his unorthodox rider's shenanigans, and Mac couldn't imagine why.

"You okay?" Chase asked.

His anger had been replaced by open concern, and Mac found he was far less willing to deal with Chase nursemaiding him than he was with Chase yelling at him.

"I'll let you know when I'm not," he snapped.

He began loosening the girth, working one-handed. The task he'd set for himself wasn't any easier than the awkward dismount had been, but it was easier than the saddling up. At least this time he didn't have to resort to using his teeth.

"Why don't you—" Chase began.

"I rode him. I'll take care of him," Mac said succinctly. His own voice was the one now filled with anger, but it wasn't directed at Chase. Of course, his brother could have no way of understanding that.

He had almost fooled himself into thinking none of this mattered, Mac thought. At least he had felt that way for the ten minutes he'd spent with Jenny this morning. But this was reality, the day-to-day frustration of his body's weakness that he'd dealt with for five years, and as he struggled with the task he'd set for himself, he acknowledged that reality was an unforgiving taskmaster.

He took a breath, thinking now about having to lift the saddle off and carry it into Samantha's immaculate stable. At least there was no one around but Chase. If he dropped the damn thing, he knew his brother wouldn't laugh.

Or maybe it would be better if he did, Mac admitted. That would have been more natural in their previous relationship than Chase's damned hovering concern was.

"Don't you have something else you ought to be tending to?" Mac asked, his gaze still on the smooth leather of the saddle and Harry's broad back that he had to lift it over.

"Not a thing," Chase said. "And if I did, I'd let it wait. I wouldn't miss seeing you make an idiot of yourself for anything in this world. I always knew you were the most stubborn, muleheaded, ornery—"

In the midst of Chase's tirade, Mac lifted, with his right hand under the saddle, but his left arm having to do most of the work, of course. The heavy saddle cleared, but barely. The weight of it when it did was far more than he'd expected. More than he had remembered a saddle weighed. But then he hadn't ridden in over five years.

There were a lot of things you could forget in five years, he thought, carrying the saddle toward the open door of the stable. Suddenly, picturing the laughing commendation in Jenny's brown eyes when he'd managed to get back on Harry without ending up on his ass in the cactus, Mac McCullar also acknowledged that there were a whole hell of a lot more of them that he had never forgotten. And never would.

Chapter Three

When Jenny approached the old cottonwood that stood in the yard of Chase's place, she could see her brother-in-law's familiar figure near the stables. Harry had already been unsaddled, and Chase was running a practiced hand over the stallion's neck. There was no sign of Matt Dawson.

"Looks like Harry survived his outing," Jenny said when she had ridden close enough for comfortable conversation.

"It wasn't Harry I was worried about."

Chase was angry. Jenny knew him well enough to recognize that from the cold blue steel of his eyes, which had briefly cut up to meet hers. They had already returned to their examination of the stallion before she had time to read whatever else had been in them.

"You surely weren't worried about *him*," Jenny said softly.

Evidently, that comment made perfect sense to Chase, for his eyes lifted again, this time holding hers.

"He looks capable of dealing with just about anything to me," Jenny continued. "In *spite* of," she added, acknowledging and dismissing Matt Dawson's handicaps at the same time. "A friend of yours?"

"Is that what he told you?"

She was aware that Chase was avoiding giving her any additional information. "That's what *he* said," she agreed.

"Then I guess that's right." The blue eyes met hers openly now, almost daring her to probe further.

"Did you really think he was going to fall off?" Jenny asked. She didn't try to conceal her amusement over the idea of Chase worrying about Matt Dawson.

"I thought it was a distinct possibility."

"And you were afraid you and Samantha would be held responsible?"

"Hell, it wouldn't be my fault if he's too bullheaded for his own good," Chase said, his anger finally breaking through his control.

"I told him he didn't look like that big a fool," Jenny said. "He didn't seem to be too concerned with hearing *my* opinion, either."

"Maybe he had just decided, 'Nothing ventured, nothing gained,'" a deep voice suggested.

Matt Dawson was standing in the shadows of the doorway that led into the stable, watching them. At least, Jenny thought he had been watching. Obviously he'd been there long enough to have overheard part of their conversation.

"And what did you gain?" she asked, fighting the urge to smile at him.

"Probably nothing more than a few aches and pains in places I'd forgotten I have."

"It would have served you right if he'd thrown you off on your ass," Chase said.

"In my opinion," Jenny said, "that seemed the furthest thing from Harry's mind."

The left corner of Matt Dawson's mouth lifted minutely and then settled back into place. Despite the number of times Jenny had now seen that movement, something fluttered inside again, shifting deep within her body, warm and undeniably intriguing.

"Sheer, blind luck," Chase suggested.

"Obviously, you two are old friends," Jenny said, smiling.

"Obviously," Matt agreed.

It was only what he had already told her. *All* he had told her. *Nothing ventured, nothing gained,* she decided. "A friendship from when you worked together in DEA?" she asked politely.

There was a small silence. Chase hadn't looked at the man standing behind him, but he had wanted to. Jenny knew him well enough to have recognized that desire as well as she had recognized his anger, even before it was expressed.

"Aunt Jenny! Aunt Jenny's here!"

The childish shout distracted Jenny, at least momentarily, from her pursuit of the shared past of Matt Dawson and Chase. She turned in the saddle and saw that Chase and Samantha's daughter Amanda was already running down the steps of the porch to join them. Jenny dismounted quickly and prepared for the little girl's always-enthusiastic welcome.

She bent down just in time to catch the small body that came hurtling toward her. Small, softly rounded arms fastened around Jenny's neck, and the sweet talcum-fragrance of the little girl surrounded her. She lifted Mandy in a hug and swung her around and around in a circle.

Jenny gradually slowed and then stopped the circle, setting the child down on her toes, carefully holding on to her forearms until Mandy got her balance.

"I slept in Mama and Daddy's room last night 'cause we have company," Amanda announced. She was still wearing her nightgown, and her voice was full of self-importance.

"You did?" Jenny asked, smiling at her.

Mandy nodded, her blue McCullar eyes widened with the pleasure of having news that exciting to share with her beloved Aunt Jenny. "On a pallet on the floor by their bed."

Jenny glanced at Chase's face, and his expression was more revealing than he had intended, she was sure. Her gaze moved automatically to Matt Dawson and found the same quick amusement she had felt at Mandy's words reflected in his harsh features.

"That's...wonderful," Jenny said. She had had to fight answering Matt's amusement, had had to force her eyes to return to the little girl. Mandy's hair was loose, tangled from sleep, blond curls trailing over the thin white lace-trimmed gown. Her eyelids were still just a little puffy with sleep and her feet were bare.

Amanda always looked just exactly as a little girl should look, Jenny thought. Small and sweet and infinitely happy. She didn't think she could have loved a child of her own any more than she loved this one. Maybe that was because Mandy looked exactly like the babies Jenny had always dreamed she and Mac would have.

Jenny McCullar's lips tilted slightly in remembrance of those long-anticipated babies, and then suddenly, the unexpected and unwanted surge of emotion caused by that memory caught her by surprise, making her eyes sting.

Disgusted with her seemingly constant urge these days to cry every time she thought about Mac, she looked up, determinedly blinking away the hated moisture. Her eyes met and then locked with the dark intensity of Matt Dawson's.

There was no amusement in his features now. There was something there, some emotion, but it had been too quickly hidden for her to be certain what it had been before it disappeared.

"That was Samantha's idea," Chase said.

Jenny knew from his tone that it certainly hadn't been his. "Mandy's more than welcome to stay with me," she offered sincerely. She put her hand on the small blond head and glanced down to smile at her niece.

"Can I, Daddy?" Mandy begged.

"We'll see," Chase hedged, his expression softening as he looked at his daughter, a daughter he hadn't even known existed for almost four years. "Run on back inside and get some clothes on," he suggested. "It's too cold out here to be running around barefoot."

"Yes, sir," Mandy said. "Mama said to tell you to come in for breakfast in fifteen minutes. You and Mr...." The child paused, obviously having forgotten the unfamiliar name Samantha had told her.

"Mr. Dawson," Jenny supplied.

Mandy's gaze swung upward to meet her aunt's. "Do you know my daddy's friend?"

"We've met," Jenny explained.

Involuntarily, her eyes sought the tall, scarred man standing in the shadowed doorway. She hadn't thought about Mandy's eyes automatically following hers, and she was the only one who could possibly have heard the child's sharp intake of breath when they did. Jenny put her hand around Mandy's shoulders and squeezed her upper arm reassuringly. She hoped Samantha's training in good manners would stand the little girl in good stead.

"Mandy, this is Mr. Dawson," Jenny said softly. "He's your daddy's friend."

The little girl's hesitation was only a fraction of a second too long to be put down to shyness. "'Lo," she managed, her normally confident voice almost a whisper.

Matt Dawson's gaze was on the child and no longer on Jenny. She should have been relieved, but she wasn't. She had no doubt, despite Mandy's gallant effort at maintaining the politeness she had been taught, that he knew exactly what the child was thinking. He didn't respond verbally to her greeting. The tightening at the corner of his mouth was minute, and he then simply nodded.

Mandy shrank a little closer to Jenny's jeans-covered leg at his almost-forbidding silence. "Go on inside," Jenny urged her softly. "Mind your daddy. It *is* too cool out here for bare feet."

Apparently grateful for permission to leave, Mandy turned and ran toward the small house. The three adults watched as, carefully holding up her nightgown, she climbed the low steps and disappeared through the screen door.

"That's a pretty little girl," Matt said into the uncomfortable silence she left behind.

Jenny turned to smile at him, but he was looking at Chase.

"She took after her mother," Chase said.

"Then you should thank God for His favor," Matt responded, his features absolutely expressionless.

Chase's laughter in response to the insult reminded Jenny of Mac's, and that memory, too, was painful, but at least Matt's teasing comment had broken the tension Mandy's unease had caused.

"DEA?" Jenny asked again. Her voice was pleasantly inquiring as if she were only picking up the thread of the conversation they had been having when Mandy interrupted them. Both men turned to look at her, but neither answered.

"That *is* what you're doing down here, isn't it?" she prompted.

"Ma'am?"

"You're here to find out who's running drugs across this ranch."

Dawson held her gaze, but he shook his head slowly.

"I don't have anything to do with that anymore, Jenny, and you know it," Chase said.

She held Matt's dark eye for a second longer before she turned to Chase. "Not with drugs, maybe," she agreed. She glanced back at the tall stranger. "Maybe he doesn't, either. Not anymore. But he's here for something. He's not exactly the 'visiting' kind."

"I don't know what you're talking about, Jenny," Chase said. "Obviously you don't, either, or you wouldn't—"

She didn't even look at her brother-in-law as she interrupted his denial.

"You don't fool me, Chase McCullar. I've known you way too long. And he doesn't fool me, either," she said, nodding slightly at the man in the shadows. "If you're not looking for evidence that somebody's using this ranch for drug running, then explain to me what you *are* doing here. Explain to me what you were doing down by the river this morning."

"Not hunting traffickers," Matt said. "You have my word on that."

She believed him. Just as she knew he had been lying earlier, she knew that he was now speaking the absolute truth. Which meant...

"You're here about Mac." She breathed that sudden realization aloud. "Chase asked you to come down here to help him find out who killed Mac."

Again, neither man answered, but Matt's gaze unlocked suddenly from hers and shifted to her brother-in-law.

"That's it, isn't it?" she asked, her eyes following the direction his had taken. "You asked him to come down here to help you find out who put that bomb in Mac's truck."

"There's one thing I can tell you for sure, Jenny-Wren," Chase said softly. As she had with Matt Dawson, she knew without a doubt that what he was about to tell her was the truth. "The fewer people who even think about *why* he's down here, the better."

Jenny's head tilted, considering. "It seems to me," she said, "that that's not the way you ought to play it. But maybe the two of you know more about what you're doing than I do."

"Not the way to play it?" Matt questioned.

She looked at him, wondering why Mandy had reacted as she had. The more Jenny was around him, the less disconcerting his features had become. The faded scars and the black patch seemed to be now only a natural part of the man. "Not if you're trying to flush out whoever killed Mac," she said. "It seems to me that in that case..."

She hesitated, trying to decide if what she had been thinking might sound naive to these two ex-lawmen. There was no doubt in her mind that she was right about that conclusion, either. Whatever else Matt Dawson was, he was almost certainly—or at least had been at one time—involved in law enforcement.

"In that case," she continued finally, having discovered no flaw in her logic, "I would think you would want everybody to know what you're here for. Shake the tree and see what falls out,'' she suggested. That had been one of Mac's favorite expressions. She must have heard him say it a thousand times.

"Jenny—" Chase began, only to be cut off by Matt Dawson's question.

"And if something does?" Matt asked her.

"Then you just hope it doesn't hit you on the head," she said. That had always been her comeback to Mac's analogy. "And if it doesn't, then you might, you just might, find out who murdered my husband."

"WHO DO *YOU* THINK he is?" Jenny asked.

She and Samantha were standing together before the kitchen sink, looking out its window at the two men who were still engaged in conversation outside—obviously a serious conversation, judging from their expressions.

"I don't know. Chase wouldn't tell me anything. DEA, maybe?"

"That's what I thought," Jenny said. "They both evaded the question, but…"

"It fits, doesn't it. Except for whatever's wrong with him."

"Maybe he's retired. On disability," Jenny guessed. "But he's somebody Chase trusts. Somebody he respects. That's obvious if you watch them together."

"God, Jenny, I don't want Chase mixed up in that again. I was afraid that after Doc's murder Buck Elkins would ask him to be his deputy. I had just convinced him that we could make it without the money from his security business. I don't want Chase doing anything as dangerous as that ever again."

"I think Chase is trying to find out what happened to Mac," Jenny said softly.

"To Mac?" Samantha repeated. Her green eyes moved from their contemplation of the men outside to examine her sister-in-law's profile.

"Now that he knows Rio's innocent, I think Chase feels

like he owes it to Mac to find out who was really guilty."
Finally Jenny turned to meet Samantha's gaze.

"And you *want* him to try to find out," Samantha said.

"I didn't think it mattered to me anymore. I thought... I
don't really know what I thought. Maybe that Mac was gone
and knowing who killed him wouldn't bring him back. Except
now..." She hesitated, and her eyes returned to the window.
"Now I think I need to know. Just to put all the ghosts to
rest. If I'm going to move on with my life, if I'm going to
marry Trent, then I think it's important to find out what happened five years ago."

"Even if that's what Chase is up to, you realize we may
never really know what happened," Samantha said. "Five
years is a long time, an almost-impossible length of time when
you're talking about solving a crime. Even a murder."

"I know. But I also understand how Chase feels. If there *is*
still the slightest chance, then it seems that we owe it to Mac
to try."

"I SWEAR THERE WAS nothing else," Chase said. "Buck and
I tried everything. There was never anything linking anybody
else to that bomb."

"So you went after Rio."

"He had come over here earlier that night spouting some
kind of crap about giving you a message. Tell you pesos or
bullets, he said. When the truck exploded, I figured Rio was
the one sent to issue the threat for whoever planted the bomb."

"You made sure he went to prison for that."

Chase's mouth flattened, but he told Mac the truth. "He
spent almost five years at Huntsville."

"And it took you this long to figure out that Rio didn't
have anything to do with it?" There was a thread of derision
in Mac's deep voice.

"I had a few other things to worry about at the time. If you
remember." Chase's voice was defensive, but his blue eyes
were again filled with anger.

"I remember," Mac said softly. "I'll never forget." The taunting quality that had been apparent in his question had disappeared. "You think she's right?"

"Jenny?" Chase asked, his own tone lightening in response. "Hell, she usually is," he admitted. "Right about what?"

"Shaking the trees," Mac said. His single eye had tracked toward the small house into which Jenny McCullar had disappeared.

"That might be dangerous," Chase warned.

Mac's laugh was dismissive. "That never stopped us before," he said.

He put his left hand over Chase's shoulder and squeezed. The touch of those long, brown fingers was light and quickly made. No one watching the two of them could possibly have realized that these men had just made a decision to pursue the stone-cold trail of a five-year-old murder.

BREAKFAST WASN'T A pleasant affair. Jenny had stayed because Samantha had asked her to and, she was honest enough with herself to admit, because she had wanted to. She had deliberately sat down by Amanda, but that had been a mistake, she realized.

It meant Matt Dawson was sitting directly across from the little girl, and Mandy seemed engrossed in watching his every move. It was the same absorption, Jenny recognized, that most people afford snakes, comprised of about equal parts of fascination and revulsion.

At least the child hadn't said anything, and Jenny relaxed enough midway through the meal to even taste the food. Samantha was handling the conversation with the ease of someone who had grown up entertaining people she didn't know. They were talking horses, and to give Samantha credit, she didn't seem the least perturbed to learn that Matt had ridden Lighthorse Harry down to the river this morning.

It was in the middle of one of those natural lulls in conversation that Mandy asked her question. She had probably wanted to ask it out in the yard, and since Jenny had been expecting something like this then, she had managed to divert the little girl's attention by sending her back into the house. She hadn't been expecting it this time.

"What did you do with your eye?" Mandy asked.

There was silence at the table for a long heartbeat, the question seeming to echo through it.

"Mandy," Samantha and Chase both said, their admonition almost in unison.

"It's all right," Matt said.

Jenny found herself holding her breath. Waiting, anticipating his answer probably more than Mandy.

"I hurt my face in an accident," he said. His dark eye was on the little girl's face.

"And your hand?" Mandy asked.

The child had apparently watched his almost-unobtrusive efforts to manage the meal one-handed, just as Jenny had.

"And my hand," he agreed.

"Does it hurt?"

How Matt Dawson handled that question would probably be the key to his future relationship with the child, Jenny suspected. Amanda was so kindhearted that such a confession would probably make her his champion. Somehow, however, Jenny didn't expect him to admit to ever being in pain, even if it was true.

"Sometimes," he said quietly. "But not much anymore."

His gaze had shifted, Jenny realized. That brown eye was focused on her face, watching her reaction.

"Is your eye gone?" Mandy whispered. In her voice was the natural horror that thought created, as the thought of any mutilation would produce in a child's mind. "Is that why you've got it covered up."

"That's why," Matt Dawson said.

"Because it's ugly," the little girl continued, reasoning her way out loud to that conclusion.

"That's enough, Amanda McCullar," Samantha said sharply. "You apologize to Mr. Dawson right now."

"Mrs. McCullar—"

"Right now, Amanda," Samantha demanded, overriding Matt's attempted protest.

"I'm sorry," Mandy managed. Her eyes filled with tears of embarrassment over her mother's unusual public chastisement. "May I be excused?" she asked, the tears in her voice also as she whispered that rote phrase, which now represented a much-desired escape.

"When you've finished your breakfast," Chase said.

Jenny wanted to protest. The little girl was normally both polite and sensitive, but if Jenny, a grown-up, had been fascinated by the story behind Matt Dawson's appearance, how irresistible must be the urge for a four-year-old to ask questions about it.

Mandy managed a few more bites in the strained atmosphere before her mother gave her permission to leave the table. Jenny suspected that Samantha was as sorry for the little girl as she was.

When the uncomfortable meal was finally over, the men rose as Jenny began to help Samantha carry the dishes to the sink. Chase had already disappeared through the back door when Jenny realized that Matt Dawson was still there, standing near that door, holding his hat in his hand.

"Thanks for breakfast, Mrs. McCullar," he said. "I enjoyed it."

"Well, I doubt if you did, but thank you for saying that. I'm sorry about Amanda's questions. Children are just naturally curious about anyone who's..." Samantha hesitated, searching for the right word.

"Different?" Matt suggested, that hint of amusement in his voice again.

"A stranger," Samantha suggested instead.

"I'll be out of your house by this afternoon, Mrs. McCullar. Mandy can have her bedroom back."

"Because of what happened this morning?" Samantha asked.

"I never intended to put you out," he said. He smiled at her, that small upward movement of the undamaged corner of his mouth. "Thanks for putting up with me last night."

"I didn't *put up* with you, Mr. Dawson. Any friend of Chase's is always welcome in our home. You're welcome to stay as long as you wish. I really mean that," Samantha added.

"Thank you, ma'am, but we both know that's not really an option. But...maybe you know of somebody nearby who has a room I could rent."

Samantha glanced at Jenny. The main McCullar house was big and empty. Rio had stayed there for several weeks. He had done a lot of work around the ranch, and Jenny had commented more than once on how much she missed having him there.

Jenny didn't offer a room to Matt Dawson. She thought about it, and she knew Samantha was halfway expecting her to. But that wasn't an option, either, she acknowledged. There was just too much about the way Matt Dawson affected her that she didn't understand.

"I don't think so," Samantha said finally, her eyes moving back to Matt's face. "I'll try to think of some place, though. In the meantime, I meant what I said. You're more than welcome to stay here."

"I guess I could bunk with Harry," Matt said. His amused gaze was on Jenny instead of his hostess. Again that slow, intriguing tilt disturbed the line of his lips.

"You probably could. Harry seems to like you," Jenny said, thinking about the stallion's calm reaction to his rider's awkwardness this morning.

"I guess it's a good thing horses *don't* judge by appearance," he said. "Thanks again for the breakfast, ma'am."

As Matt crossed to the kitchen door, for the first time Jenny noticed a slight hesitation in his stride. Almost a limp, she decided. She wondered if that was permanent or the result of his abduction of Harry this morning—one of those aches and pains he'd admitted to. Maybe if she waited long enough, she thought, Mandy would ask him about that, too.

"YOU KNOW AS WELL AS I do this bag means less than nothing."

With his tanned fingers Sheriff Buck Elkins poked the crumpled plastic sack Jenny had laid on his desk. Mac's desk, she had thought, as she put it there. Or at least it had once been Mac's desk. A long time ago when he had been sheriff of this county.

"It means drugs. You and I both know that, Buck. Especially around here," she argued

"I could probably find a hundred of these things up and down the river. Illegals are always carrying stuff across tied up in plastic."

"'Stuff'?" Jenny repeated derisively. "Taped like this? Drugs, you mean, don't you, Buck."

"Yeah. That, too. But that little bit isn't enough to make any difference. Not even enough to be interesting to the feds, Jenny. That river's always been used for smuggling everything from candle wax to animals."

"How can you be so sure this is just illegals bringing a 'little bit' across?"

"Half the drug rumors that get started on the border have their roots in illegal immigration. Somebody sees a truck on their property at night, and all of a sudden we got trafficking going on, or so they say. That river teems with life, come sundown, and I'm not talking fish."

"Neither am I," Jenny said, feeling her temper begin to rise at Buck's condescending attitude. She had grown up in this county just as he had. She had been born less than twenty miles from the Rio Grande, and she was well aware of the endless human traffic that crossed through the shallow warmth of its waters. The same traffic that had used the river for hundreds of years, despite the laws of both countries.

"Drugs, Buck," she said softly, almost daring him to contradict her. "Here in this county. Mac told us that."

"Jenny," Elkins said, shaking his head, his voice full of resignation and denial at the same time, "you know we never could find—"

She pushed the plastic sack across the desk and closer to him. "I found," she said, interrupting. "Somebody approached Mac. Somebody dropped these sacks on my property. You're the sheriff of this county. I want something done about it. I want you to investigate whatever's going on out on my ranch."

"If somebody was using your property to bring in drugs, you can bet they're thinking twice about doing that now that Chase is back. Maybe with just you and Samantha living there these last few years, somebody saw an opportunity to do a little smuggling. Illegals or drugs or whatever."

He pushed the plastic toward her and leaned back in his chair, lifting the front legs slightly off the floor and balancing on the back ones with the ease of long practice.

"I don't really know what this contained, Jenny, but I don't think whoever left it there is going to chance anything with a former DEA agent living on the place. They find out Chase's back, they'll go somewhere else. That border's way too wide for smugglers to hang around if somebody's willing to give them grief. There are too many other stretches where nobody gives a damn what they do."

That was the same argument Mac had made. *"They're not going to try anything where the law has bowed its back against them."* Only...

"If that's the case, Buck, then why did somebody kill Mac?"

Sheriff Elkins's mouth thinned as his hazel eyes, half shrouded by his lids, examined her face. "Is that what this is about, Jenny? Mac's murder?"

"Maybe," she said softly. "You never found out who did it."

He lowered his chair to the floor and tapped the brown plastic sack twice with one finger, as if he were pointing at it. "I have to tell you that I don't think this is related," he said.

"How can you know that?"

"I don't *know* it. It's just..." He took a breath and then started again. "Look, Jenny, what happened to Mac happened a long time ago. Most of the people who were involved in trafficking back then are more than likely already in prison or dead. The rate of attrition in that business is fairly high." There was still an edge of condescension in his voice, hidden just under the pleasant south-Texas drawl.

"That must be real convenient to believe. *If* you believe it. You were Mac's friend. Don't you ever think about what they did to him?"

"Every day of my life," Buck said softly, and the words had the undeniable ring of truth. "There's not a day that I unlock that front door over there or sit behind this desk, that I don't think about Mac. But I'm sorry, Jenny. That doesn't mean I think this has anything to do with what happened five years ago. I wish I did. I wish I still thought we had a snowball's chance in hell of catching the bastards who did that to Mac."

Apparently, however, Chase *did* think they still had a chance, Jenny remembered. Why else would he bring Matt Dawson down here? Suddenly, the real regret in Buck's eyes made Jenny want to assure him that someone, at least, seemed to believe there was still a chance. She wanted to tell the sheriff what Matt and Chase were up to, but she hesitated, remembering Chase's warning.

"Chase is your best bet," Buck continued, almost echoing what she'd been thinking. Surprised, she shook her head, a small crease forming between the smooth, dark wings of her brows.

"Nobody's going to use your ranch anymore for anything illegal with Chase out there. Whatever was going on when this was discarded is surely *not* going on now."

It was dismissal, polite and reassuring, but dismissal just the same. There wasn't much else she could do, Jenny knew. She had made the local authorities aware of the situation. Maybe Buck was right. It would be incredibly risky to use the ranch for trafficking with Chase living there.

"Thanks for your time," she said. There was a hint of frost in her politeness. Somehow she had expected Buck to be more concerned, but she knew the realities of the border as well as he did. There wasn't much to go on. These plastic bags, whatever they had once contained, represented less than a drop in the ocean of the drug traffic. Buck was probably right about it all.

"Any time, Jenny. You know that. You know how I felt about Mac. How we all felt. Believe me, if there was anything I could do…"

"I know," she said softly. This time there was sincerity in her agreement. She did know how close Mac and Buck had been. She also knew how long the sheriff had tried to find his murderers after her husband had been killed.

"You let me know, now, if you have any more trouble."

"I will."

"You did tell Chase, didn't you?" Buck asked just before she reached the door.

"His friend was with me when I found this," Jenny said. That wasn't exactly going against Chase's advice, and it might represent the slight shaking of those trees she'd recommended.

"His friend?" Buck questioned.

"Someone who's staying with him awhile. An old friend, Chase said."

"Then Chase knows about what you all found."

"I'm sure Chase knows," Jenny agreed. She closed Buck's office door behind her, again trying not to remember that it, too, had once been Mac's.

Chapter Four

"I'd about forgotten how primitive this place is," Chase said, looking around.

Mac, too, surveyed the interior of the small shack that stood on the line between the two McCullar properties. It was obvious that it hadn't been used in years. But there was a pump for the well, he remembered, and once they started the motor, he would have water. There was also firewood for the iron stove that would fight the chill of the desert night and allow him to cook if he wanted. And there were beds.

"Hell, Mac," Chase said, shaking his head. "You can't stay out here."

"Why not?" Mac asked. He picked up his suitcase and laid it on top of the first of the bunks. A small cloud of dust rose when the suitcase made contact with the blanket that covered the mattress.

"It's pretty isolated, for one thing."

"I'm not sure that's bad."

"Rio stayed here one night when he first came back," Chase said. "Somebody came out and beat the hell out of him because they thought he'd had a part in killing Doc Horn. Or maybe because of you. We never did find out who was responsible for that beating."

"I've got no enemies. Nobody's out for Matt Dawson's hide."

"But they may be eventually. *If* we do what Jenny said."

"You think somebody might come after me."

"It's a possibility. Something you ought to be aware of."

"I thought that was the whole purpose of Jenny's plan."

"To use you as bait?" Chase asked mockingly.

"To flush somebody. You can't flush game without making noise. That's your job. *You're* the one who's going to attract attention by announcing what we're up to. Watch your back, little brother."

"I don't like you being out here by yourself."

"You can leave me that Winchester you got in the truck."

"I left *Rio* the Winchester. It didn't do him a whole hell of a lot of good."

"Yeah, but you forget. I'm a lawman," Mac said. His voice was full of amusement. It was unclear whether he was mocking Chase's worrying about him or mocking himself. "We're always prepared for the unexpected."

"Somebody wanted you dead five years ago. They came pretty damn close to getting what they wanted."

"And I have to tell you, I'd really like to find out who that bastard was," Mac said. There was no amusement in that and no mockery. "Jenny's right. The only way we're ever going to find out is to give whoever it was a reason to surface again. The best one I can think of is to make them think we know more than we do about Mac McCullar's murder and that we're determined to find out the rest."

"And when we do?" Chase asked. Mac's questioning gaze came up from the suitcase he was unpacking to find the troubled eyes of his brother. "What are you planning on telling Jenny?"

"Maybe nothing," Mac said softly.

"I thought that's why you came home. Because of Jenny."

Mac smiled, the movement of his damaged mouth almost twisted. "Because of Jenny," he agreed. "But that doesn't mean that telling her who I am is the right thing to do. Or that it's what I'm gonna do when this is finished. I just want to make sure Jenny's happy. Make sure that somebody's taking care of her.''

That had been his intent—at least at the beginning. Just to check out the man Jenny was in love with. But Mac admitted to himself that those good and honorable motives had somehow become hopelessly entangled with his memories. All the old memories that had been battering at him since he had seen Jenny dancing in someone else's arms at the wedding.

"You really think she'll care about any of it?'' Chase asked, interrupting his mental admission that it wasn't going to be easy to leave Jenny alone.

"No,'' Mac agreed softly, "but I'm still pretty damn sure I will.''

His gaze fell again to the clothing in the suitcase, which he continued to lay out on the bed. Chase watched the careful movements of his brother's long fingers for several minutes in the stillness before finally he went out to the truck to bring in the rifle.

"BECAUSE IF RIO'S *NOT* guilty, then it stands to reason somebody else is,'' Chase McCullar said.

His eyes circled the familiar faces that surrounded him, searching them for reaction. He was in Cochran's, a small convenience store/service station about halfway between the McCullar land and the town of Crystal Springs.

The store was an unofficial gathering place for the ranchers in the county, and Chase had timed his early-Sunday-morning arrival in order to be here when the largest crowd was in attendance. People would drift in and out all day on their way to and from church or just to socialize, and he knew that whatever he said would be repeated endlessly throughout the long, lazy day.

"You really think Delgado didn't have nothing to do with Mac's death?'' Ben Pirkle asked. "You really believe that bastard's story?''

Chase had long suspected that Pirkle had been one of those

who had come out to the line shack that night and almost beaten his half brother to death. Ben had been open about his hostility when Rio returned. He had demanded that Buck lock Delgado up when Doc was killed, despite the lack of evidence linking Rio to the crime, despite Chase's unwillingly provided alibi for his half brother, and despite the undeniable fact that Anne Richardson had been with Rio at the time Doc was murdered.

"I do now," Chase said.

"You sure as hell didn't believe him back when Mac died," Dwight Rogers said, his voice full of disgust.

"I was wrong," Chase said, "and I hope I'm man enough to admit it when I am."

"If you think Delgado's innocent, then who the hell you think put that bomb in Mac's truck?" That question was from Bobby Thompson, his weather-beaten face furrowed with the realization that whoever had killed Mac might still be here, still living in this county.

"That's just what I intend to find out," Chase said. Again, his eyes examined their faces, looking for some telltale response.

"After five years?" Ben asked.

"After a hundred, it that's what it takes. Mac was my brother. Now that I'm back, I don't intend to let the people who did that get another night's sleep, believing that they got away with murdering a McCullar."

"Buck never could find out anything about who did it," a voice reminded him. Chase was able to put a name to the face after a couple of seconds of thinking about it. Phillip Warren had taken over the running of his family's run-down spread after his father's death, and from county gossip he was making a real success of it. Much more of a success than his father ever had.

"But Mac wasn't Buck's brother," Chase said softly.

There was a small silence while the men digested that. It was something they would understand, Chase knew. These were family men, and the ties of blood in Texas, as in the rest of the South, were incredibly strong.

"You going below the border?" Dwight asked. His mouth was slightly pursed in thought, reminding Chase of his powerful father-in-law, Sam Kincaid.

Kincaid might be a good place to start his search, Chase realized. There was very little that went on in this neck of the woods that the old man didn't know something about. Sam had liked Mac—better than he'd ever liked him, Chase admitted ruefully. Sam had made that abundantly clear.

"If I have to," Chase said. "But from what I know now, I think whoever killed Mac was from right around here."

"What makes you think that?" Warren asked, the doubt in his voice obvious.

"The way it was set up. The phone call that got Mac out that night was local. They knew which vehicle Mac would take. Add that to the fact that they set it up at his house, in his front yard—something too risky for strangers, it seems to me. And then…" Chase deliberately hesitated. "Then there are some other things I've found out about the situation since then."

"What about Ray Morales?" Pirkle suggested. Buck's deputy had been running an illegal-alien operation, supplying workers for the meat-packing plants in the American heartland, when he was killed.

"He came in response to Buck's advertisement for a deputy. Ray wasn't even here when Mac was killed."

"Maybe he had some hand in it, though," the old man persisted.

"He kills Mac just so he could get hired on as deputy? You must not know how little this county pays, Ben."

There was laughter and a brief relaxation, at least until Chase continued.

"Ray wasn't involved, but we've got a pretty good idea who was. We're just going to have to prove it."

"We?" Warner questioned.

"An old friend of mine's come to help me."

"Somebody who was with you in the DEA?" Warren asked.

Chase's eyes met his and held for a few seconds before he answered. "Somebody who knows what he's doing," he said, being deliberately cryptic, but he knew they would take that as confirmation.

"You really think you can catch Mac's killers after all this time?" That was Rogers again, his voice full of doubt.

"Don't you put any money on me *not* catching 'em, Dwight. Don't you make any bets against it," Chase warned. "Those folks think they got away with murdering my brother. Now that I'm living here again, I find that I really don't like that idea very much. It makes me damned uncomfortable."

"Buck know what you're up to?" Pirkle asked.

"He will. I'm going on into town and tell him what I've learned. Buck's in charge here now, and I plan to operate within the law. I don't believe in night attacks or trying to beat somebody to death 'cause you *think* they're guilty. I'll get my revenge in a courtroom."

Chase didn't miss the reactions this time. At least they recognized themselves, he thought. Damn cowards. He had hated Rio Delgado with every ounce of emotion he was capable of feeling, but he would never have thought about doing what some of these upstanding citizens had done that night.

"Y'all take care, now," Chase said. He picked up the sack Maggie Cochran had put his unneeded purchases into, nodded to her, and then walked out.

The silence he left behind him, which lasted at least until he had closed the front door, was all the proof he needed that his first attempt at getting out the word that he was determined to find Mac's killer had had an effect.

Now it would just be a matter of stirring things up a little further, putting out the same message he'd just delivered here to the rest of the far-flung community. Then he and Mac could sit back and see what happened.

And something would, he knew. That cold finger of fear and premonition, which his brother had long ago labeled "lawman's instinct," had been running along his spine all morning.

The trees were shaken. Now they would just have to protect their heads from whatever fell out. And watch each other's backs. He thought again about Mac sleeping alone out at that line shack. He had worried about it last night, but he knew now he had to do something about it. And he would. Before tonight, he promised himself. Just as soon as he got back to the ranch.

JENNY KNEW THAT WHAT she was doing wasn't wise, but she had lived her entire life doing what was wise, doing the acceptable thing. Even marrying Mac McCullar instead of going on with her nurse's training had been considered by most people in this county to be the right thing to do. After all, why would any woman need a profession when she had a good, strong man like Mac to look after her?

She slowed the pickup as she approached the line shack. The building was really a small bunkhouse, a remnant from the days when the McCullars had run cattle over this arid expanse.

She had fought the urge to come out here since Chase phoned yesterday to tell her that Matt Dawson was going to be staying in the shack. She had protested—not his presence, of course, but the lack of hospitality putting a McCullar guest up in such a place represented.

"We don't have room, and he knows it," Chase had told her. "He won't stay here another night. I don't think Mandy's reaction did anything to help that situation."

"I don't think he should be out there. Remember what happened to Rio."

"Rio has lots of enemies. Nobody around here even knows Matt."

"Is he eating with y'all?"

"He's invited," Chase said, but she knew from his voice that that was something else Matt Dawson had decided to avoid.

"I just don't think it's a good idea—"

"You got a better one?" Chase challenged.

She thought about it. She had plenty of room, of course, but for some reason, she couldn't imagine living in the same house with Matt Dawson. Unlike Amanda's, her hesitation had nothing to do with his looks.

Or maybe it did, her honesty suggested—but his appearance certainly didn't affect her the way it apparently affected the little girl. It was her attraction to Matt Dawson that Jenny feared. An immediate sexual attraction that she couldn't understand, couldn't explain in any rational way.

"I don't have a better idea," she said softly.

"Then that's where it stands," Chase agreed. "I went into town today. Did what you suggested."

"What I suggested?"

"Shook a few trees."

"And?" Jenny asked, beginning to wonder about the consequences of what she had urged Chase to do. She had already lost Mac to those bastards. What in the world had she been thinking when she'd suggested Chase and Matt try to stir them up?

"I guess we just wait and see what falls out," Chase said quietly. He was also remembering Mac, she knew. "I'll talk to you later on tonight or tomorrow."

"Okay," Jenny said, almost reluctant to let him hang up. "Kiss Mandy for me."

"She probably needs a swift pop on the bottom instead, judging by the way she acted at breakfast yesterday."

"And you're going to do that?" Jenny teased. Chase was the biggest soft touch imaginable when it came to his daughter, and he had been since the first time he'd met her.

"Probably not," he replied, a matching humor in his voice. "Samantha handles the discipline, but I have to tell you, there's been some hand-wringing around here after yesterday's fiasco. A lot of 'Where did I go wrong?'s.'''

"Tell Samantha to stop worrying. I don't think Matt thought too much about it."

"Matt?" Chase repeated.

Jenny knew what her brother-in-law was questioning.

"Mr. Dawson seems a little formal," she said. She could hear the slight defensiveness of her explanation.

"What do you think of him?" Chase asked.

She hesitated too long, conscious suddenly of the slight moisture in the palm of the hand that held the phone.

"He seems very nice," she said finally.

"Well, that's sure the kiss of death," Chase said, making no effort to hide his amusement.

"Are you trying to fix me up, Chase McCullar? May I remind you that I don't need a boyfriend."

"Yeah, I forgot. You've already got one of those."

"What's *that* supposed to mean?" Jenny demanded, feeling anger surge at his sarcasm.

"Not a thing, Jenny. It just always seemed to me that after Mac…" He hesitated, adjusting his tone to be less offensive. "Trent Richardson never seemed to be your type."

"I think I'm a little more qualified to decide *my* type than you are," she said angrily. "And your mysterious friend certainly isn't it."

"Don't get riled. I'm not trying to fix you up. I just wondered what you thought of him."

"I think… I think I want you both to watch yourselves," she admitted. It was the truth. Not the whole truth, but certainly part of it. "You be careful, Chase."

Chase laughed. "Matt's got my back, Jenny-Wren, and I've got his. Nothing's going to happen to either one of us. Talk to you tomorrow."

When the connection was broken, Jenny had stood with the phone in her hand for almost a minute, reminded by Chase's words of Mac's promise that night five years ago. *"Nothing's*

going to happen to me.'' Then, for some reason, she had
headed for her kitchen and begun cooking the meal that rested
beside her on the seat of the pickup, carefully covered to keep
it warm.

It was only now, when she had arrived at the line shack,
that she allowed herself to question why she was here. Neigh-
borliness, she suggested reasonably. Traditional Southern hospitality. Human decency.

Uh-huh, she mocked herself. All of the above, maybe. But
also maybe because of the way Matt Dawson's damaged
mouth moved when he smiled. The way she felt when she
knew he was looking at her. The breadth of his shoulders or
the way his long legs fit into those worn Levi's. Just normal
human decency.

She cleared those images and climbed down from the truck.
She deliberately slammed the pickup's door, knowing Matt
would hear it, that it would give him a little warning that he
had company. Then she walked around to the other side of the
cab. She was lifting out the laden tray when she became aware
that Matt Dawson was standing in the open doorway of the
shack, watching her. A little unnerved by that realization, she
pushed the truck door shut with her hip and began walking
toward him, carrying the tray.

"Chase said you aren't eating at their house," she explained. "So I brought you supper."

His gaze dropped quickly to the covered containers and then
rose again to her face. He was wearing those same jeans, and
he had his boots on, but his tan shirt wasn't tucked in and it
was unbuttoned. Even as she walked toward him, he was
working on rebuttoning it. His progress was slowed by the
fact that he was using only his left hand, the big fingers struggling with pushing the buttons through the holes.

She thought about how many everyday tasks required the
use of two hands. And then, as her eyes followed the downward movements of those long brown fingers, she realized that
the lower edges of the shirt gaped slightly, exposing a taut,

ridged stomach. And a thin line of dark hair that led down
into the top of his jeans, which rode low on his hips.

Her mouth went dry, and her lower body began to ache
with memories that crowded, unwanted, into her head. Memories of running her fingertips along a similar line of dark hair
on Mac's stomach. Or following it with her tongue. Tracing
its pathway to the inevitable end. And then...

She jerked her eyes away from that flat expanse of belly
and back to his face. He knew what she had been thinking.
He knew exactly what she was feeling. And as she had that
dawn by the river, she waited for him to react to the almost-
blatant acknowledgment of her attraction to him.

"You didn't have to do that, Mrs. McCullar," he said.

She was at a loss. The sudden, cruelly evocative images of
Mac's strong, living body had been too powerful in her brain,
pushing out any memory of what she had said that had
prompted that remark.

"I brought some provisions out," he added. His gaze was
as intense as it had been before. As penetrating. As if he could
read every nuance of her expression. As if he knew her every
thought.

And yet he was a stranger. A total stranger. Someone she
had just met.

"I like to cook," she said. She lifted the heavy tray, as if
to verify that claim.

He didn't look at it, but that slow tilt disturbed his lips.
Disturbed her. Almost against her will, she smiled at him. His
half smile widened slightly, and then he moved back out of
the doorway to allow her to enter.

IT WAS TWILIGHT, almost dark now in the small house, so dark
that she had finally lit the oil lamp that stood on a table across
the room. They were sitting at the wooden table that had been
pushed out of the way against the wall. She had helped Matt
pull it out, and she had sat across from him, watching him eat.

Jenny had found that she liked watching him eat her cook-

ing, liked watching him enjoy food she had fixed with her
own hands. She supposed that made her some kind of throw-
back, and she wasn't sure she would have confessed that satisfaction to anyone else, but the fact that this man had obviously been hungry and that he had enjoyed the supper she'd
brought had given her pleasure.

Matt glanced up from the nearly empty plate. She was surprised when a slight flush reddened the skin of his cheeks. He
wiped his mouth on the napkin she'd brought—a cloth one,
because Mac never liked paper so she had quit buying them.

"Sorry," he said.

"For what?" she asked, smiling.

"Ignoring conversation and manners while I wolfed down
your chicken."

She laughed. "That's Mac's mother's recipe. You dip the
pieces in buttermilk before you flour them, and then you let
them sit for a couple of hours."

She didn't know why she had told him all that—information
he couldn't possibly be interested in—but she had thought
long and hard before she'd finally settled on the famous
McCullar chicken. It was one of her specialties, but the deciding factor had been that everyone ate fried chicken with his
fingers, no knife and fork required, and it was easily managed
with one hand.

"Mac because of McCullar?" Matt asked.

He was just making conversation, she knew. Trying to make
up for eating rather than talking before.

"His name was really Drew," Jenny said, smiling, remembering again. "But nobody ever called him that. I suppose
because it was his father's name, too."

"I guess Mac's better than Junior."

"It fit," she said softly. It had been perfect. He was just
Mac.

"How long has your husband been dead, Mrs. McCullar?"

"Jenny," she corrected automatically. "I thought Chase

might have told you. It's been almost five years. Five years this December.''

That was always a conversation stopper. People never knew what to say. In the silence, Jenny watched her fingers rub a path along the rough edge of the table.

''I understand you're engaged now?''

Her eyes lifted from the aimless movement of her hand. He was watching her, waiting for her reaction, just as Chase sometimes did. Another old lawman's trick.

''I'm not engaged. Did Chase tell you that?''

''I thought somebody mentioned it. Maybe I was mistaken.''

''I'm seeing someone, but there's nothing official. Nothing's settled.''

He nodded slightly, almost as he had at the wedding. She didn't know why she felt compelled to explain her relationship with Trent to him. It was none of his business. A lot of people thought she and Trent were engaged. One more shouldn't matter.

''That man you were dancing with at the wedding?'' he asked.

''Trent Richardson. He's Anne's brother.''

''From around here?''

''He lives in San Antonio. He's a state senator.''

''I guess you'll be moving there eventually.''

''If I decide to marry. If not, I'll stay here.''

''Ranching's a hard life for a woman alone.''

''Chase and Samantha are next door. And I don't really ranch anymore. But I've been thinking about asking Rio if he'd like to manage the place for me, maybe breed horses like Samantha does. Rio could make a go of that. It seems a shame for the land not to be used for something.''

Suddenly, she wished she hadn't told him about that idea. It was true that she'd considered the possibility, but only if she married Trent and moved away, and that was something she still had a hard time imagining.

"Rio is Chase's half brother?" he asked.

"And Mac's."

"The one Chase sent to prison?"

"Chase wanted to punish somebody for Mac's death. Just to make somebody pay."

Again he nodded, his dark eye still studying her face.

"I never really believed Rio had anything to do with it, not after all Mac had done for him, trying to keep him out of trouble," Jenny continued. "I didn't see how Rio could want to hurt Mac after that. How anybody could. But Chase was so sure."

She took a breath, thinking about Rio, about those long five years spent in prison for a crime he didn't have anything to do with. That was still cause for regret.

"It was so hard for Chase when Mac died. I don't think any of us realized how hard," she said softly. "He tried not to let anyone know, I guess."

"It's hard to lose a brother," Matt agreed.

"Especially when it's someone like Mac."

She looked down at her fingers, which were suddenly restless again. She didn't want to talk about Mac to this man. For the first time in her life, Jenny realized, she didn't want to talk about Mac at all, and that scared her. It made her feel as if being here with Matt was wrong. A violation, somehow, of what she and Mac had had. The most frightening thing was that she had never felt this guilt when she was with Trent.

"I'll help you gather up the dishes," he said.

She looked up quickly, a little surprised that the questions had stopped. Matt Dawson had already pushed back the wooden chair he was sitting in. He stood and began to place the dishes on the tray. Jenny sat and watched him.

And she knew why. She had known as soon as she had felt that small shiver of guilty fear. She hadn't come out here to deliver Matt Dawson's supper. That wasn't what being here was all about. It hadn't been about anything like that from the first time she'd met him.

"Mrs. McCullar?" he questioned, his deep voice very soft.

"Jenny," she said again. "My name is Jenny. No one ever calls me Mrs. McCullar."

She looked up, forcing her eyes away from their fascination with the sure movements of his good hand, up to his face, a long way up. She kept forgetting how tall he was, maybe because she remembered other things. That tantalizing glimpse of flat brown stomach. The way the thin material of his worn jeans hugged the muscles in his legs. His tilted smile. The way his hands felt, moving...

"I'll be glad to take these out to the truck for you," he said, interrupting that impossible image. "But I have to warn you. If this is your grandmother's antique china, these dishes are probably safer if you carry the tray."

"As a matter of fact," she said, his prosaic tone breaking whatever spell she had been under, "these *are* part of my grandmother's wedding china. I'll carry it." She got to her feet, leaning across to take the handles of the tray he'd filled.

"Thank you for supper," he said. "Thanks for bringing it out here."

Suddenly he seemed very close. So close she could smell him. Male. Warm skin. Soap. Maybe some kind of aftershave, but she couldn't be sure. Very pleasant. She *was* sure of that.

She had the urge to lean forward a little farther across the separation of the table, a matter of only inches now, and put her lips against the scarred skin of his throat. To put her face there and breathe in the scent of his body. To try to absorb the very essence of his skin.

She did nothing of the kind, of course. She lifted the tray with hands that trembled—again. And she wondered if she would be the one to drop her grandmother's china. It seemed a distinct possibility.

"I'll get the door for you," he said.

He led her across the small room to the open doorway of the shack. The desert landscape that stretched beyond the door appeared faded, almost eerie in the gathering night. The low, distant hills were purpled with shadows, and the first stars were beginning to appear against the clear, dark charcoal of the desert sky.

He followed her to the truck and opened the passenger-side door. The plastic bag she'd taken into Crystal Springs to show Sheriff Elkins was still on the seat. She had forgotten to take it out yesterday, and this afternoon she had just set the tray down on top of it. She was about to do that again when Matt Dawson stopped her.

"This came from down by the river?" he asked. He stepped into the opening beside her and reached inside the truck, pulling the bag toward them. The action put them together in the narrow space between the cab and the opened door. Nearer than they had ever been before.

Again, she could smell him. And again, she fought the urge to move closer, the urge to touch him in some way. To let him know what she felt.

"Jenny?" he said.

His voice was so low. So quiet. Only the peace of the desert surrounded them. There was nothing else out here. No one else. She had known that when she came.

He put his hand over hers and guided the tray down onto the passenger seat, but he didn't move out of the way. He didn't move at all, and it seemed to take an enormous act of will for her to raise her eyes to his face.

The lines and angles of it were as harsh as before, but the darkness softened the rest. She lifted her face, her lips opening slightly. Wanting. Wanting his damaged mouth over hers. Wanting his hands on her shoulders pulling her to him. Wanting. God, she had wanted him for so long. Such an endlessly long loneliness of wanting.

Her eyes must have told him. Or he had simply known, as he had seemed to know before what she was feeling. His head began to lower. His lips parted also, and her breathing quickened. Anticipating their touch. His touch. His head tilted to one side, aligning itself to fasten over hers.

Then suddenly it lifted. Moved away from hers. And he turned, his gaze directed over the empty, barren expanse that surrounded them. Only—it wasn't empty any longer, she realized.

A familiar black pickup was approaching from out of the darkness. The truck's headlights were on, and it was near enough that Jenny knew that she, too, should have heard it, should have been aware long before she was of its approach. But her concentration had been on something else, her hearing deadened by desire. By excitement. Anticipation.

Matt Dawson stepped away from her, out of the narrow space inside the opened door. His big body turned toward Chase's approaching truck.

Jenny drew in a deep, probably audible breath, trying to quell the torrent of need that was still flooding her body. Trying to prepare herself to face Mac's brother without the hunger she had just felt for another man's body being obvious in her face.

Chase blew the horn, a quick tap, and Jenny knew that he had seen them. She wondered *what* he had seen, and then she realized that it was none of Chase McCullar's business. Whatever she did, whatever she felt, she didn't have to explain to anyone, not even to Mac's brother.

By the time Chase pulled the truck up next to hers, she had managed to get her breathing under control, if not her emotions. She felt deprived, deserted. And unreasonably angry at Chase for showing up out here right now.

Chase stepped out of his pickup and, leaving the driver's-side door open, he began walking around the front of the two vehicles and toward them. He didn't say anything when he got there, but his eyes, almost luminous in the growing darkness, moved searchingly from one face to the other. Jenny fought to hide what had happened, but like Mac, Chase was very good at reading faces, almost too good at reading people.

"Jenny," he said, but he only nodded at Matt. "What are you doing out here?"

"Bringing me supper," Matt said.

His voice revealed no trace of the frustration she still felt. She wondered briefly if she could have been mistaken. She replayed the last few seconds of what had happened between them in her mind, up to the point where his mouth had begun to lower to find hers. No mistake. No doubt about what he had intended. Maybe he hadn't been as moved by it as she had been. Maybe to him it had been simply...

"Jenny?" Chase said questioningly. She fought to find her equilibrium, struggled for some shred of control, of sanity.

"Fried chicken," she offered, although she knew that wasn't what Chase was questioning. "Since Matt wasn't coming to yours and Samantha's place to eat."

"I see," Chase said.

And then no one said anything. The sudden silence was uncomfortable, full of tension. Or guilt.

"Well, it's good you're out here," Chase said finally. "It'll save me a trip by your place. I wanted you both to know that I did what we talked about. I spread the word pretty wide that Matt and I are unofficially reopening the investigation into Mac's murder."

"Unofficially?" Jenny questioned.

"Officially it's never been closed. But even Buck admitted that he'd stopped looking a long time ago."

"Get any reactions?" Matt asked.

"Nothing that I'd call out of the ordinary. Interest. Speculation. But folks around here like to talk, even if they don't know a thing about what they're talking about. There wasn't anything that set off any alarm bells," Chase said.

"Something will," Matt said. "Somebody's not going to like the idea."

"That's what I came out here for. I don't think you ought to stay out here. It's too dangerous."

Matt's mouth tightened in response to that. Not enough to be a total dismissal of Chase's concern, but enough to indicate he wasn't amused by it.

"I'm not afraid," he said.

"Yeah, well, maybe you ought to be. We're talking about a murder here. About people more than willing to do murder again. Maybe you *ought* to be afraid."

"You want me to come back to your place?" There was a hint of disbelief in the question.

"I think that would be the smart thing to do. But if you're too stubborn to realize—"

"I know what you're worried about," Matt said. "I just don't think that's an option."

"Because of Mandy. You're letting a four-year-old's reaction to—"

"This has nothing to do with Mandy," Matt interrupted again, anger creeping into his voice. "I'm not looking for anything to happen quick, Chase, and if you are, then I think you're bound to be disappointed. I can't stay with your family for a long period of time, and you know it."

"My *family*," Chase repeated bitingly.

There was anger in that, too, but Jenny didn't understand it. She thought again about offering to let Matt stay at her house, but given what had almost happened between them tonight, that didn't seem to be an option either. And if Chase were concerned about Matt's safety, then it seemed that he should be at Chase's. *"Matt's got my back,"* Chase had told her, *"and I've got his."* If they were going to work together, then it made sense to her that they should be together.

"I don't need a bodyguard. Or a nursemaid," Matt said quietly. It was clearly a warning that Chase shouldn't pursue this any further.

"What you need is your head examined. Just like riding that damn stallion yesterday. What the hell do you think you—"

"I think you've said just about enough," Matt interrupted. His tone was different than it had been before, and its soft, menacing coldness stopped the flow of Chase's invective.

Chase stood for a few seconds, lips flattened with the pressure he was exerting to keep from arguing further. When he turned and began to retrace his path around the front of the two trucks, his fury was apparent in his stride.

"Chase," Matt said, but Chase didn't turn around. He had reached the front of his pickup, was caught briefly in the headlights, when Matt began to follow him.

Jenny hadn't moved, knowing she had no part in this, but she could see their figures, silhouetted against the darkness on the other side of the parked vehicles. Their faces were illuminated slightly by the dome light in Chase's truck. She could hear Matt's voice, softly reasoning now.

Chase had gotten to the driver's-side door, when Matt grabbed his arm, half turning him. "I know what you're thinking, and I appreciate it, but you have to understand—"

The quiet words were suddenly interrupted by an echoing report. It seemed distant and removed, an unexpected crack of noise, instantly fading away into the darkness like the last of the light. It took a moment for Jenny to realize what the sound she heard had been—a realization made in the eerie silence that followed the rifle's report.

By the time she had identified the noise, she was already running around the trucks that separated her from the two men, unthinking of the danger that exposing herself on the other side might represent.

The scene that she found when she arrived beside the open door of Chase's pickup was horrifyingly familiar. One of the men knelt over the body of the other, which lay sprawled on the ground. It was too reminiscent of running out of the house that night to find Chase bending over Mac's burning body, trying to beat out with his bare hands the flames that engulfed it.

Not again, Jenny found herself praying. *Oh, please, dear God, not again.*

Chapter Five

He didn't think there was anything that could evoke the horror of what had happened five years ago more than the smell of a hospital. The unmistakable medicinal odor made him almost physically ill, even today. This one was no worse than any other, he supposed, and he had had experience in a lot of different ones.

Just never much experience at this—not at seeing things from this perspective. He had never been the person waiting outside that blank expanse of wall, outside the unmoving glass-topped doors, endlessly waiting for someone to come out and tell him what was going on.

Mac leaned against the tile wall and put his head back against its coolness. He closed his good eye, which was burning with fatigue. It had been hours since the chopper had brought Chase here, the trauma center nearest the ranch, and in all that time no one had told them much of anything. Nobody had time to issue progress reports. Mac understood that. At least, intellectually he understood it.

Somehow that didn't help worth a damn. He opened his eye and lowered his head, allowing his gaze to settle on the two women who sat, almost huddled together, on the cold vinyl of the hospital's uncomfortable chairs. *Waiting room,* Mac thought bitterly. What a hell of an appropriate name.

He probably no longer even heard the bell that signaled the

elevator's frequent arrivals and departures, but he recognized the distinctive figure that stepped out of this one immediately. Mac was facing the corridor and the bank of elevators, so he saw Sam Kincaid long before the women could. He guessed he should have been expecting the old man to show up.

Samantha was Sam Kincaid's only child and, like it or not, Chase McCullar was the man she had chosen to marry, had chosen to love—half a lifetime ago, it seemed. It was a love she had never given up on, despite the years and the circumstances.

Automatically Mac straightened, pulling his aching shoulders away from the wall, and began to walk across the waiting room to greet Kincaid. Mac was the head of this family, had been since his father's death, and in situations like this, greeting visitors was his job.

Sam Kincaid's eyes, sharp and piercing under the white brows, focused on Mac as he walked toward him, limping a little more than usual from standing most of the night. The hazel eyes considered his face, rested a heartbeat on the black patch and the scarring, and then moved away, dismissing him.

He was no one Sam knew, Mac realized. No one he would recognize. *And therefore no one who had any rights here,* he acknowledged bitterly. No more rights than any other friend of Chase McCullar would have had in this situation.

Mac stopped, forced by that unwanted realization to simply watch as Sam Kincaid walked over to his daughter. When she saw her father, Samantha stood and was enclosed in the old man's arms. Sam hugged her fiercely, rocking her slender body gently in his embrace.

"I'm so sorry, baby," he said.

Even from here Mac could hear the rumbling baritone. Despite the realization he had just made, he moved again, irresistibly drawn by the tableau the three of them made: Sam and his daughter holding each other; Jenny still seated, watching them, her dark eyes full of pain.

Finally Sam pulled away and looked down into Samantha's face. "You got the best folks taking care of him?" he asked.

She shook her head—not a denial, but an acknowledgment of ignorance. Her eyes found Mac's face, pleading for him to answer that.

"There wasn't time to call anyone in," Mac explained. Again the old man's gaze focused on him, considering. Kincaid was listening to what he was saying, but just as obviously he was reserving judgment on whether or not it deserved his approval. "We just barely got him here. I didn't think..."

Mac hesitated, reluctant to confess that he really hadn't believed Chase would make it. Remembering again the seemingly endless wait for the helicopter while Jenny had tried to keep his brother alive. Remembering the looks on the paramedics' faces as they made their first assessment of Chase's condition. But his brother *was* still alive. He had to believe that. Surely to God someone would have told them by now if he wasn't.

Sam's assessment hadn't stopped when Mac's explanation faltered. Most people were embarrassed to make a prolonged appraisal of his face, but the old man seemed to be scrutinizing every centimeter of the damaged skin. For a second, Mac wondered if it was possible that Sam suspected; but if Jenny didn't recognize him, he reasoned, then it seemed impossible that Kincaid could.

"Who are you?" Sam asked bluntly.

"This is Matt Dawson. He's an old friend of Chase's," Samantha said.

"You were with him when it happened?" Sam questioned.

"Yes, sir."

The old man's mouth pursed and his eyes were still cold, still judgmental, but he didn't ask the other question that had clearly been in his tone. Thankfully that had remained unexpressed.

It was, of course, the same question that Mac had been asking himself throughout this endless night. *Then how come*

you let him get gunned down like that? How come you didn't
protect him?

"What do they tell you?" Sam asked.

Mac assumed the question was for Samantha, but the hard
eyes were still on his. "Not a damn thing," he admitted softly.

"Bastards," Sam said succinctly. "They never told me
nothing when Betsy was dying. They don't ever tell you nothing."

"I'm sure that as soon as they know something definite…"
Jenny suggested softly.

Mac was a little disconcerted to find that Jenny was standing
beside him, almost against his elbow. While his attention had
been focused on Sam, she must have risen. He resisted the
still-familiar urge to put his arm around her shoulders and pull
her protectively against his body, just as Sam was holding his
daughter.

"Where's Cupcake?" Kincaid asked.

Her mouth lifting into a slight smile for the first time tonight, Samantha nodded toward the upholstered bench against
the wall. Chase's daughter was asleep, her tiny thumb securely
in her mouth.

"I know she shouldn't be here," Samantha said, "but I
didn't have anyone to leave her with."

"I'll get somebody to take her to the ranch," Sam promised. "Rosita can look after her."

Samantha seemed to be considering the idea, without much
enthusiasm, given her constant struggle to live her own life
without Sam's interference. Her options here, however, were
obviously limited.

"I can take her home with me," Jenny offered, reading and
understanding Samantha's hesitation. "Or I can stay at your
house. Maybe Mandy will feel better, safer, at home. This is
bound to be traumatic for her, no matter what we do, but I
think if she's at home…" Again, Jenny let her sensible suggestion trail off.

"Mrs. McCullar," Sam said, holding out his hand.

Jenny's small fingers slipped inside the firm grip of the big, liver-spotted fist he'd offered her. "It's good to see you again, Mr. Kincaid," she said.

"You staying out there?" Sam asked. He was still holding Jenny's hand, but his attention had refocused on Mac.

"I'm staying," Mac agreed.

Sam nodded. "Then I guess that's all right. You know you're *all* welcome to come to my place."

Sam Kincaid's "place" was the biggest ranch in this part of Texas, immense and immensely successful. The casual invitation was heartfelt, however, as sincerely south-Texas hospitable as it would have been coming from any of their less exalted neighbors.

"I think it might be more...profitable," Mac suggested, "if I stay at Chase's." He thought the old man would understand what he meant by that. More chance to investigate who had done this to Chase.

"Any idea what was behind it?" Sam asked. The shrewd eyes, now clouded with age, were still pinning him.

"Some," Mac said.

"You *know* why somebody shot Chase?"

That was the other question Mac had been thinking about most of this endless night. "I'm not sure they were trying for Chase," he finally admitted.

"Not sure?" Sam's mouth had pursed again, considering.

"We were standing together. It was dark enough that...they could have been trying for me," he confessed. The nightmare idea that Chase had taken a bullet meant for him wasn't much worse than the other possibility, but because it *was* the worst of the two possibilities, he offered it first.

"Why?" Sam asked.

"Chase had let it be known that we were investigating Mac McCullar's murder."

The old man didn't say anything. His eyes were still hard, but there was something else in them now. Something besides speculation. "And you think somebody may have been gunning for you because of that?" he asked finally.

"It's possible," Mac acknowledged. Kincaid was known for his shrewdness, but Mac couldn't believe that the old man had figured this out. No one else seemed to suspect he wasn't who he claimed to be, but there was something in that considering look which indicated that Sam Kincaid understood more about what was going on than he should have.

"That doesn't make any sense," Jenny said. "At least, no more sense than someone targeting Chase for that same reason. And besides…" she began, but her voice faltered. She tightened her lips briefly and then went on, forcing herself to finish the painful confession she had begun. "*I'm* the one who urged Chase to tell people what you two intended. I'm the one who said he should shake the trees."

Her dark eyes were on Samantha, apology and confession in them. And apparently all the guilt Jenny had felt through these terrible hours—a guilt that was surely as strong and as painful as his, Mac realized.

"Oh, Jenny," Samantha said. Only that, but she moved away from her father and put her arms around her sister-in-law, pulling the smaller woman close. "This isn't your fault. None of this is your fault. We both know Chase well enough to know that once he made up his stubborn McCullar mind to do something, he wouldn't consider anything else. Not the danger. Not anything. Chase needed to know what happened to Mac. We all need to know."

The reassurances were low, murmured against the softness of Jenny's cheek, but the circle in which they stood was small enough that they all heard them.

Again Sam Kincaid's eyes were on Matt Dawson's scarred face, watching his reaction. And considering.

WHEN THEY FINALLY received it, the news was far better than what they had been dreading throughout the agonizing night. The angle at which Chase's head was turned when the powerful bullet struck had saved his life, the doctors suggested, keeping it from plowing into his brain. Instead it had cut a deep gash along the side of his head. The bad news was that Chase was still unconscious.

Sam had begun calling specialists almost from the moment he'd arrived, using his cell phone with the same expertise he was reputed to have had at one time with a rope and a branding iron. So there was no doubt that Chase McCullar would, from now on at least, have the best care money could buy. Kincaid had a lot of that to spread around, and apparently he wasn't opposed to spending it on his son-in-law.

They were allowed to see Chase only briefly. He was surrounded by tubes and monitors, seeming almost a stranger. What if he hadn't grabbed Chase's arm, Mac thought, turning him around at the last second...?

Mac's nausea returned, slamming into his gut with all the memories—the uncertainty of life and death, of course, but also all the memories of the seemingly endless pain and the frustrating disability that had followed it. All remembered. All endlessly despised.

The others began to file out. Mac touched his brother's limp fingers, remembering their strength, remembering them fastened around his during the darkest days of his life. Remembering how they shook as they gripped Lighthorse Harry's bridle a couple of mornings ago. And the promise Mac McCullar made to his brother before he left his hospital room, only Chase would have understood.

WITH THE DAWN, HOWEVER, all the practical considerations of life pushed their way into their anxiety. One of those considerations was Mandy, of course. Another was the care of the animals at both ranches. Someone had to see to those things, and no one expected Samantha to leave the hospital.

Mac didn't want to leave, either, but staying at Chase's bedside was another right he had given up five years ago. Unless he was ready to reclaim it openly now, it would make no sense to anyone for him to let Jenny and Mandy drive back home by themselves and tend to those necessary chores.

All the logic in the world, however, didn't make walking out of that hospital, leaving his injured brother behind, any easier. It hadn't felt like logic. It had felt like desertion. Betrayal. And cowardice.

Mandy was on the seat of the pickup between them, her head in Jenny's lap and her feet and legs across Mac's. She had been too tired and perhaps too disoriented to pay Mac much attention. And that was a relief. He wasn't sure he was up to dealing with the little girl's revulsion this morning.

He had known from Mandy's reaction that he'd only been fooling himself in thinking that his face wasn't all that bad anymore. Obviously it was still bad enough to frighten children. Maybe even women and children.

Except... The remembrance of Jenny's lips opening, her face lifting in undeniable invitation had also stayed with him during the hours of this long night. It was still there, still cherished, even if it had been pushed aside by what had happened to Chase.

And what did that really mean? he wondered. Maybe only that it had been dark enough out there that she'd forgotten what he looked like. He knew there was nothing else the plastic surgeons could do. He thought he had learned a long time ago not to worry about his appearance. He *thought* he'd learned a lot of things. Unconsciously he shook his head, his breath sighing out in a small hiss of self-disgust.

''He'll be all right,'' Jenny said. She glanced away from the road as she said it, meeting his eye quickly, before her concentration returned to the heavy morning traffic. ''Chase is strong. He's going to make it. We have to believe that.''

He turned to look at her, the classic features profiled against the thin light of morning. She was so damn beautiful. She always had been. All her life. When she was old enough to start dating, old enough for him to finally ask her, he hadn't been able to believe she was willing to go out with him. And then she had never dated anyone else.

Until Trent Richardson. Until…

"Matt?" she questioned. Her eyes flicked toward his again. "You okay?"

"You don't have to worry about me, Jenny," he advised quietly. He had never wanted that. Never wanted Jenny going through what Samantha was going through this morning. That endless waiting. Wondering. Worrying. Just learning to deal with it all.

She laughed softly. "I guess I'm a worrier by nature. I try to take care of everybody." Her eyes went back to the highway and the speeding cars. "Except Mac," she added softly when he didn't respond. "Mac always took care of me."

He turned his head away, his unseeing gaze seeming to focus on the scenery that flew by outside the window. *"Mac always took care of me." And that was why, my Jenny-Wren, I left five years ago. You will never understand that, never forgive it, I know, but that was exactly the reason why.*

BUCK ELKINS WAS AT Chase's house when they got there. The McCullar stock had already been tended to, he told them. He and a couple of the neighbors had come over to do that as soon as they'd heard.

"I knew Samantha had let her help go when Chase came back home. We've been over at your place, too, Jenny," he said.

"Thanks, Buck. You don't know what it means to have neighbors at a time like this," Jenny said. She had come around to get Amanda, but Mac had already begun awkwardly lifting the little girl out of the truck when she arrived.

"I can carry her," Jenny offered.

"*I* can carry her. Don't worry," he added. "She's still asleep."

"I didn't mean that," Jenny said.

She moved out of his way, allowing him room to maneuver

the little girl out of the truck. Mac lifted her against his left side, holding her with his good arm, settling it under her small bottom. Mandy stirred in her sleep, and then put her arms around Mac's neck, nuzzling her face into his shoulder.

"Daddy?" she said. She raised her head slightly to look at him, and Mac waited for her reaction, his stomach knotted. Nothing happened, except the small blond head settled again onto his shoulder. Settled and stayed.

"Door's unlocked," Buck said. "I guess Mrs. McCullar left it that way last night. I checked to make sure everything was cut off inside. Folks sometimes forget and leave appliances on in an emergency. I didn't want to go until somebody came home."

"Thank you," Jenny said again.

"What the hell happened, Jenny?" Mac heard Buck ask as he began walking away from the pickup. "Why didn't you call me? I didn't know anything about it until I heard it on the scanner."

"There wasn't time. We were all at the shack—"

"We?" Buck interrupted.

"Chase, Matt and I," Jenny explained. "We were all standing outside the line shack, and the shot just came out of the darkness. There was no warning. No noise before or after. Nobody around. As soon we realized how badly Chase was hurt, Matt drove home to call for the medical chopper. We never thought to call you."

Mac stopped at the screen door, shifting Mandy's body to make his hold on the sleeping child more secure. When he bent his knees slightly to reach the handle with his good hand, he heard Jenny say, "I think I'd better help get Mandy tucked in. Come on inside. I'll make some coffee."

Mac had managed the screen door and was already inside when she arrived. He heard her footsteps behind him, but he didn't wait. He knew the way to Mandy's room. It was where he had slept the one night he had spent here.

He carried the little girl into the bedroom, but once there

he did wait for Jenny to pull down the covers on the narrow bed. When he carefully deposited the child in it, she opened her eyes and looked up at him. Mac stepped back, afraid she'd be frightened, and turned to leave, letting Jenny take over.

He could hear her murmuring reassuringly to Mandy as he made his way to the kitchen. He had also heard Jenny mention coffee outside, and after the tasteless, colored water he'd been drinking at the hospital all night, the thought of real coffee sounded impossibly inviting. Maybe his brain would work a little better, and he could figure out where he ought to start looking for the bastards who had shot his brother.

Mac was surprised to find Buck Elkins had accepted Jenny's invitation. More surprised to find the sheriff was already putting fragrant ground coffee into the filtered cone of the coffee maker.

"Jenny offered me a cup of coffee," Buck said, looking over his shoulder. He slid the cone into the pot and pressed the switch before he turned around, holding out his hand.

"Buck Elkins," he said. His expression was pleasant, but his eyes were as considering as Sam Kincaid's had been.

Mac ignored the hand. That had been hard to learn to do, but he'd had years of practice now. He nodded instead. "Matt Dawson."

"Jenny said you and Chase are old friends."

Apparently he had trained Buck pretty well, Mac thought. That was exactly the question he would have asked. Elkins had been his deputy at one time, after Chase had left to go to work for the DEA, driven off by Sam Kincaid or maybe by his seemingly hopeless love for Samantha.

"That's right," Mac said.

"You ex-DEA, too?" The sheriff's arm had finally dropped, but his eyes had dropped also, briefly examining Mac's unmoving right hand.

"No," Mac said. *Next question,* he thought, again almost amused by their careful duet.

"But you were in law enforcement?" Elkins asked.

His eyes were on Mac's face, avoiding the patch and the scarring. Mac found that he preferred Sam Kincaid's open assessment to the pretense that there wasn't anything to stare at. To be fair, however, this was the way most people looked at him.

"Looks like one of you beat me to the coffee," Jenny said from behind him.

At least it saved him from having to tell another lie, Mac thought. That was about all he'd done since he'd come home. Lie to people. To friends and to his family. Only with Chase had he been able to be honest, to be himself, and now…

"You both looked like you could use some," Buck said.

He smiled at Jenny. She took three mugs out of the cabinet, apparently very familiar with Samantha's kitchen. She poured the coffee, and they stood in silence for a few seconds, drinking the scalding brew Buck had made.

The coffee was as strong as that he used to make at the sheriff's office, Mac thought. They used to joke about having to cut it with a knife. If Buck's interrogation skills had improved through the years, apparently his coffee making hadn't.

Buck set his cup down on the counter while it was still half-full. He didn't ask any more questions, but before he left, he apologized to Jenny.

"I guess I was wrong about that plastic bag, Jenny. Wrong in thinking the traffickers would just give up with Chase living here."

"You think…" Jenny began, and then she paused.

Just as he had been, Mac knew, Jenny had been convinced last night that Chase had been shot because of his notice to the county that he intended to catch his brother's murderers. Now the sheriff's words gave them another possibility to consider.

A possibility that Mac, guilt-ridden, hadn't even thought of through the hours he'd spent regretting telling Chase he needed to know who had put that bomb in his truck five years ago. Hours he'd spent blaming himself for what had happened to his brother.

"You think whoever left that sack out there had something to do with this?" Jenny asked.

"Don't you?" Buck asked.

His voice was puzzled, and Mac realized that it probably *was* a far more likely scenario than imagining a murderer who had gotten away with a five-year-old homicide would panic at the first hint that someone was reopening the case.

The fact that Chase, an ex-DEA agent, was now living on McCullar land would surely be enough to give whoever had been using this ranch for trafficking a lot of reason for concern.

"I guess I just wasn't thinking too clearly," Jenny said softly.

Her gaze moved to Mac, but he controlled his features, not even meeting her eyes. He didn't want Buck to think he was anything more than an old friend who had come to visit and had ended up in the middle of all this.

"You're the one who told me somebody was running drugs across your property. I don't know why anybody else would want Chase dead, Jenny. Do you?" Buck's eyes had followed Jenny's and his question might have been addressed to Mac, as well. If so, Mac didn't answer it.

"No one," Jenny said. "I can't think of anyone who would want Chase dead."

Buck nodded, his eyes still on Mac. "Well, I'll go take a look around out at the line shack, see if I can find anything. We might get lucky. You call me when you hear something from the hospital. I'd like to know how Chase's doing. I'd also like you to call me if you think of anything else about last night that I ought to know."

"Okay," Jenny agreed.

When the door closed behind the sheriff, Jenny's brown eyes met Mac's. "*Could* it have been about drugs and not anything to do with Mac's murder?" she asked.

"I don't know. But he's right. It sure as hell is something else to think about."

IT WAS A COUPLE of hours after Buck's departure. During their slow passage, Matt Dawson had been acting like a caged bear, Jenny thought. He flinched every time the phone rang, and it had rung off and on all morning. One call had been from Samantha, reporting that there was no change in Chase's condition. The others had come from neighbors and friends who were just finding out Chase had been shot.

"Would you trust me with your pickup?" Matt asked her finally.

"Of course," Jenny said, agreeing to his request without any hesitation, without even having to think about it. Her truck was an automatic and he'd had no trouble driving it last night.

"I appreciate that," Matt said. "I won't let anything happen to it, Jenny."

She remembered Chase's anxiety the morning Matt had taken Harry. She knew just how he had felt. "It's not the truck I'll worry about," she said softly.

His eyes skimmed over her face, settling briefly on her mouth. She wondered if he were remembering last night. *Before* Chase had interrupted them.

"I'll be careful," he promised. "I'll just feel better if I check things out for myself."

"At my place?" she asked, puzzled.

That hadn't been his intent. That much was clear when he didn't respond to her question. Finally, however, he nodded, picking up the keys from where she had left them on the table.

He went out the back door without any other explanation, and she watched through the kitchen window as he started the truck and drove it out of the yard. It wasn't until he had it out on the dirt road that she realized she'd been holding her breath.

She released it, listening to the sound sighing out into the stillness. Mandy was still asleep, and suddenly, once again, Jenny was aware of being alone. Disgusted with herself, she picked up the phone and stood for a minute, considering exactly who else she needed to call about Chase.

She should call Trent. He had probably been worried if he'd tried to call her last night, and he usually did—every Sunday night. Only the fact that she had seen him at the wedding two days ago might have kept him from making that habitual call.

She didn't want to talk to Trent right now, and she knew why. *Later,* she thought. *A lot later.*

Instead she asked the operator to connect her to the hotel in Galveston where Anne and Rio had gone for their honeymoon. That trip had been her wedding gift to them. She was probably the only one who knew how little money Rio had. It had seemed something that she could do for him that he wouldn't be able to refuse. Thankfully, he hadn't.

Now she was going to be the one who would destroy the joy of their trip, but Rio would want to know about Chase. She was as certain of that as she was certain he had had nothing to do with Mac's death. *"Mac was my brother,"* he had told her, and what that relationship meant to him had been evident in his quiet voice. So was Chase, of course, no matter what enmity had been between them in the past. Rio would want to know.

As she listened to the distant ringing, Jenny found herself hoping that she wouldn't have to leave him a message. She glanced at her watch. It was still early enough that surely they wouldn't already be up and out. Then she smiled, remembering her own honeymoon. They wouldn't be up and out.

Rio answered, his voice fogged with sleep.

"Rio," she said softly, trying to think, now that she'd reached him, exactly what she wanted to say. "It's Jenny."

"Jenny?" he questioned. More awake now, more in command, more Rio. "What's wrong?"

He had known at once that she'd never have called him unless something was wrong—something serious. That made it a little easier to get the words out.

"It's Chase. Chase has been shot. He had surgery last night, but…"

The silence at the other end of the line was too long. *"Mac was my brother,"* Jenny thought again, remembering exactly what had been in Rio's voice.

"We'll be right there," he assured her. "A few hours, Jenny. I'll be there."

"Rio, you don't have to—"

"Where are you?" he interrupted.

"I'm at Chase's."

"I'm on my way," he promised, and the connection was broken.

She held the phone for a moment, wondering if she had done the right thing, but there had been no hesitation in Rio's response. He was coming home, and she wanted him here. She needed him. All the McCullars together again.

She shook her head, wondering why she had thought that. Then she realized for the first time that if Chase died, there would be no McCullars. The line would end. Mandy would marry, of course, but her children would bear someone else's name. And she and Mac…

She pushed that thought aside, swallowing the lump of pain and loss that always resulted. She and Mac had never had children. If Chase died, only Rio, who was not even a McCullar—who had never been acknowledged by his father and didn't bear his name—would be left of that strong line.

She shook her head, unable to imagine this land passing out of McCullar hands. That was what Trent wanted her to do, she knew. To sell the ranch and its memories, destroying, he believed, the ties that kept her here.

But that isn't it, Trent, she thought again. *It isn't this land. That isn't what you have to fear. It's the memories. All my memories.*

Even as she thought that, she realized that those same memories had not interfered with whatever she felt for Matt Dawson. That, too, was something Trent didn't yet realize. Something that she knew would be almost impossible for him to understand when she finally had to explain.

Chapter Six

As he climbed out of the pickup at the line shack, Mac found himself wishing Jenny hadn't told the sheriff as much as she had about what had happened here last night. He needed to look around without wondering whether what he was finding were traces of Buck's search or signs left by the person who had shot Chase.

It took him only a few seconds to decide on the exact spot where they'd been standing last night. After all, Chase's black pickup was still here, parked in the same spot where he and Jenny had left it. They had ridden to the hospital together, Jenny driving her truck, as she had this morning.

And there was the blood on the ground, of course, although if he hadn't known what he was looking at, he might never have recognized the dark stain as blood. But it was, and that was how Mac knew he was standing where Chase had been when that single shot was fired. He made himself picture their positions, reliving the split second before he heard the sound of the rifle, trying to remember the angle at which Chase's head turned when he reached out and grabbed his arm.

When he had his own body in that exact position, Mac slowly turned his head to the left. Despite the low brim of his Stetson, his eye narrowed against the glare of the desert sun. In his direct line of sight, the trajectory perfect, was the low bluff that looked down on the McCullar houses.

He should have remembered it last night, he realized, because it also looked down, of course, on the line shack. A sniper with a rifle and a good scope could easily have made that shot, despite the poor light. Mac could have made it. At least at one time, he could have made it, he amended.

He needed to get up there and look around. He wondered again if Buck had done what he'd said he would. Whether the sheriff, too, had come out here and made these same calculations. If he had, he might already have been to the top of that bluff.

Except Elkins hadn't known the details Mac knew. He hadn't questioned Jenny long enough to be able to figure this out. He would eventually. Buck was too good a lawman not to.

Mac knew that the sheriff had been cutting Jenny some slack this morning, acting out of kindness, considering her tiredness and her natural distress, as a friend would do. But in giving her that consideration, he had also delayed his own investigation, and that was always a mistake.

I didn't teach you as well as I thought I did, Buck, Mac thought, smiling. *And this time I guess that means I got lucky.*

His eye fell again to the stain on the grayish tan soil. His brother's blood. *Blood is thicker than water.* He remembered telling Rio that. It had been a long time ago, but nothing ever changed about the truth of those words, about what they meant.

His vision blurred with the thought of losing Chase, a thought whose horror he had fought against through these long hours. Chase had been the rock he had clung to five years ago. The only person Mac had known he could trust to do what he'd asked. Despite his misgivings about the course his brother had chosen, Chase had never let him down, never betrayed him. And now...

Reining in emotions that threatened the control needed to do this job, Mac lifted his gaze from the blood on the ground and fastened it again on the bluff. That was where he needed to be. Up there. Once, he would have driven the pickup to its base and clambered easily up that rocky slope. Five years ago he would have done that without even thinking about it. But not now.

Instead, he'd have to go around and connect with the main road. That should take him within four or five miles of the top of the bluff. He could drive part of that, and then he'd have to walk, a couple of hot and inevitably painful miles. Not that he minded those, but when he got there, he was well aware that there would probably be nothing that would be helpful. No clue to whoever had shot Chase.

That was the way law enforcement worked. You checked out every possibility, every lead, knowing that ninety-nine percent of them wouldn't amount to a hill of beans. And then every once in a while you got lucky.

Luck and persistence. He had always believed those were the keys to good police work. He would damn well have the persistence. His mouth flattened as he remembered his brother lying in that obscene nest of tubes and wires that were keeping him alive. What he really needed now, Mac McCullar thought, was just a little bit of the other for a change.

IT WAS LATE AFTERNOON when Rio and Anne arrived at Chase's house. When she heard the car pull into the yard, Jenny thought it might be Matt. She hadn't heard from him since he'd left this morning. She had called her house a half-dozen times, but no one had answered, and her anxiety had increased throughout the long hours of the day she'd spent entertaining Amanda, answering the little girl's unanswerable questions about where her mama and daddy were and when they'd be coming home.

Samantha had called a couple of times, but there was really nothing to report. Nothing had changed about Chase's condition. *At least he's still alive,* Jenny thought, but somehow that anxiety had become so mixed with her worry over Matt's disappearance that she had even thought about phoning Buck

Elkins and asking him to go out to her place to check on Dawson.

Except she knew how much Chase's enigmatic friend would hate that. There was no doubt in her mind that Matt Dawson would resent the hell out of her sending somebody out to look for him.

So when she heard the car, she had rushed out onto the narrow porch. She had been glad to see Rio and Anne, of course, but she had to admit that she had also been disappointed. Disappointed that it wasn't the tall, scarred man she'd been worrying about through most of the day.

Rio hadn't said anything. He had taken one look at her face and, as Sam Kincaid had done with Samantha this morning, he had simply enfolded her in his arms. The arms that held her were far younger and stronger than Sam's, but they were just as welcome. Jenny hadn't realized how much she needed someone to hold her. Someone she could depend on.

"Tell us what happened, Jenny," Anne said. "And then tell us what we can do to help."

Jenny stepped back, pushing gently out of Rio's embrace, but before she moved away from him entirely, she stood on tiptoe to touch her lips to his dark cheek. The kiss was sisterly, just like the quick peck Chase had given her a few days ago, and as unusual between them as Chase's had been. No matter that they had grown so close during the weeks Rio had lived with her, Jenny had never before dared to show him how she felt about him.

"It's going to be all right, Jenny," he said. "Chase will be all right."

"I know," she agreed. Habit and not conviction. "I also know that you both must be exhausted, but…" She hesitated to ask, but she needed to know so desperately, and Rio was the ideal person to send. She even had a legitimate excuse for asking him to make the trip—his beloved black stallion.

"If you're going over to see Diablo," she asked, "would you do me a favor?"

"You need something from the house?" Rio suggested.

She knew he was expecting a request for a nightgown or a toothbrush maybe, certainly not the one she was about to make of him. "Not exactly. I need you to…find somebody."

"Find somebody?"

"Chase's friend, Matt Dawson. He went over to my place this morning to check on things, and he's not back. I've called a few times, but I'm getting a little concerned."

"You want to explain why?"

Rio's dark eyes were questioning, but she knew that despite his questions, he would do what she'd asked. He would naturally be the one to go over to check on the horses, and he might as well check on Matt at the same time.

"Come on inside," Jenny invited, delaying that explanation as she tried to think exactly how to phrase it without giving away too much of what she felt about Matt Dawson. "I'll tell you everything that happened. At least…everything I know."

WHEN RIO PULLED THE CAR up before Jenny's house, nothing seemed to have changed about the ranch since he'd left a few days ago. Of course, around here change came slowly, if it came at all. Rio didn't know why he would have expected anything to be different. Maybe because his own life was so different now than when he'd come here that night to find his black. And had found Anne Richardson instead.

He could never have imagined the changes that had resulted from that discovery, not even in his wildest dreams. He had arrived on McCullar land with nothing, and in the few weeks he'd spent here, all that had changed. His entire life had changed.

Now he had Anne's love and Jenny's friendship. His beloved Diablo had been returned to him. Even Chase McCullar seemed almost accepting of his innocence, maybe even accepting of him. At least there had been a beginning there. The beginning of a relationship, he remembered, that might now go no further because some coward's bullet, flying out of the darkness, might have destroyed it before it could become anything more.

Denying that possibility, Rio got out of the car, looking around. There was no sign of Jenny's truck. No sign of Chase's friend. He'd check in the house before he left, but it looked as deserted as the rest of the place. He knew where Jenny kept her spare key. The other one was on the key ring she had given Dawson.

He wondered about the normally levelheaded Jenny doing that, trusting a stranger enough to give him the keys to her house and her truck. He wondered momentarily if this mysterious Dawson could have cleaned Jenny out and then driven her pickup off into the sunset. Or below the border.

Except he was Chase's friend, he reminded himself. Whatever Dawson was, he had apparently achieved something Rio wasn't sure he ever would—Chase McCullar's friendship.

He shrugged off that regret and moved toward the corral. He whistled softly, a melodic two-note trill, knowing that wherever he was, Diablo would come. He would put Jenny's horses in the barn, he decided, since no one might get back out here tonight to see about them. They'd be safer there, and there was already a chill in the November twilight.

RIO STOOD FOR A MOMENT in the pleasant dimness of the barn after he'd fed and watered Jenny's horses and Diablo. He ran his hand over the gleaming coat of the black, allowing himself to remember. His and Anne's first kiss had taken place in this barn. As had his confrontation with Chase that led to a bare-knuckled fistfight, which, if Anne hadn't intervened, had seemed destined to continue until one of them killed the other.

He also remembered Anne the first time he'd seen her, standing in the double doorway of this building, holding Mac McCullar's big gun pointed steadily at him. And he remembered Mac. It was the oldest of those memories. That of his dead brother standing in that same dark doorway.

Rio's eyes lifted to that opening. It was darker in the barn now than it was outside, despite the gathering twilight. Almost as dark as it had been that night. And then, as Rio watched, a figure moved again into that doorway.

The hair slowly rose all over Rio's body, the most primitive human reaction to that which cannot be explained by logic. He shivered, his brain trying to deny what he was seeing.

He closed his eyes. It was only a trick of the fading light, he argued with himself, but when he opened them again, the broad-shouldered figure was still there, clearly silhouetted against the faint, ghostly twilight of the dying sun. Rio had dreamed about this, had remembered it, too many times to be mistaken.

Mac McCullar was standing in the doorway of his barn, just as he had stood there more than fifteen years ago when Rio had first come to this ranch, a bitter, lost thirteen-year-old, skirting dangerously close to going bad.

"Who the hell are you and what are you doing in here?"

Not Mac. That wasn't Mac's voice. He would have recognized his brother's voice anywhere, anytime, despite the passage of years, despite the fact that they had had only that one conversation. But he had never forgotten what Mac had told him that night. The soft words had been engraved on his memory. On his soul.

"I don't have enough brothers," Mac had said to his father's unwanted bastard, his deep voice gentle with undisguised amusement, *"that I can afford to lose track of them."*

It had been the long-awaited acknowledgment of kinship Rio had never received from his father. A precious gift, freely given by a brother he had never known. A brother he had come to steal from. And he had never forgotten it or forgotten the debt he owed to Mac McCullar.

"A better question might be what the hell you're doing here," Rio demanded.

He could clearly see the gun the man was holding. It was just as big and was handled as competently as the one Anne had held on him the night he'd gotten out of prison. And as it had been that night, it was pointed straight at his heart.

"My name's Matt Dawson. Jenny sent me over here to check on things," the man in the doorway said.

Rio was surprised Dawson had taken time to explain. He might just as well have chosen to shoot first and ask questions later, especially considering what had happened to Chase last night. Given those circumstances, Rio wasn't sure that, finding an unexpected and unidentified intruder in a dark barn, he would have been that restrained.

"I'm Rio," he said simply.

"Chase's brother."

"Half brother," Rio clarified. He wasn't sure Chase would want to claim any closer relationship to him than the one he couldn't deny, the one that had always existed between them.

"Sorry," Dawson said, lowering the gun. "I didn't know you were back."

"Today."

"Jenny sent you over here to check on me?" There was a trace of amused resignation in the question.

"I think she was a little concerned when you seemed to have disappeared. I guess that's natural, considering what happened to Chase last night."

Rio led Diablo into the stall as he talked, fastening the door on the stallion. Since the gun was no longer focused on his midsection, he had taken that as permission to move. He shook his head a little as he double-checked the stall lock, thinking about that eerie sense of déjà vu he'd felt when he had looked up and found Matt Dawson standing in that doorway.

He still didn't understand the strength of that feeling. This man was as tall as Mac and his shoulders were as wide, but he was much leaner, his body almost too finely pared down. And his voice was nothing like Mac's.

"Did Samantha call?" Dawson asked.

"Nothing's changed," Rio acknowledged.

Dawson had moved into the barn now, coming much closer,

and for the first time Rio got a good look at him, despite the dimness. If he had been able to see his face before, Rio realized, he never would have made that mistake. Mac McCullar had been a good-looking man, and this poor bastard…

But he didn't let his eyes avoid the man's scarred visage. Beauty was only skin-deep, as Rio Delgado had ample cause to understand. It didn't have anything to do with the quality of a man. If Chase McCullar thought enough of Dawson to offer him his friendship, then Rio knew there was character here, hidden beneath that marred exterior.

He held out his hand. Dawson's gaze didn't release his, but he didn't reach out to take the hand Rio had offered. *Because of something Chase had told him?* Rio wondered, as he allowed his own hand to fall. Because this man was Chase's friend, and Rio was only his bastard half brother, an unwanted McCullar connection?

Matt Dawson's thin lips moved, the left corner of them tilted slowly upward. "Bad hand," he said softly. "Nothing else. Not what you're thinking, anyway." Without another word he turned and retraced his steps to the open doorway and disappeared through it into the growing darkness outside.

Behind him, Rio found he had stopped breathing. *How the hell…?* he wondered, and then, shaking his head again, he followed Chase McCullar's friend out into the twilight.

WHEN THE TWO VEHICLES drove into the yard at Chase's, Jenny again came out onto the porch. She watched Matt Dawson walk across the yard, moving through the broken pattern of light and shadow the rising moon cast through the limbs of the old cottonwood tree. He brushed Mandy's rope swing as he passed by, touching it into gentle motion.

He was limping again, the hesitation in his long stride much more noticeable than she had ever seen it before. Her eyes followed his progress up the two low steps, and then he stopped in front of where she was standing and looked down at her.

She shook her head, questioning the intensity of that look.

"Nothing," he said softly, the word loud enough only for her ears. "I didn't find anything, Jenny. Not even a footprint."

She nodded, fighting the urge to touch him, to reassure herself that he was really all right, other than the obvious exhaustion she could read in his face.

"Is that where you were?" she asked. "Looking for footprints?"

"He said you were worried," Matt said. His head tilted back toward Rio, who was walking across the yard toward them. Matt's voice was still low, still intimate, but she knew they would have only these few seconds alone.

"I was worried," she admitted. She made no apology. Maybe she had no right to be concerned about him, but she had been. And after last night...

"I'm sorry," he said, the words almost a whisper. "I didn't mean to cause you any more worry." His left hand touched her arm, cupping her elbow lightly, and then he added, "Offer to drive me out to the line shack after supper," he said. It wasn't a request. And he seemed to take her agreement for granted.

Suddenly her heart was hammering as it had last night. Just as it had when his mouth began to lower to cover hers. There was more to that command, she knew, than the need for someone to provide transportation. Rio would have done that. This was something else, and she understood that.

She nodded again, her eyes holding his. His fingers squeezed her arm gently, his thumb moving slowly across the soft skin, almost a caress, and then he released her. He opened the screen door and disappeared inside just as Rio arrived at the foot of the steps.

"Any word?" Chase's half brother asked.

He was standing on the bottom step, so they were almost the same height. His dark eyes were concerned. For her or for Chase? she wondered.

"Nothing's changed," she said.

Rio nodded and then he, too, climbed the steps and opened the screen door. He left Jenny alone in the moonlight, watching the shifting shadows and the slow, uneven drift of Mandy's swing.

"THE SHOT CAME FROM the top of the bluff," Matt said. "I should have figured that out last night."

"Even if you had, even if you'd gone up there then, whoever it was would have been long gone," she reminded him.

She was driving slowly, although the narrow dirt road was infinitely familiar. She could have driven it blindfolded. But there was no hurry. She was glad to be in the dark interior of the truck. And glad to be alone with him. It was almost as if they were isolated in here, protected from whatever evil was in the desert night that had once seemed so safe to her.

"There wasn't a casing or a print, and no tire tracks."

"So you think whoever did it walked in?"

"Or climbed up," he agreed.

"Why?"

"Less chance of being seen."

"Seen by whom? There's no one for miles."

"By me, maybe. I wish I knew who Chase told I was staying out here."

"I can't imagine that he'd tell anyone. Why would he?"

"Then how would they know to stake out that bluff?" Matt asked.

It made sense, Jenny realized, and it also explained why he had thought that bullet might have been meant for him. He was the one who was living out here.

"If they knew you were at the shack, then they'd know Chase would come out eventually," she reminded him.

"I guess you're right."

"Besides, there's no reason to think Buck's not right."

"About it being traffickers?"

"I can't think of a single thing that might have a chance of driving Samantha and me off of this land, other than Chase being killed.''

"You think somebody wants the ranch? There are a lot of other places on the border that nobody owns. Why expend so much energy acquiring this one?''

"The ford, maybe. You can just about walk across the river there any time of the year. And if they're bringing in drugs—''

"Hell, Jenny, they bring in drugs by the truckload. El Paso, Laredo, Brownsville—anywhere there are bridges. Why come way the hell out here where there's nothing? Where you have to drive across that river and take a chance on being seen or heard?''

"Because things are tightening up. They X-ray entire trucks now before they let them cross those bridges. Maybe it's beginning to have some effect.''

"Not enough,'' Matt said. "Shooting Chase to get access to that ford makes no sense. It's got to be the other.''

"Mac's murder.''

"It's the only thing that *does* make any sense,'' he said again, maybe continuing their argument in his own mind.

Jenny pulled her truck up beside the black shadow cast by Chase's. Neither of them said anything for a moment, but Matt made no move to get out. Nor did he invite her to come inside with him. And so she waited, her heart again beating loudly enough that she was really afraid he might be able to hear it.

"Then…'' she began, knowing where the word would lead. Resisting, and yet not wanting to resist. And besides, she was right. "Then if that's true, you're in as much danger as Chase was,'' she said.

"What makes you think that?''

"Because that's what he told everybody. That you'd come down here to help him find Mac's murderer.''

"Then maybe they'll come after me,'' Matt said softly.

He wanted them to. It was in his voice. All he wanted was a chance to get at whoever had shot Chase. That's what he'd been doing all day, Jenny realized. He'd been out here at the shack and crawling around on top of that bluff all day looking for something that would lead him to them.

"You can't stay out here," she said. She had just realized that he couldn't, no matter what he wanted.

"I'm not sleeping on that damn couch at Chase's," he said. Whatever had been in his voice before—the deadly menace—was gone. Or hidden under his amused denial. "It's just about big enough for Mandy."

"You can stay at my place," Jenny heard her own voice suggest. She hadn't intended to say that. She knew all the reasons why that wasn't a good idea, but none of them seemed to matter when she remembered last night. Any part of last night.

"I can't stay at your house, Jenny."

"Why not?" she asked reasonably, working at keeping her voice even. "If you're worried about the neighbors, don't be. There aren't any. And what I do is my business."

"I'm not sure Rio would agree with that," he suggested. "He seems pretty protective."

"Rio doesn't make my decisions. You can't stay here, and you won't stay at Chase's. That doesn't give you many options."

When the silence stretched, she realized he was thinking about it. They were still sitting in the quiet darkness of the truck's interior. And so she waited.

"You're going to stay at Chase's?" he asked finally.

"I'm going to sleep in my own bed," Jenny said decisively. She hadn't been aware that she had made that decision, but it was in her head, already analyzed, all the logical reasons for it prepared for articulation. "Mandy's asleep. She won't miss me. My things are all at my place. I'm too tired to pack a suitcase. I can call Rio and Anne and explain what I'm doing. Besides, I'll sleep better in my own bed."

She was on dangerous ground with that assertion, she knew. Would she sleep better? Would she sleep at all with Matt Dawson in her house? Again the silence expanded into the surrounding darkness. When she glanced at Matt, he wasn't looking at her. He was staring out the front windshield, but in the moonlight, she could see the muscle in his jaw knot and then slowly unknot.

Maybe because he could sense her eyes on him, Matt turned his head. In his face was what had been there last night. And what had been there earlier tonight when he had touched her arm. Again, he said nothing, but he nodded his agreement, the movement slow and somehow deliberate.

Finally she remembered to breathe, remembered to smile at him, but beneath those surface conventions was undeniably the other. That surge of incredible anticipation.

"We should take Chase's truck back with us," he said.

Matt was no longer making eye contact. He was looking beyond her now into the night, and she knew that, too, was deliberate. She wondered how much he understood about what she had just felt. How well he could read what was happening to her.

"I'll drive it," she offered. Chase's truck wasn't an automatic, she had remembered.

He nodded again, and reached across his body to open his door. She watched him walk around the front of her pickup, enjoyed watching him without him being aware of what she was doing. He opened the driver's-side door for her and helped her out, but he held her elbow only for the few seconds that required and then he released her. There was no slow glide of his thumb over her arm this time. No unnecessary contact.

He slipped his fingers instead into the pocket of his jeans, fishing for Chase's keys. He'd put them there last night, and she realized that, just as she had, he had been wearing the same clothes for almost thirty-six hours.

At least she'd had a chance to grab a shower at Samantha's, while he'd been out here in the heat trying to find something that might help Buck catch whoever had shot Chase. She remembered Rio's opinion of Buck's skills and acknowledged that the sheriff would probably need all the help he could get.

"You must be exhausted," she said, reaching for the keys he'd finally gotten out.

"I don't think I'll have any trouble sleeping," he admitted.

"Me either," she said.

That was all that was behind his agreement to stay at her house tonight. Just an arrangement that made more sense than any other. An arrangement for a place for two very tired people to sleep. Whatever else she had been imagining was only that—her imagination.

"I'll follow you," he said.

But she didn't move. They had been standing like this last night when he had almost kissed her. Only a single step separated them. She wondered what would happen if she took that step. If she raised her face to him as she had done then. If she put her hands on those broad shoulders and leaned against him. Would he hold her as Rio had, her breasts crushed against the muscled wall of his chest?

She knew it would be nothing like when Rio had touched her. Matt's touch would be something else. Something that she would respond to as she had always responded to Mac, melting into his embrace without any thought of resisting.

"It's late, Jenny," he said quietly.

His dark gaze was softened by the moonlight, and it was caressing her face like a lover's fingers, but in his voice was denial. He didn't want what had almost happened between them last night to happen again.

So Jenny McCullar, who had never thrown herself at a man in her entire, practical life, walked around him to Chase's truck. And as she drove it home in the darkness, she was almost unaware of the tears.

Chapter Seven

Mac McCullar came awake suddenly, heart pounding and mouth dry, his lungs struggling for air. *Just a nightmare,* he thought, trying to fight his way out through the black terror.

It was the old dream. The same one that always brought him awake like this—cold, sweat-drenched sheets wrapped around his body, holding it helpless and shivering against the forces of his memories. *So damn helpless,* he thought, trying desperately to pull his mind away from the remembrance of the months he had spent like that, dependent on somebody else for everything. For every bite of food. Every sip of water. Every...

He banished that litany, deliberately destroyed the hated images. Most of the time he succeeded in not thinking about those days when all he *could* do was think. Those agonizing days when he'd made the decision that had put him and Jenny in the situation they were in now. A situation that was becoming harder and harder for him to deal with.

Jenny had wanted him to kiss her tonight. He had known what she wanted, but that was hardly surprising. He had always known when Jenny wanted him. He could see it in her eyes or maybe in the faint underlying flush of her skin. Or maybe he could just sense it—that invisible aura of desire, so strong that he was never in any doubt. He always knew when she wanted him. Just as he had known tonight.

He rolled over onto his side and pushed the pillow under his head with his fist, trying to find a more comfortable position for his aching, trembling body. He thought about Jenny sleeping in the room next door, curled into that near-fetal position she always assumed when the night was chilly, as this one was.

Not just chilly, he realized. Cold. It was damn cold in here. He glanced at the window he had opened before he crawled between the lavender-scented sheets. Their familiar fragrance had almost been evocative enough, despite his intentions, to drive him into that bedroom next door.

The same room where he and Jenny had slept together, had made love, had tried to make babies, for more than five years. Now she was sleeping there alone, and he was lying here nude, shivering and wanting. Left with nothing but memories. Memories that were as cold as the night air that drifted through the open window, gently billowing the gauze curtains inward, like ghosts in the darkness.

He didn't want to get up. He knew that after yesterday his hip and leg would hurt like a son of a bitch until he'd loosened them up. For at least a couple of hours, he'd be stiff and aching like an old man. He closed his eye, burrowing a little deeper into the quilts, trying to get warm, trying to forget the images of the nightmare and go back to sleep.

He forced himself to lie there, unmoving, for a long time. He ordered his brain not to think, not about any of it. Not about Jenny. Not about what the bastards had done to Chase. He forced his breathing to even and pretended he was watching the sullen movement of the river. He lay there for a long time, trying to relax back into the oblivion of sleep. Trying to forget.

It didn't help. None of it destroyed the memories or lessened the tight, aching hardness of his groin. Finally, annoyed by his lack of control, he pushed the covers off and sat up on the edge of the bed. His hip protested, the pain sharper than he could remember it being in a couple of years.

Of course, it had been a long time since he'd tried anything like what he'd done yesterday. All that damned therapy was a far cry from crawling around over a bunch of sand and rocks, searching every inch of them for any trace of a killer. Attempted killer, he corrected himself.

Buck was right about that. There was no proof that whoever had shot Chase had had anything to do with Mac McCullar's murder. When he realized how he'd phrased that last thought, he laughed, a breath of sound, very soft and a little bitter.

He had been thinking about himself in the third person. That was almost how it had felt since he'd come home. Like he really *was* someone else. Someone who had lived a different life. And he guessed that wasn't so far now from the truth.

He pushed himself up, off the unfamiliar, too-soft mattress, and walked barefoot to the window. He didn't work at pretending not to limp. There was no one here to see, and so he favored the aching hip, leaning heavily on his good leg to protect the other.

He already had his hands on the top of the sash, about to push the window down and cut off the flow of cold air, when he became aware of what had probably awakened him. Maybe even what had produced the nightmare. He wasn't sure whether it was the acrid hint of smoke that he noticed first or the smudged glow shooting upward into the darkness from just below the horizon.

The line shack that sat on the boundary between the two McCullar houses was on fire. It was far enough away that he couldn't really see the burning building, but because he knew every inch of this property, there was no doubt in his mind what was burning. Someone had set fire to the shack where he was supposed to be sleeping. Where he *would* have been sleeping, had Jenny not convinced him to come back here.

Jenny, he thought. Anxiety pushed into his chest, ballooning suddenly, as hard and tight as his aching arousal had been. But there was no reason to doubt Jenny was sleeping safe and sound in the room next door. No logical reason.

And no reason not to check on her, he told himself. He limped back to the bed, picking up the jeans he'd thrown across the chair when he'd come out of the shower. He sat down on the edge of the mattress again and pulled them on. When he stood to zip them, he didn't take time to fasten the metal button at the top. He grabbed his shirt as he walked around the bed, struggling to get his arms into the sleeves as he opened the door to his room and started down the dark hall.

Jenny's door was closed. He knocked a couple of times before he reached down and turned the knob. Jenny McCullar didn't have anything he hadn't seen a million times before, he thought. Despite the grim purpose of this predawn visit, he fought an urge to smile. At *least* a million times.

Jenny was already sitting up in bed in response to his knock. He could see her face, white in the darkness, framed by the short hair, which was disordered from sleep. Her eyes were rounded with surprise that he would come into her room.

"What is it?" she asked.

Her hand had drawn the sheet to her breasts. She held it there, almost hiding the low neckline of the blue silk gown she was wearing. He had chosen that nightgown. It was the last thing he'd ever bought for her. It had been a Christmas present, already wrapped and lying under the tree on that December night—

"What's wrong?" she said again.

"The line shack's on fire," he said.

"The line shack?" she repeated disbelievingly. "Are you sure?"

"You can see it from here," he assured her. As he had in his room, he limped across to the window and pushed back the curtains. The fire seemed to have diminished a little, but the glow was still there. As the smell of smoke would be, he knew, if he opened this window.

"Oh, my God," Jenny said softly.

She was standing beside him. She put her hand on his arm,

and he looked down into her face, her eyes wide with fright, the pupils dilated. "You would have been out there," she said.

"But I'm not," he soothed. As he had wanted to do in the hospital, he put his arm around her shoulders and pulled her against the warmth of his body. She fit as if she had been created to stand beside him. And she had been, he thought.

As she leaned into his embrace, he felt her arms slip around his waist, the left one slipping inside his open shirt, warm against his skin. The feel of it so damn familiar. *Nothing more,* he thought. *I won't ever ask for anything more. Just to hold Jenny. Just this once. Just to know that she's safe.*

"You could have been killed," she said. And then she shivered.

"It's all right," he whispered.

Without thinking, seeking only to reassure, he turned his head and put his chin on the top of her head, resting it against the gleaming darkness of her hair. It smelled of flowers. It smelled like Jenny. Just as it always had. His small, brown-haired Jenny-Wren. Still acting from the seemingly unbreakable force of habit, he lowered his head and pressed his lips against that fragranced softness.

"It's going to be all right," he whispered again. "I promise you, Jenny." He felt her nod, the movement small, brushing lightly against his mouth.

"I should call Rio," she said, the inflection questioning.

"He can't do anything tonight. Morning's soon enough to hear bad news." That was something his mother had always said, Mac remembered, but it didn't matter. Jenny had never known his mother, who had died while Mac was a teenager. Long before he had loved Jenny.

"What should we do?" she asked.

She was still standing in his arms, and he wanted her there, of course, but this wouldn't make anything any easier, he knew. He had foolishly allowed himself to hold Jenny again, and now he didn't ever want to let her go. It had been too hard to let her go the first time, to free her, and he wasn't sure he could find the strength to do it again.

Using every ounce of willpower he possessed, Mac removed his arm from her shoulders and shifted his body a little to the side. Her arms fell from around his waist, and as he had, she moved back, increasing the distance between them. They were no longer touching, no longer standing together against whatever was out there. Against whatever evil had again touched their lives.

"Wait for morning, I guess," he said, "and then we call Sheriff Elkins."

Her eyes had been on his face. He made himself look back at the glow on the horizon. Definitely smaller now and darker. By morning, nothing would be left out there but a smoldering pile of ashes. And maybe, just maybe, he thought, a print or two.

Just a little luck, dear God, he prayed silently again, *before this all goes wrong. Just give me a little bit of luck.*

RIO ARRIVED SHORTLY after dawn. Jenny hadn't called him, but since she and Matt hadn't gone back to bed after they'd discovered the fire, they were dressed and in the kitchen when the car came screeching into the yard. Jenny met him at the door.

"You're all right?" Rio asked. His face was white and strained, its perfection almost stark with terror.

"We're all right," she said. She put her hand on his arm and stood on tiptoe to put her cheek against his.

"We?"

"Matt slept here last night," she said. She stepped back, out of the doorway, to reveal Matt Dawson sitting at her table, the long fingers of his left hand wrapped around the warmth of his coffee.

"Thank God," Rio said. "They burned the shack last night. I just got back from out there. I thought…" His eyes shifted again to Matt. "There's nothing left."

"We saw it," Jenny said.

"As soon as I smelled the smoke, I knew what they'd done," Rio said.

"What *who* had done?" Matt asked.

Jenny glanced at him, surprised at the tone of the question.

"You knew what who had done?" Matt repeated.

The horror had begun to fade from Rio's eyes, but his mouth tightened at the question and suddenly a muscle ticced at its corner. He shook his head. "I don't know. I just thought that it might be whoever came out there before."

"When somebody beat you up?" Matt questioned.

Rio nodded. "They had gasoline that night. They poured it around the shack. They were going to try to burn me out. I knew if they lit that gas off, I'd never get out of there. Not alive."

"You think this fire was set by those same people?" Matt asked.

"That doesn't make any sense," Jenny interrupted. "You weren't even here. No one even knew you were coming home last night, Rio."

He smiled at her, despite the anxiety still reflected in his eyes. "No one knew I was coming home," he agreed softly.

She understood why he had smiled and why his voice had softened into tenderness. That had been in response to her unthinking words. *Coming home.* To her, this, the McCullar land, was now Rio's home and always would be.

"And after all," she continued, "you weren't the one who was supposed to be out there. If that fire was deliberately set— and we still don't know that it was—then you couldn't have been the target. Matt was."

"Matt? Why would anybody...?" Rio's question faded and his dark eyes moved from one set face to the other.

"For the same reason they shot Chase," Jenny said. "Whoever shot Chase set that fire." Her comments were directed at Matt. "You know that. They were trying to get rid of you, just like they tried to get rid of Chase."

"You think that means this is all happening because of your husband's death?" Matt asked.

"Not drugs. Not what Buck thought," Jenny said. "Just Mac. Just because you were trying to find out what happened to Mac."

"Is that what you and Chase were up to?" Rio asked.

"Chase needed to know who killed his brother," Matt explained.

"You put the word out that that's what you were doing?"

"It seemed like a good idea at the time," Matt said. His voice was cool, obviously reading the implied criticism.

"It was my idea," Jenny said. "I thought it might make them react, bring them out into the open."

"I guess it worked," Rio said bitterly.

"I never meant for Chase to be hurt," Jenny protested. "You know I wouldn't want anyone to be hurt, not even to catch Mac's murderer."

"I know, Jenny. I'm sorry. I know you didn't think somebody would go after Chase. But…you believe whoever killed Mac is behind this, too?" Rio's question was to the stranger seated so comfortably at Mac McCullar's table.

"Maybe," Matt said.

Rio's dark head slanted, questioning Matt's lack of agreement with that idea, especially given the evidence.

"Buck Elkins thinks it's all about drugs," Matt explained. "He thinks that somebody has been using this ranch as a transfer point and it became too dangerous with Chase back."

"Except Chase has been 'back' for a while now and nothing's happened."

"Not until I showed up. Is that what you're suggesting?" Matt asked quietly.

"I'm *suggesting* that I don't have a whole hell of a lot of faith in Elkins or his opinions."

"And you don't like him," Matt said. It wasn't a question.

"I don't like him," Rio agreed. "But I also lived on this

ranch for several weeks. I didn't see any evidence that anyone was using it for trafficking.''

"You think you'd know?'' Matt asked softly.

"I'd know.'' There was a hint of challenge in Rio's clipped answer.

"Does that mean you've got some experience with drugs?''

"I don't have any experience with trafficking, if that's what you're implying. I don't know any more about running drugs than anybody else who's lived along this border for a while.''

"You've always walked the straight and narrow, I guess,'' Matt said.

"Most of the time.'' The old bitterness was in Rio's voice. "*All* of the time, when it comes to that. Whatever you've heard—''

"I haven't heard anything. Jenny found some plastic bags. Down by the river. I thought you might take a look at one of them and see what you think.''

"Okay,'' Rio said. His voice was still hard, despite the fact that Matt appeared to be backing off any accusation.

"Jenny,'' Matt said.

She had put the bag and the tray on the counter when she came in last night. She hadn't even remembered that they had transferred them to Chase's truck when they had taken hers to the hospital that night. The supper dishes and the plastic sack had both still been on the seat when she drove the black pickup back here last night, so she'd brought them in.

She didn't like the tone or the direction of the conversation between the two men, but she picked the sack up and carried it over to the kitchen table. Maybe Rio *would* know something that could help. After all, a man could learn a lot of things in prison or living the kind of life Rio had lived before, skirting so close to the edge of the law.

"Was that used to carry what Jenny thinks?'' Matt asked.

"Drugs,'' Rio agreed. He, too, would know exactly what kind of packaging was used to transport contraband across the river.

"Want to take a guess about what kind?"

Matt was watching Rio's face intently, trying to read his reaction to that question, Jenny realized. Rio hesitated for a moment, his black eyes assessing Matt Dawson, and then he walked across the kitchen, his boot heels echoing.

He picked up the plastic bag and turned it so that the opening was toward his face. "Not marijuana," he said. There was no hesitation in voicing that opinion. Then he carefully turned the bag inside out.

There didn't appear to be much residue, as if whatever had been carried inside the sack had been wrapped in something else—something that would provide double protection from the river or make for ease in distribution, maybe. Rio stuck the tip of his forefinger on his tongue and rubbed it across the snow-white powder that lined the bottom seam of the sack. Then he touched his finger to the tip of his tongue.

His dark eyes lifted suddenly to Matt's, widened a little with surprise. "You knew what this was," he said accusingly.

Matt nodded. "I did what you just did last night. I guess I should have done it sooner."

He might have, Jenny realized, had it not been for her. He had been reaching for the plastic bag when she had tilted her face up for his kiss. Then Chase had arrived and, as she had, apparently Matt had forgotten about this until last night.

"What is it?" she asked. It was almost as if they had forgotten she was here, as if what they had discovered was so important, it blocked all the other considerations.

"I know what I *think* it is and even, given the color, where it came from, but we'll have to have it tested to be absolutely sure about that. It's heroin," Matt said.

Which shouldn't have been such a surprise, she thought. Why they would react as they had to that discovery? "There's a lot of heroin brought across the border," Jenny said.

"A lot of black tar," Rio corrected. "Mexican brown. Not anything like this. At least—not that anybody knew of."

"I don't understand," she said, shaking her head. What did

it matter what kind of drug was being carried across that ford on Chase's place? The important thing was that it was obvious now that something had been.

"This is very white, so it's probably not Mexican," Matt said. "And the odds are that in this location, it's *not* coming in from Asia."

"Then…"

"Colombian heroin," Rio said. "I heard they've gotten into this. A new crop, easy to grow, and they produce a very potent product. Pure enough to be sniffed. They haven't been growing it in a great enough quantity to make much of a dent in the Asian stranglehold. At least not until lately. Maybe the last three years."

"So that means this has nothing to do with Mac?" Jenny asked. "Is that what you're saying?"

"The cartels don't even handle this stuff," Rio said. "Not like cocaine. So far it's been handled by the independents, by the little dealers in Colombia. They use mules—individual carriers—and they fly it in, mostly to New York, in suitcases or in somebody's stomach. Once there, they distribute it in the States. That way, even if the carrier gets caught at the airport, their loss is minimal."

"And now… You think this means someone is trying to bring it in through Mexico?" Jenny asked in disbelief.

"Why not?" Rio asked softly, obviously thinking about the possibilities. "Everybody's focused on the major entry points, on the bridges, focused on stopping the flow of cocaine and marijuana from the big Mexican cartels. And in the meantime—"

"Someone is bringing this across the river here," Jenny said.

"It's worked for years for the Colombians," Matt explained. "They fly their cocaine into Mexico, sell it or trade it to the Mexican middlemen for distribution, and let the Mexican organizations worry about getting it into the States. Any loss after its arrival in Mexico is theirs, not the cartels'. It speeds up the traffic and cuts the chances of a disaster for the Colombians.''

"Apparently somebody had a good thing going bringing heroin across here until Chase moved back," Rio suggested.

"Maybe," Matt hedged again. "Or maybe this has *nothing* to do with Chase getting shot. Why wouldn't they just go somewhere else? Why take a chance on getting folks stirred up around here by shooting people? That's the real question."

"You got an answer for it?" Rio asked.

"Not yet, but I will have," Matt vowed softly.

"I still don't understand what you think this means. Could these be the same people who killed Mac?" Jenny asked again.

"Probably not. It's been too long. This stuff wasn't even being grown down there when Mac was killed," Rio explained. "At least not in any quantity. And remember, as far as anyone knows, this still isn't being brought across this border.''

"But...it is. At least, it's being brought in here," Jenny said.

"Maybe only here," Matt agreed.

"Why?" Rio asked.

"I don't know," Matt said. "Convenience, maybe. You ought to be able to supply some information about that. You lived right across the river from this ranch."

"I've 'lived' in prison for the last five years," Rio said. The excitement of discovery had faded from his eyes, and the frustration of again being the accused had returned. "I wasn't in any position to know what's been going on around here. I don't have any way of knowing who's mixed up in this. But I can tell you one thing. I'm not involved, if that's what you're thinking."

"I heard you and Chase didn't get along too well," Matt suggested quietly.

Rio took a step closer to the table, eyes glittering. "Just what the hell are you suggesting, you son of a bitch?''

"I'm suggesting that somebody who knows this land pretty well has been using it to bring Colombian heroin into this country. Somebody close to this side of the border or the other."

"Not me," Rio said. "And I didn't have anything to do with shooting Chase."

"He wasn't even here, Matt," Jenny said. "And besides..." *"Mac was my brother."* She remembered those words and the tone of Rio's voice when he'd said them. Rio wouldn't hurt Chase.

"Am I going to have to fight this battle all over again?" Rio demanded.

Jenny looked up to find his face tight with anger. She realized that he was asking the question of her.

"No," she said, shaking her head. "Not with me. I know you had nothing to do with what happened to Chase."

"And you?" Rio asked, his eyes on the seated man again.

"Prison can change a man," Matt said. He didn't flinch from the fury in the black eyes. "I needed to know."

"Now you do," Rio said caustically. "I didn't have *anything* to do with that ambush."

Matt nodded. "I accept that. I'd like your help to find whoever did."

Jenny waited for Rio's agreement, waited as his eyes studied the marred features of Chase's friend. Finally, long after the silence had grown uncomfortable, Chase's half brother shook his head.

"I'm not tying up with you or with Elkins. I've had enough of people who doubt my motives, and more than enough of somebody accusing me of something I didn't do."

"Rio," Jenny protested, putting her hand on his arm again.

He shook it off, but he looked at her, his dark eyes still hard and cold. "You're mighty trusting of a stranger, Jenny. A stranger who's throwing accusations around pretty damn freely. Maybe you ought to think about the fact that nothing happened here until *he* arrived. Chase lived here for months without any trouble. Then *he* shows up and all hell breaks loose. It's something to think about,'' Rio warned her.

He turned and crossed the room quickly and was gone, slamming the back door behind him. Jenny waited for a moment in the sudden silence before she turned to look at Matt.

"Why did you do that?" she asked.

He met her eyes openly, but his face was as hard as Rio's had been. "Just what I said. Prison can change a man. I needed to know if it had."

"He should never have been in prison. That was Chase's fault."

"You're sure Chase was wrong?"

"Of course, I'm sure. How in the world can you believe—" She stopped because she realized that Matt had no way to know what kind of man Rio really was. Just another ex-con, she realized. That was all he would seem to Matt Dawson.

"You're wrong," she said softly.

"I hope so. But he had lots of opportunity to set this up while he was living here. And a lot of reason to hate Chase McCullar."

"You're wrong," Jenny said again. "Rio had nothing to do with this. Not with the drugs *or* with Chase. If you're *really* looking for whoever did those things, then you'd better start looking somewhere else."

"I'm not ruling out any possibilities, Jenny. I promise you that."

The phone shrilled suddenly, not breaking the tension that had been between them, but escalating it. *Word about Chase?* she wondered, and she knew from Matt's eyes that he was thinking the same thing. Dreading the answer as much as she was.

She picked up the receiver on the second ring and said hello, expecting to hear Samantha's voice. Hoping now for the same frustrating message she had given them yesterday. *At least no change,* Jenny found herself praying. If this was not good news, then at least let there be no change.

"Jenny? Thank goodness, I caught you."

Not her sister-in-law, but Trent Richardson. Jenny glanced at Matt and found that his eyes hadn't left her face.

"Trent," she said and watched the dread disappear, to be replaced by something she didn't have a chance to evaluate before Matt looked down at the mug he held cupped in his left hand. She watched the muscle knot in his jaw as it had last night.

"I just heard about Chase," Trent's voice said in her ear, interrupting that examination. "Anne called me. I wondered why you hadn't let me know about what's going on down there."

She wouldn't have attempted to answer that, but he paused, obviously waiting for some explanation.

"It was just too...sudden. Unexpected. I'm sorry. I should have called, but..." She let the sentence trail away. There *was* no excuse for not calling him, and Trent was too intelligent to be fooled by any she devised. There was only the truth. She hadn't *wanted* to call him. But she couldn't tell him that. Not now. Not with the man who was responsible for her reluctance to talk to Trent sitting in her kitchen. Matt was listening to every word she said to the man she was supposed to be in love with, the man she had once been contemplating marrying.

"How is he?"

"They say they won't be able to tell us anything for a while. Not until he wakes up."

If he wakes up, she thought, and then she destroyed that idea, deliberately denying it a place in her mind.

"I'm coming down," Trent said. "You shouldn't be there alone."

She didn't want him here, she realized. There were too many things happening that she didn't understand, too much going on, internally and externally. She didn't want to have to deal with Trent right now.

"I'm not alone," she said softly. Matt's gaze came up at that, holding her eyes briefly before he let his drop again.

"Who's there?" Trent asked. He was trying to figure it out, his deep voice puzzled. If he had talked to Anne, he knew that she and Rio were staying at Samantha's.

"A friend of Chase's," she said, reluctant for some reason to give him any other information.

"Who is it?"

"A man named Matt Dawson," she said softly.

"And he's staying there with you? At your house?" There was surprise, maybe a touch of outrage in those questions.

"He *was* staying at the line shack…" Jenny began, and then she realized that if she told Trent about the fire, there was no chance he'd stay put in San Antonio.

Trent waited through her silence for a few seconds before he repeated what she'd begun. "He was staying at the line shack and…"

"Someone burned it down."

"Burned it *down?*"

His voice was loud and sharp in that repetition, loud enough that Matt looked up again. Silently she shook her head, trying to signal her unhappiness with the way the conversation was going.

"Are you telling me that someone burned the place deliberately?" Trent demanded.

"It looks that way," she admitted.

"I'll be down there after lunch," he said.

The connection was broken before she had an opportunity to try to dissuade him. Not that it would have done any good, she knew. She realized that Matt was still watching her.

"He's on his way down here," he guessed.

"Considering…" she began, and then she hesitated. *Damn it, I don't want him here, either,* she thought, *but there's not much I can do about it.*

"I guess it's natural that he's worried about you. Or maybe he's just coming down to protect his interests," Matt suggested.

"His interests?"

"His...territory, maybe."

"I'm not *anybody's* territory," she said, angered by the quiet hint of contempt in his voice. That mocking assessment of her relationship with Trent Richardson seemed almost familiar, somehow. Déjà vu. It was almost as if she had heard him make that very same appraisal before.

"And I promise you Trent's interests don't *need* protecting," Jenny said, allowing her anger to show. Anger with him not only for his treatment of Rio, but also for his sarcastic comment about Trent, a man he didn't even know. She put the phone back on the counter and left the room, leaving Matt Dawson sitting alone at her kitchen table.

And what the hell did I accomplish by that? Mac wondered when Jenny had gone. Her departure had been a little more restrained than Rio's, but not by much. He had driven a wedge between himself and Jenny, and although that might offer some protection, a buffer against what had been happening between them, he had also alienated his half brother.

He hadn't believed Rio had anything to do with whatever the hell was going on on this land, but he had had to ask. Unlike Buck, he was still too good a lawman not to remember that you had to ask the hard questions. And accept the result if people didn't like you asking them.

He also knew he needed to get out to that line shack and take a look around. But even more than that, he needed to drive to the hospital. He needed to see Chase, just to reassure himself that his brother was still alive.

The hours were slipping away, and he had accomplished nothing. Nothing except the alienation of the two people who should have had the most reason to want to help him find whoever had shot Chase.

Maybe he *had* been a lawman at one time, he acknowledged bitterly. Maybe he had even been a pretty damn good one. All he was now, it seemed, was a broken-down, washed-up has-been who *thought* he could still function like a sheriff.

Somewhere, whoever was directing all this mayhem must

be laughing. Having a real good laugh over the idea of some-body like him ever getting to the bottom of the cesspool his county had become.

My county, Mac thought bitterly. Yet on some level it still was his county, and he'd be damned if they were going to get away with destroying it and the people he loved.

He slid the nearly useless hand across the wooden table until it was next to the coffee cup. He positioned his palm against the side of the mug and watched the unresponsive fingers re-fuse to fasten securely around it. Testing again, testing himself as he always did. Always pushing the limits of what he had accomplished. Which, when he thought about it, didn't seem like a hell of a lot today.

Poor, pathetic has-been, he thought again. The quick McCullar temper, which he usually was able to control, boiled upward suddenly, acting in combination with the familiar frus-tration.

He pushed himself up, his left hand flattened against the top of the table. At the same time, he swept his right arm across its surface, catching the coffee cup in its wide sweep, hurling it and its contents across the kitchen. The mug crashed into a cabinet and fell, shattered, to the floor.

Mac McCullar didn't even look at it. He grabbed the plastic bag from the table and limped across the room and out the back door. He never looked back at the broken pieces he left behind. After all, he didn't need to look. He'd had nothing but broken pieces to think about for the last five years.

Chapter Eight

Nothing had changed. That was obvious by the slow, steady beeps of the monitors and by the unnatural stillness of his brother's once-strong-and-vital body.

Mac hadn't walked over to Chase's bed this time. He hadn't allowed himself to touch his brother's hand or look down on the tracery of veins that marked the waxen eyelids. Instead, he had stopped just inside the glass door that separated Chase from the other patients in the ICU, nausea and fear again clawing for equal space in his stomach.

He had gone by the line shack on his way to the hospital. He had found nothing but ashes, gently swirling in the desert wind around the burned-out shell of the building where he was supposed to have slept last night.

Samantha and her father had been at the hospital when he'd arrived. Mac hadn't told them about what had happened at the line shack. That would be only another anxiety for two people who had enough to worry about. He had told them, however, that Anne and Rio were back and were taking care of the beloved horses. Sam had nodded his approval, his age-clouded eyes again assessing.

"You got anything else to tell us?" Kincaid had asked.

Mac knew what Sam was hoping for. Some information about who had shot Chase. Or why. Those were questions Mac still didn't have answers to—at least, not any he was willing to share yet with Sam Kincaid. Not until he'd done a little more sorting through what he'd learned. However, thinking about what he had found reminded him of the favor he needed.

"You have any connections with the DEA?" Mac asked the old man and watched the shrewd eyes stretch a little in surprise.

"I probably know somebody who does," Sam said. "But I thought *you* might be better connected there than I am."

Mac shook his head, offering no other explanation.

"Then that's not where you and Chase tied up?"

"No," Mac agreed. That had happened long before his brother's employment with the federal agency, he thought.

Sam nodded. "What do you need from the folks at DEA?"

"I need to get something analyzed." He glanced at Samantha and realized she was listening. He hated to worry her, but he made the request anyway because he didn't have a choice. He had too few allies in this battle, and Sam Kincaid had connections he could use. "I need to know its origin."

"What kind of 'something'?" Sam questioned.

"Heroin."

"Has this got something to do with what happened to Chase?"

"Maybe. I'll know more about that when I find out where it came from."

"I don't understand," Samantha said.

"Somebody's running drugs on Chase's property," the old man suggested.

"Or on Jenny's," Mac clarified.

"You get me a sample, and I'll find out for you," Sam promised.

The old man would be as good as his word, Mac knew. Sam had even walked with him out to the parking lot to get the sack he'd brought, but he hadn't asked any more questions.

Sam would give him the results as soon as the lab could check for the South American signature, Mac thought, as he watched the slow, measured rise and fall of Chase's chest. If he was right about the heroin's place of origin, it might not mean much, but it would at least be a starting point.

"Somewhere to start, Chase," Mac said softly to his brother. There was no response. Nothing but the quiet monotone of the machines.

He wasn't accomplishing anything standing here, Mac knew. Whoever had shot Chase wasn't going to be discovered in this hospital room. There wasn't anything he could do about whatever was going on inside his brother's body. There might, however, be something he could do back home. That was important to him right now—just to be doing something.

MAC KEPT THINKING on the way back to the ranch about Trent Richardson's expected arrival. Logically, he couldn't blame the senator for his decision to come down here. No one would understand that protective response better than Mac. Still, he found he was resenting the hell out of the idea that Richardson was coming down here to look after Jenny. That was Mac's job. It always had been.

He almost missed the turnoff to Crystal Springs, picturing Richardson and Jenny together. Or thinking about the natural way Jenny had put her arms around his own waist last night. The way she had leaned into his embrace, melting against his body, just as she always had.

Mac slammed on the brakes just before he passed the turnoff, the back end of Jenny's truck slewing in response. He knew he needed to tell the sheriff about the fire last night and about the heroin. This was Buck's county now, and he might even have some information about drug traffic on this stretch of the border that could save Mac some time. It sure wouldn't hurt to ask.

He found he was wrong about that. It had hurt. At least it had hurt to open the door to the sheriff's office and find Buck Elkins sitting behind his desk.

Mac had brought that desk over here from the ranch. It had belonged to his grandfather, but it had been too big for the house. Jenny hadn't protested when he'd carried it to his office in town. Hell, she'd probably been glad to get the thing out of the house, although she hadn't been insensitive enough to say that.

Now Buck Elkins looked pretty much at home sitting behind it. He had lowered the front legs of his chair to the floor when Mac opened the door. The thought ran through Mac's mind that it might be more appropriate for the county sheriff to be out looking for whoever had shot Chase instead of sitting comfortably in his air-conditioned office.

Of course, maybe Buck had already done all that. To be fair, Buck knew as well as he did that chances would be slim-to-none of him finding anything valuable. Mac hadn't. But at least he'd been out there trying.

"Dawson, isn't it?" Buck asked. "Chase's friend."

"Matt Dawson," Mac agreed.

"What can I do for you, Mr. Dawson?"

"Maybe I can do something for you," Mac countered, deciding suddenly that he'd like to see Elkins's response to what he'd found—his unprepared response. "You know anything about somebody bringing Colombian heroin across the border here?"

"Heroin," Elkins repeated. And then, "*Colombian* heroin?"

There was nothing but surprise in that repetition—at least, nothing else Mac could read. "That's right."

"Here?" the sheriff said. The surprise was still evident in his tone, but it seemed mixed now with a touch of amused disbelief.

"You heard anything about that?"

"Not a thing. Occasionally cocaine, plenty of marijuana," Elkins admitted. "Probably even some Mexican heroin. Nothing else. Not anything else that I know of. What in the world makes you think somebody's bringing Colombian heroin in *here?*"

"Jenny McCullar found a plastic bag down by the river—"

Buck's face cleared, the puzzlement relaxing, as he interrupted. "I *told* Jenny that bag could have held anything. Or it could have held nothing."

"It held heroin," Mac said, pronouncing each word distinctly. He remembered that Buck had originally dismissed what Jenny had brought in here to show him. Dismissed also Jenny's good common sense and her intelligence. "Some very *white* heroin," he added.

"There's a lot of heroin brought over the border these days. It's a popular drug. Not much here, though. Not much of anything here."

"I'm having this analyzed. I don't think it's Mexican."

Buck nodded, his hazel eyes assessing again. "I guess you got the connections to do that."

"I asked a favor from a friend."

"When do you expect to have some results?"

"I'll let you know. I always believed local officials need to know as much about what's going on in their jurisdictions as the feds do."

"Is that a fact?" Buck said softly, but there was suddenly a flush—resentment or anger? Mac wondered—across his cheekbones. The color was visible even beneath the deep tan. "Well, we do appreciate your consideration of us *locals*, Mr....?"

"Dawson," Mac said. Buck had remembered his name when he'd walked in the door. Apparently his memory was selective or else it was just Mac's day for saying the wrong thing, for ruffling feathers. "I just thought I'd let you know what I'd found."

Buck nodded, almost contemplatively, as he held Mac's gaze. The flush had deepened slightly. "Well, I'm much obliged for the information," he said finally.

The usually friendly eyes were almost cold. Buck didn't like to be told how to do his job, and Mac couldn't blame him. He wouldn't have, either.

"Can you think of anybody around here who's suddenly

gotten prosperous? Maybe in the last couple of years? Or even in the last few months?''

"Prosperous," Buck repeated, amusement returning to his voice, relaxing it. "There's not many folks down here that I'd call prosperous. Not in *any* year."

"How about somebody who suddenly seems to be doing a lot better than they used to?'' Mac suggested, ignoring the sarcasm.

Buck appeared to think about it for a few seconds before he shook his head. "Not that I know of."

"Well, I'd appreciate you letting me know if you think of something."

"Sharing information, you mean," Buck suggested, the edge back in his voice, a little more openly sarcastic this time.

"Solving a crime," Mac reminded him softly. "Or trying to, anyway."

He turned and headed toward the door. He stopped with his hand on the knob and looked back. Elkins was watching him.

"Nice desk," Mac said softly.

"I inherited it," Buck said. His eyes had narrowed, but they hadn't moved from their focus on Mac. "It kind of came with the job. You let me know what you find out about that heroin, you hear?'' he reminded.

"I'll let you know," Mac said. Then he opened the door and stepped out into the fall sunshine.

It came with the job, he thought, finally allowing the left corner of his mouth to creep upward into the smile he'd been fighting for the last few minutes. *Just like all the rest of the stuff that came with this job,* he thought. The endless paperwork and the long hours. The criticism. Too much danger for too little money. Always a lack of resources.

He knew he should be glad that the sheriff's job and all that went with it belonged to Buck Elkins now. However, as he left the office that had once been his, Mac McCullar also knew that, despite those remembered frustrations, he really wasn't.

"WHAT ELSE DO YOU KNOW about him?" Trent asked. "Other than the fact that he claims to be Chase's friend."

"He didn't *claim* to be Chase's friend," Jenny corrected, holding on to her patience. "Chase *said* he was. That's all I know. He's Chase's friend, apparently an old friend."

"Who shows up here and all hell breaks loose," Rio said.

The four of them were sitting at Samantha's kitchen table, eating a late lunch, which consisted of sandwiches and a salad. Neither Anne nor Jenny had felt like cooking. Anne had fed Mandy earlier, and the little girl was taking her afternoon nap, but the adults had delayed eating until Trent arrived.

Samantha had called from the hospital, but there was no change, still no news except that Matt Dawson had come in to see Chase this morning. Given the direction the conversation was taking, Jenny was beginning to wish she hadn't shared that.

"Are you trying to blame this on Matt?" she asked her brother-in-law.

"It felt like he was trying to blame it on me," Rio said.

"He doesn't know you. He watched Chase get shot, went for help, and then worked with me to keep him from bleeding to death out there. Now he's trying to figure out why it happened."

"You think he's DEA?" Trent asked. "Is that where he knew Chase?"

"Neither of them would say. I asked, but..."

"But what?"

"They avoided the question." She shrugged, poking her fork into her salad.

"I wouldn't think even former agents would want to advertise that fact," Anne suggested quietly.

"Why not?" her brother questioned.

"Safety, maybe. Anonymity. I don't know. It just doesn't seem unreasonable that you might not want to talk about it."

"Especially if something terrible had happened to you because you *were* an agent,'' Jenny added, grateful for Anne's intervention.

''What does that mean?'' Trent asked.

Neither she nor Rio, the only ones who had met Matt, rushed to answer.

''Jenny?'' Trent asked.

''It's obvious that if he *were* DEA, he's retired. Maybe on disability.''

''Disability,'' Trent repeated.

There was a note of what seemed to be relief in his voice. At least it had sounded that way to Jenny, and she didn't like hearing it.

''He's been pretty banged-up somewhere,'' Rio said.

Jenny looked up at his comment and found Rio's black eyes on her, and not on Trent, whose question he'd been answering.

''But despite what Jenny says, I'd like to know more about Mr. Dawson,'' Rio continued. ''About exactly where he knew Chase. If he *is* ex-DEA, that puts a different complexion on things.''

''That would make you more willing to accept him,'' Jenny suggested.

''Maybe. To accept his right to ask questions, I guess.''

''I don't know how we could find that out,'' she said. ''Not if he's not willing to tell us.''

''I could do some checking,'' Trent offered. ''I have a few contacts within the law-enforcement community.''

''I'm not sure that's a good idea,'' Jenny protested softly. ''It's an invasion of his privacy, for one thing. Matt's done nothing wrong. He was only trying to help Chase find out who killed Mac.''

''Is that what this is about?'' Trent asked. ''Mac's murder?''

''Or maybe drugs,'' Rio said.

''Drugs?'' Again those notes of shock and displeasure were clear in Trent's normally pleasant voice.

"Jenny found evidence that somebody's been transporting drugs across the river."

"Here on this ranch, you mean?"

"At the ford," Jenny admitted.

"You didn't think it was important to tell me about that?" Trent asked. "You didn't feel it was something I needed to know?"

"I knew what your reaction would be."

"To try to convince you again to get rid of this place. If Chase dies—"

"Trent," Anne said softly. Her brother stopped the unthinking, and unthinkable, words.

"I just want you safe, Jenny. And you're damn well not safe on this ranch. Not living way off down here by yourself. Especially not given the state of this border these days."

"I'm not by myself," she said. It was an old argument, but the things that had happened in this county lately had certainly given Trent added ammunition for his side of it. "Chase and Samantha live next door," she said. "This is our property—"

"Somebody just shot Chase and *burned* your property," Trent interrupted. "Now I find out that somebody's running drugs here. How much more do you need, Jenny, to convince you to give up the worthless piece of desert? Just because it belonged to Mac—"

"That has nothing to do with it. This is *my home*. It has been for more than ten years. That's not easy to walk away from, no matter what's going on. No matter what you think about it."

Trent took a deep breath and then expelled it. He certainly knew her well enough to know that pushing her would just make her dig in her heels. He smiled instead and put his big hand over her fingers, which were playing with a fold of the tablecloth.

"I know it's not easy, sweetheart. I just want to give you a *new* home, a safer one. How do you think I feel having to worry about you all the time? Wondering what the hell else is going to happen down here?''

"I know," she admitted softly. "But maybe…"

"Maybe what?" he asked, rubbing his thumb across her wrist.

Jenny fought the urge to pull her hand away and hide it in her lap. To put it out of his reach. And then she felt guilty for wanting to do that. "Just don't do this right now," she begged. "Not when we're all so worried about Chase. We can discuss it later. Please."

Trent nodded, reluctantly she thought, but at least he'd agreed. She needed some time to think about everything— about the dangers he worried about, which were real dangers, she knew. Most of all she needed time to think about the other—about how she felt about Matt Dawson.

"Sure I can't convince you just to go back with me for a few days? You look exhausted."

"I didn't get much sleep last night," she said. She looked up to find Rio's eyes on her, and it was only then that she realized how that statement might be interpreted.

"How about if we drive in to the hospital and see Chase?" Trent invited.

"I promised Samantha I'd look after Mandy, and I really haven't done very much of that."

"Mandy's fine," Anne assured her, smiling. "She's been busy telling Rio how to tend to the horses. They like each other. I think it must have something to do with the fact that they speak the same language." She glanced at her husband and smiled. How much she loved the dark, incredibly gentle man she had married was clearly revealed in that look.

And it was painful for Jenny to watch. "They speak horse," she suggested, fighting her jealousy of what Anne and Rio had.

Anne turned back to smile at her. "Something like that, I guess. Go on. Let Trent take you in to the hospital. You'll feel better after you've seen Chase and talked to Samantha.

She probably will, too. Tell her not to worry. Things are fine out here. Everything's being taken care of.''

Anne was right, of course. She would feel better, and Anne and Rio would look after Mandy as well as she could.

"I'll run you back to your house if you want to change," Trent offered. "Throw whatever you'll need into a suitcase."

"I'm not going to San Antonio with you," Jenny said. "I thought you understood that."

"I'm not going back tonight. Anne says I can sleep on the couch. I meant you can get whatever you need to bring back over here. You are planning on spending the night here, aren't you?"

"You can sleep with Mandy," Anne suggested.

"We'll see," Jenny said softly. She pushed back her chair and stood, beginning to gather up some of the dishes they'd used, hoping to forestall any other questions. Especially the ones she didn't have answers for.

MATT WAS BACK AT the ranch when they pulled up in the yard. He had taken Jenny's truck this morning without asking her permission, and now it was parked near the kitchen door. She remembered the broken cup and the coffee splattered on the cabinet and the floor, which she had found after he'd left. She still didn't know why that had happened.

"Matt's back," she said. "Maybe he can tell us something about Chase."

"Good," Trent responded. "You can introduce us."

She tried to think of some logical reason for Trent *not* to come into the house with her. Tried and failed. But it didn't really matter because about that time Matt walked out onto the back porch. He was wearing the denim shirt he'd worn that first morning by the river, tucked into those same skintight jeans.

Jenny got out of the car, not waiting for Trent to come around to open her door. She walked up the steps, feeling the intensity of Matt's dark eye focused on her face again. She heard Trent's door close and then his footsteps behind her, but she didn't even turn around.

"Trent, this is Matt Dawson," she said. "Chase's friend."

"Matt," Trent said. He held out his hand. "Trent Richardson. Glad to meet you."

Matt's hand wasn't extended, and he didn't respond to the greeting. His gaze had moved to study Trent's handsome face, and his mouth tightened.

"I don't shake hands," he said simply.

Trent let his arm fall, but then, before she realized what he intended, he put it proprietorially around Jenny's waist.

"I've heard a lot about you," Trent said easily.

Trent was so good at this, Jenny thought. At meeting strangers. Making everyone feel at ease. It was part of his profession, and he had refined it to an art. Only, it didn't seem to be working with Matt Dawson. Nothing had changed in the tightness around his mouth or in the coldness of his dark eye.

"We're going in to see Chase," Jenny explained. "Samantha said you'd been there this morning."

Matt nodded, but he didn't look at her. He was still focusing on Trent's handsome features.

"How is he?" Trent asked, still relaxed, despite the near hostility that was emanating from the tall, scarred man.

"Still the same," Matt said softly.

"I need to change clothes," Jenny said, speaking into the almost-solid force of the tension that shimmered between the two men. She moved slightly, away from Trent's arm.

"I was going out to check on the horses," Matt said.

She nodded agreement, although she knew as well as he did that it wasn't necessary. He still didn't move, however. She didn't understand what was in his face, what had been there since she and Trent had gotten out of the car, but she recognized that it was probably good he'd thought up that excuse. At least she wouldn't be leaving the two of them together while she dressed.

Finally, she turned and opened the back door. She was relieved when Trent followed her inside without saying anything else to Chase's friend. Nothing really unpleasant had happened, but somehow what *had* happened had reinforced her feeling that she didn't want Trent down here. Except she wasn't quite sure what to do about the fact that he was here. Or about the fact that she, herself, had given him the right to believe he belonged.

"HE'S AWAKE."

Sam Kincaid's greeting had been so unexpected that Jenny's eyes filled with tears, tears she could do nothing about. Somewhere deep inside, she realized, she had expected the evil to win again. She had expected to lose Chase as she had lost Mac.

Trent hugged her, smiling at the old man. "That's nothing to cry about, sweetheart," he said softly. "That's great news. Isn't it?" he asked Sam.

"About the best we could expect," Kincaid agreed. "At least that's what the doctors say. A lot more than they expected to happen this soon, I can tell you. You two want to see him?"

"Will they let us?" Jenny asked.

"Sure, they will," Samantha's father assured, his relief and near euphoria infectious. "I'll promise to donate a wing or something," he said. He winked at her, and put his big, gnarled hand against the small of her back, guiding her toward the glassed-in room where Samantha was sitting by Chase's bed.

She glanced up to smile at them when they entered.

"How is he?" Jenny asked softly.

"Groggy," she said. "Disoriented. But he knew me. He said my name." As Jenny's had, Samantha's emerald eyes filled suddenly with tears at the unexpected joy of that.

"That's wonderful," Jenny whispered. She walked across the space not taken up by the monitors and put her arm around her sister-in-law's shoulders. "I'm so glad."

"Jenny," Chase said. His voice was hoarse, distorted, probably a result of the throat tube they'd recently removed. But it was strangely familiar, reassuring somehow. "Tell Mac," he said softly.

She took a breath. The whispered name caught her off guard. Still disoriented, Samantha had said. Jenny stepped closer to the bed, so Chase could see her, and then she smiled at him.

His eyes were swollen and unfocused. "Hey, Chase," she said. "Welcome home."

His head turned minutely and the blue gaze settled approximately on her face. "Tell Mac," he said again.

"I will," she whispered, fighting the tightness in her own throat, fighting tears again. She reached down and touched the strong brown fingers of the hand that lay, limp and unmoving, against the white sheet. She was surprised when they closed around hers.

"Careful," Chase said. He moistened cracked lips with his tongue, the blue eyes locked on hers, trying so desperately to tell her something that made no sense.

She nodded again, not trusting her voice.

"Tell Mac to be careful," he whispered. His eyelids drifted downward, slowly. He lifted them again, but even that small effort seemed to take more strength than he now had. Strength he would need for getting well. They closed again, hiding the inarticulate urgency that had been in his eyes, and then she felt his fingers relax suddenly, releasing hers.

"He's still a little confused," Samantha said.

An apology, Jenny knew, for reminding her that she could never tell Mac anything, not ever again. Whatever warning Chase had intended for his brother was five years too late.

"I know," Jenny said. "It's all right. He's never forgotten Mac. Maybe never forgiven himself for what happened. I guess it's always on his mind. Or maybe the hospital reminded him. The sound of the machines. I guess we'll never know what prompted that."

She realized it wasn't important. What was important was that it seemed Chase would be all right. She turned and put her arms around Samantha, who returned the tight embrace before they stepped apart, almost embarrassed, it seemed, by that display of emotion. Maybe they'd been married to those strong and silent McCullar men for too long, Jenny thought.

"How's Mandy?" Samantha asked.

"She's fine. She's telling Rio how to tend to your horses."

"I'll bet she is," Samantha said, laughing. Her eyes were still a little damp, but the laughter was good. So welcome after the dark night they had all passed through. "She's too much like a certain man of my acquaintance, who shall remain nameless."

"Chase," Jenny guessed, thinking of that stubborn Mc-Cullar nature.

Again, Samantha laughed. "Actually, I was thinking of Sam. But you know..." She paused. Her eyes, filled with an ineffable tenderness, fell to caress the face of her husband, sleeping naturally now. "You may not be very far wrong, at that."

JENNY WAS SO TIRED when they got back to the ranch that evening, she wasn't sure she could get out of the car. She could probably count on one hand the hours of real sleep she'd had during the last two days. All she wanted to do now was to fall into her own bed and pass out.

With the knowledge that Chase was going to recover, the adrenaline and anxiety that had carried her through this crisis were no longer flooding her body. Instead, she felt as if she might not have the strength to climb the back steps and make it down the hall to her bedroom.

Except she still had to deal with Trent. And with Matt Dawson, she thought. And tonight she really didn't feel like playing referee between the two of them.

"You wanted to get some things to take over to Samantha's," Trent reminded her. He had turned in the seat and was looking at her, compassion for her tiredness in his eyes. He took her hand, brought it to his mouth, and pressed a kiss against the palm.

"I'm not going to Samantha's," Jenny said. "I'm going to sleep in my own bed tonight." She remembered saying that last night, the words echoing suddenly in her head. She *had* slept there, at least the few hours she had managed to sleep.

"Then I'll stay with you," Trent said. His voice was agreeable, almost mellow with the thought. "I don't like the idea of leaving you here by yourself."

"I'm not by myself," she reminded him softly.

"Dawson," he said. Then he smiled at her. "Somehow, that's not real comforting, Jenny."

"Why not?"

"Because he might have been the target of that fire last night. Or even when Chase was shot. And...because you know nothing about him."

"He's Chase's friend. I trust Chase's judgment," she said stiffly. *And my own,* she thought, but she refrained from saying that out loud.

"I repeat. You know nothing about him."

"I'm not going to argue with you. Matt is Chase's friend. He has nowhere else to stay. And this is my home. I don't intend to be run off by whatever's going on around here."

"Attempted murder, arson, drug trafficking," Trent enumerated softly. "Most people wouldn't want to stay where those things are happening, no matter how long they'd lived there. It's dangerous, Jenny, and you're smart enough to know it."

"I know that this is my home. I don't intend to give it up to the cartels or to the people who shot Chase. That's what's wrong. Too many people just give in. Just give up."

"So you're determined not to? That's just sheer bullheadedness," Trent argued.

"Maybe I've been a McCullar too long," she said softly. "I still am. I guess I always will be."

She met his gaze and held it, trying to tell him what she felt without having to put it into words. There was a slight narrowing of his eyes.

"What the hell is that supposed to mean?" he asked softly.

"I guess that…I'm just not really ready."

"Ready for what?"

"For anything else," she admitted.

"For me? Is that what you mean? Not ready to give up this worthless ranch? Or not ready to give up Mac?" There was bitterness in that question, and she knew she deserved it.

"I never meant to make you unhappy," she said. "I really thought I was ready to move on, but…" Again she waited, hoping that she wouldn't have to say anything more, hoping he'd understand.

"You know what I think, Jenny? I don't think this has anything to do with the ranch or with Mac. I think this is about something else. Maybe…*somebody* else."

She didn't deny the accusation because she couldn't. Not in all honesty. It *was* about somebody else. She had been ready to settle for marrying Trent. To settle for companionship. Maybe just for safety and security. All of which he could provide.

But that was only because she had forgotten the other. She had almost forgotten what it felt like to want a man's mouth over hers or his tongue trailing, hot and wet and demanding, over the skin of her throat. Over her breasts. To have his hands moving against her body, their callused strength brushing tantalizingly against her softness, touching places that only he knew. Evoking responses that belonged only to him.

She knew now that those hands didn't belong to Trent Richardson, and neither did she. She had only been fooling herself to think that she ever could.

"Jenny?" Trent said. For the first time since she'd known him there was a note of pleading in his deep voice.

"To somebody else," she agreed softly. She didn't even realize she had rephrased his question.

She opened the door and climbed out of his car, and she didn't look back as she walked up the steps of the house where she knew with absolute certainty Matt Dawson would be waiting.

Chapter Nine

Mac heard the car. He had been consciously listening for the sound of their arrival since he'd gotten out of the shower and dressed in the clean clothes Jenny had laid on the foot of the bed he'd slept in last night. He had needed to shower and change because he'd gone back out to the line shack again after Jenny and Richardson had left for the hospital.

He had discovered he couldn't stay in this house alone. There were too many memories, too many ghosts. He had lived here all his life except for the last five years. Now that he was home again, he knew he hadn't been living at all while he'd been away. Away from his land and his family. Away from Jenny.

It was a long time after the car pulled into the yard before he heard the kitchen door open and close. He had tried not to imagine what was happening out there in the darkening twilight, had tried not to think about what might be causing the delay.

Maybe the senator would come in with Jenny. Maybe Richardson intended to spend the night here. If so, Mac wondered what Jenny's boyfriend would think about the peace offering he had left on the kitchen table.

Trent Richardson probably didn't need to make peace offerings. It was highly likely that polished front never slipped.

The son of a bitch probably never lost his temper, Mac thought bitterly, never breaking Jenny's dishes or friendships.

He pulled in a slow breath, trying to tamp down his building anger. He had no right to blame Richardson for being in love with Jenny. Mac was the one who had decided on this course. He was the one who had given Jenny up five years ago, clearing the way for somebody else to hold her. To kiss her. To make love to her in the warm, silent darkness of their home.

That was the thought that was unbearable, of course, and until today, he had never allowed himself to think it. Until today he had never had a face to put with that imaginary lover. The face of the man who might take his place.

Now he knew that face. He had seen it—and would see it in his nightmares. Those damn perfect features. His fingers lifted to touch the patch that covered the ugliness of the empty, misshapen eye socket. They trailed slowly over the roughness of the burned skin of his cheek. And then they fell.

"Matt?"

It was Jenny's voice, coming from the kitchen. She must have seen the flowers and the mug he had bought to replace the one he'd broken this morning. It hadn't even occurred to him that he needed to do something about what he'd done until Richardson had shown up with Jenny this afternoon, all those smooth politician manners in place.

"Matt?" Jenny called again. "Where are you?"

He realized he was sitting in their bedroom—in what had once been their bedroom. Just sitting in the gathering darkness. Waiting for Jenny to come home.

Suddenly she appeared in the open doorway. She glanced perfunctorily around the room and began to turn away. Then she turned back, her eyes locking on the chair where he was sitting.

It was in the darkest corner of this room. Mac hadn't needed to turn on the light. He knew every inch of this bedroom, just as he knew every inch of Jenny. Every centimeter of her skin. Every pore. Every atom of her being.

"What are you doing in here?" Jenny asked softly. Her voice held no anger at his invasion, only puzzlement. She was still standing in the doorway.

"Is he with you?" Mac asked.

There was a small silence, and finally Jenny stepped into the room and walked halfway across the distance that separated them. He could see her face in the faint light that filtered from the curtained windows behind him, but he knew that to her, given his position before them, he would be nothing more than a shadow, a dark silhouette. And that was good. Maybe, he thought again—as he had thought that night at the line shack—maybe she'd forget what he looked like in the darkness.

"No," she said. "I told him..." Her voice faded, but her shoulders moved upward with the depth of the breath she took. That movement was visible even in the dimness. "I told him it would be better if he didn't stay."

Mac nodded. He remembered that she might not be able to see him, but he still he didn't say anything, savoring what she'd just told him.

"Have you eaten?" Jenny asked.

He laughed, a whisper of sound. He couldn't help it. Practical Jenny. Always taking care of everybody, seeing to everyone's needs. *And who will take care of you, Jenny-Wren?* Mac thought. *Who the hell is going to look after you when I'm gone?*

"Maybe that wasn't such a good idea," he said.

"Eating?"

"Letting him leave."

"Did you want him to stay?" Jenny asked, a hint of amusement in the question.

"Hell, no, I didn't want him to stay." Again, he watched the slow rise and fall of those small shoulders.

"Well, I didn't, either," she said reasonably. "So he's gone. Are those your flowers on the kitchen table?"

Mac smiled, feeling some of the anger and the tension begin to melt away. "Your flowers," he corrected.

"You bought them for me?"

"And the cup. I broke one of your cups this morning. Damn stupid accident. I just wanted to say I'm sorry."

"For the cup?" she asked carefully.

"For the crack about *him*. For making Rio mad. For... everything, I guess."

"Okay," she said softly.

"Did you like them?"

"Violets are my very favorite flowers."

"Is that a fact?" Mac said. "I guess I must have gotten lucky." And then he asked, spoiling whatever effect that nonchalance might have achieved, "Does *he* give you violets?"

"Roses," Jenny said. "By the dozen."

"My mother loved roses," Mac said softly. Remembering other ghosts. Other times in this house. All so damn long ago.

"I guess most women do, but...I've always loved violets."

The silence built slowly in the darkness, but there wasn't anything awkward about it. It was peaceful, as peaceful as this desert had once been. And that, too, had been a long time ago.

"Chase is awake, conscious, and talking," Jenny said suddenly. "I'm sorry I didn't tell you that before. He said—"

The sentence was cut off, the words halted too abruptly.

"He said what?" Mac asked. The slow seconds ticked by until finally Jenny's voice came again out of the shadows that had lengthened into the room as they talked.

"He said that I should tell Mac to be careful," she whispered. And then her voice strengthened. "I suppose it's not surprising Mac would be on his mind. Maybe because of the hospital. The sound of the monitors. I don't really know. *Something* there reminded him of his brother, I guess."

"It's good to hear that he's better."

"They think he'll be all right. That there won't be any permanent...impairment."

Jenny had thought about how to phrase that, he realized,

thoughtful and sensitive as always. The left side of Mac's mouth lifted and then settled again.

"That's good. Chase would hate that."

"Mac would have hated it, too. Chase told me that. A long time ago. That if Mac couldn't recover, couldn't be the man he had always been, then he wouldn't have wanted to live."

"He may have been right about that."

"I'm sorry," Jenny said softly. "I didn't think..."

It took him a second to figure that out—why she was apologizing to him. Then it hit him. "Sorry about *my* impairments?" he asked. He forced amusement into his tone. "You didn't hurt my feelings, Jenny. There's not much I can do about those. Except just...live with them, I guess."

"I would have wanted Mac alive no matter what. Just as Samantha would have wanted Chase. None of it would ever have mattered. None of it."

He wondered if that quiet avowal was about Mac or about him. And then he realized that the distinction was unimportant.

"I guess men feel differently," he said.

"Mac wouldn't have. Nothing that could have happened to me would have made any difference to the way Mac felt. Nothing," she said again.

"I didn't mean that. I mean about themselves. About their own...impairments."

"I don't know," she said. "But I'm glad about Chase. He was so good to me after Mac died. If it hadn't been for Chase, I don't know what I would have done. He took care of everything—Mac's funeral, the insurance, all the endless paperwork. I didn't have to deal with any of it. And all that time he was hurting as much as I was. He just never let on. I never understood how bad it was for him. Not then, anyway."

Mac had trusted Chase, and his trust had not been misplaced. Chase had done what he had promised, but for some reason, Mac didn't want to think about that now. He didn't want to remember those days, those decisions. He just wanted to savor being with Jenny—for however short a time that would be.

"We could go somewhere," he said.

"Go somewhere?" Her voice was touched with surprise at the change of topic.

"Out to get something to eat, maybe."

"Obviously, you are *not* familiar with this county," she said. She was smiling.

"Hamburgers," he suggested. "Barbecue. There's got to be some place. I'm *not* a picky eater."

She laughed. "Would you settle for bacon and eggs and canned biscuits?"

"You don't want to go out."

"I want to go to bed," Jenny said emphatically. Suddenly the room was too silent, and it was a long time before the last word stopped echoing in the quiet darkness between them.

"Then..." Mac began, fighting ghosts, fighting memories, "why don't you let me cook. I can do bacon and eggs. If you'll crack the eggs," he added. "I never could get the hang of doing them one-handed."

"Deal," she said softly.

He pushed up out of the chair and began walking across the room. He expected her to turn and lead the way to the kitchen, but she didn't move. She watched him until he was standing directly in front of her, looking down again into her eyes. Remembering.

"You took a shower," she said, tilting her head back and allowing her lids to fall. "I can smell the soap."

Mac heard the breath she drew, the sound almost like that soft inhalation when he pushed into her waiting body. Almost a shiver of sound, as her body shivered under his hands when they caressed her skin in the darkness.

She wasn't asking for his kiss. He knew that. It wasn't what it had been before, but somehow her unpreparedness tonight was more compelling than her unspoken invitation had been.

Almost like her small hands pushing against his chest when he knew that she didn't really want to push him away.

Suddenly he was hard, the hot blood rushing into his groin, filling the strengthening arousal so quickly that he almost gasped with the exquisite torture of it. Wanting Jenny. Endlessly wanting Jenny.

He couldn't resist. He took the step that separated them and watched her eyes open in response to that unexpected movement. Her head was still tilted backward on the pale, slender column of her throat. He fitted his mouth over hers, which opened at the first touch of his lips. Opened and then replied, her tongue melding with his.

In a slow, primitive dance of desire. So evocative that it literally made his knees weak. The memories of loving Jenny invaded his head, pushing out all the cautions he had lived with since he had come home.

Somewhere inside he knew that kissing her, touching her, would only make it worse; knew that it would be a mistake, and that it wasn't fair. He knew and rejected all of that knowledge in exchange for the feel of Jenny's mouth moving under his.

He put his hand against the base of her spine, pulling her body nearer. She responded again, stretching on tiptoe, her small hands seeming to float upward to grasp his shoulders, easing into the kiss, allowing it to deepen.

He could feel her breasts against his chest now, and he fought the urge to crush her to him. To claim and possess what was his. What always *had* been his—morally, legally, physically.

And yet was not. Not any longer. Not by the rules he himself had designed and established five years ago.

Jenny, he thought, his tongue seeking hers, his body shaking with need, his loins heavy with the heat and the force of it. Forbidden. He had once let her go. A long time ago. He had freed her in order to protect her from what he had become.

And now, because he needed her, wanted her so desperately,

he was again destroying. She had created a life for herself after he chose to end the one they had shared, and he knew he had no right to destroy that which she had rebuilt from the ruins of his first destruction.

"I didn't want him here," she had whispered in the darkness. But she would have, Mac knew, if he hadn't come back. Trent Richardson would have been the one holding her. His perfect mouth would be over hers, his undamaged face and still-strong body pressed against the trembling flame that Jenny's had become.

Mac raised his head, pulling his lips away from hers. They followed, seeking still the contact he had broken. Again he retreated, denying, and finally her eyes drifted open, dark with emotion, unfocused with desire.

"What's wrong?" she whispered.

Her hand left his shoulder and touched his cheek. Her thumb brushed against the side of his mouth—the left side, so that he was able to feel the slow caress it made. Involuntarily, the undamaged corner lifted in response to that pleasure.

"Have I told you how much I like your smile?" she asked.

He laughed—doubtful, of course, about the truth of that.

"Don't laugh," she whispered, putting her forefinger against his lips, forbidding him to deny what she'd said.

She stretched again on tiptoe and pressed her mouth gently to the corner of his, the corner that still worked as it was supposed to. He wondered if she had been aware when he kissed her of the slight paralysis of the other side. He hadn't even thought about the possibility. Not when his mouth had lowered to find hers. Not until now.

"Can you..." he began, and then stopped, unwilling to voice that question, unwilling to remind her of what he was. *Impaired.* It was her word, and yet it was so damned descriptive. Descriptive about it all, he thought, because, of course...

"Can I what?" she repeated, smiling at him.

"Nothing," he whispered. "Nothing that matters."

He stepped back, allowing his hand to fall away from the

curve of her back. Releasing her. No rights. No rights to anything. Not Jenny. Not his land. Not even to his own name.

She nodded. But she was waiting, wondering maybe about what came next. And the answer to that was, of course, nothing. There was nowhere to go from here. Nowhere he *could* go. Nowhere he had any right to take Jenny. Certainly not to the bed that stretched wide and inviting almost beside them. Not even back into his arms.

"Eggs," he suggested softly, still fighting his body's aching betrayal of all his good and honorable intentions.

"Eggs?" she echoed. Obviously it hadn't been what she was expecting.

"You promised to break the eggs for me," he said.

Her dark eyes held his and then traced openly over his features. He wondered if she was comparing them to Richardson's. Her gaze lingered for a long heartbeat at the corner of his mouth before it finally came back to meet his.

"Are you sure that's what you want?" she asked. There was invitation in her voice. Need. Desire. All the things that were also within him.

What I want, Mac thought, *is your body under mine. Your legs wrapped around me. Moving. All the familiar sensations building slowly in this lavender-scented darkness. Building until...*

"I'm sure," he said softly, destroying the images of what he wanted. Destroying everything. Again.

She said nothing for a long time, and then she whispered it. One whispered word, and it was over.

"Okay," Jenny said.

She turned and led the way to the kitchen. Behind her Mac stood, fighting for control to follow her into the light. His good hand clenched into a fist that he wanted to drive through a wall. Or into Trent Richardson's undeniably perfect nose.

McCullar temper, he thought. And even as he thought it, he recognized that the person he was angriest at was dead, and out of his reach. That bastard had died in an ICU burn unit five long years ago. There was no way now he could ever come back to life. No way, even if he was willing to try, that Jenny would ever understand why he had done what he'd done. Or be able to forgive the unending hell he had put her through.

THEY HAD EATEN IN silence. He could feel Jenny's eyes on him occasionally, but he avoided making contact with them. Avoided looking for what might still be in them.

When she began to gather the dishes they'd used from the table, he stood. "I think I'll take a look around outside," he said. "Just to be sure everything's all right."

"What does that mean?" she asked.

"If somebody *was* after me last night, Jenny, then it's possible they know by now that I'm staying here."

"You think they might try something else?"

"I *think* I'm going to take a look around," he said. "That's all. And even that's probably paranoia. There wasn't enough of the line shack left to decide if the fire was deliberately set. I'm just cautious by nature."

"But you think there's reason to be cautious," she said again. "You think it's not safe."

"*You're* safe, Jenny. I can promise you that."

Again her eyes held his, questioning.

"Why don't you leave those damn dishes and get some sleep," Mac suggested. He allowed himself to smile at her. "*I like your smile,*" she had said. He wondered again if that could possibly be true.

"I think I will," she agreed softly. She turned to put the dishes she'd been holding into the sink, and she didn't look at him again. "Be sure to lock up when you come back in," she reminded, still turned away from him.

"Nothing's going to happen tonight," he promised her. He would damn well see to that, Mac thought, as long as he had Chase's Winchester and his own big old Colt. He had taken the handgun out of the bedside drawer the day he'd come home and found Rio's unknown car parked outside. He had hidden the Colt in the barn, and he knew Jenny hadn't yet realized it was missing.

He'd take a blanket and bed down outside, someplace where he could watch both the house and the outbuildings. *Nothing's going to happen,* he had promised. That was one promise he could keep, he thought, weighed against all the others he'd already broken.

"'Night," Jenny said.

"Sleep tight," Mac said softly.

Sleep tight, my Jenny-Wren, he thought as he watched her move down the dark hall to their bedroom, through same hallway where his mother's wallpaper roses still bloomed, faded now with age and the relentless passage of time.

Nothing's going to happen tonight, Mac vowed silently. *Not to this house or to this land. Not to you. And not even, my beloved, between us. I won't bring any more destruction to your life, Jenny. That, too, is a promise I can keep.*

MAC DIDN'T HAVE ANY IDEA how long he'd been asleep or what had brought him awake. Maybe just discomfort. He hadn't meant to drift off, but of course he had had as little sleep as Jenny during the last two days. That and the seeming peace of the night had finally gotten to him.

He glanced at the sky, trying to decide what time it was. What moon there was, a high-floating crescent of silver, gave far too little light. The eastern horizon was dark, no streaks pushing from beneath it to lighten the sky.

Just a few more hours, Mac told himself. If he could just stay awake until dawn, he would have kept his promise to Jenny. A safe night. He pushed himself up a little, straightening his spine and feeling the low cramping pain in his back.

He was a little too old or too "impaired" to pull this kind of duty, he thought. A little past stakeouts that involved propping his aching back against a pile of shadowed rocks or resting his damaged hip against the cold ground all night.

Against his will, his eyelids had begun to drift downward again when the noise forced them to jerk upward. It was probably what he'd heard before. Maybe the first time, he had been too deeply asleep to identify where it was coming from. Or maybe whoever was moving around in the barn had not been making quite so much noise before. Had not been quite so disturbing to the horses.

It was the stallion, of course. He was the spookiest of the lot, and Mac silently thanked the big black for reacting to whatever had entered the darkened McCullar barn in the middle of the night.

Maybe to do there what had been done out at the line shack? The thought was sudden, and it pushed the last of the fatigue-induced lethargy out of Mac's head. He scrambled up, moving awkwardly because of the stiffness that had crept into his body along with the chill of the night.

He carried the Colt in his left hand, wondering belatedly if he could hit a damn thing shooting left-handed, something he'd never tried before. Just point and shoot, he told himself. The principle was the same. Don't aim. Don't get fancy, worrying about it. Just point the gun like a finger and pull the damn trigger and keep on pulling it.

He was almost to the double doors of the barn. They were open, and Mac knew he had closed them when he'd left. He had gone inside to get the Colt and to double-check the half gate on the stallion's stall, just as carefully as he'd watched Rio do it, knowing that his half brother's caution was probably a comment on the black's temperament.

He could hear the horse now. Protesting whatever was going on in there. Protesting the presence of whoever was in the barn. Obviously somebody the stallion didn't know, somebody he didn't trust.

By that time Mac was edging carefully toward the opening. When he was close enough, he looked in, forced to wait for his vision to adjust to the heavy darkness inside.

The silhouette of the horse emerged from it first. The stallion was out of his stall, rearing against the pull on his bridle, resisting the man who held it. That man was himself only another shape in the darkness. There was nothing distinguishable about him.

Mac concentrated on size, height and build. Still nothing familiar or noteworthy. No one he could identify. He thought about shouting at the intruder to release the horse. And if he didn't obey?

Damn it, Mac thought. In the darkness even the stallion was no more than a shifting shape. Mac couldn't distinguish where one darkness ended and another began. And he found he wasn't willing to risk shooting the black to get the man holding him. Not yet, at least. That didn't make any sense, he supposed. Not unless you were a horseman.

Other possibilities flew through Mac's brain. This was the only entrance, he realized, this door he was standing beside. Which meant...

Mac leaned against the heavy door, pushing it inward. If he could get both doors closed and then locked, he'd have the intruder trapped in the barn. Except, all of a sudden as he leaned against the door, the metal hinges creaked.

Mac heard also the sharp smack of sound, the flat of a hand against the stallion's flank, with which the intruder sent the now panicked black careening toward the opening. Mac had identified the sound, but not quickly enough to get out of the way.

The frenzied horse burst through the narrowing opening like a tornado, knocking wide the door Mac had been in the act of closing and throwing Mac backward to land with paralyzing force on the ground. The back of his head hit with an audible crack and the air seemed to darken and then thin around him, as he fought to stay conscious.

Stunned, he lay where he'd fallen for a few seconds, almost afraid to move. He listened to the drumming hoofbeats of the black fade in the distance. Finally he managed to get to his knees, fighting nausea. He rested there for a moment, evalu-

ating his body's responses to that effort, trying to decide if
any of the pain was new or worthy of concern. When he made
it to his feet, he was a little surprised to find he still held the
gun in his left hand.

He must not have been down for as long as he thought
because the barn door he'd been pushing closed was still
swinging slightly back and forth from the powerful blow the
horse had struck it as he barreled through.

Mac used the door as a shield, sheltering his body behind
it while he again took a look into the interior of the barn.
There was nothing there. No dark shape and no movement.
None that Mac could see.

Whoever had been inside hadn't come out through those
double doors. Mac knew that. He hadn't lost consciousness,
so he would have heard him or seen him. *Which meant that
he had to still be in the barn.*

Mac eased inside, trying to keep his body out of the thin
stream of moonlight that edged between the doors. Once he
was inside it was easy to blend into the shadows that hugged
the walls. He leaned against the wooden planks, his head still
swimming slightly. He had the gun pointing into the blackness
in front of him, and he held his breath, listening to the silence
that surrounded him.

Listening. For movement. For the other man's breathing.
For anything. But the hay-scented darkness held none of those
noises. *Silent as a tomb,* ran through Mac's head. That eerie,
empty silence of the grave. Only, he *knew* the intruder had to
be here. There was no other way out. No way except through
these doors.

And through the loft, Mac realized. That was where he'd
gone, of course. Mac couldn't guess how many times he and
Chase had jumped out of the opening in that hayloft onto the
bales they'd thrown to the ground below. It wasn't all that
high, and even less scary if you simply hung by your fingers
and then dropped to the ground. That would be almost noise-
less. Easily accomplished while Mac had been distracted by

the horse's charge or had been picking himself up, too slowly he knew, from the hard-packed dirt.

He thought about climbing the wooden rungs of the ladder and looking out the opening. *Thought* about it and then discarded the idea. His hip had begun to burn, the fire deep within the damaged jòint. The pain was not unfamiliar, of course, but with the fall, it was sharp enough to clear his head, to insert some logic into his anger. There was no way now that he was going to catch whoever had been in here.

Too old and too damn slow, Mac thought bitterly. He limped across to the electric switch to flick on the lights and was forced to blink against their sudden glare. The barn was empty, but in the middle of the broad aisle that stretched between the stalls stood a jerrican.

Gasoline, Mac realized, feeling a shimmer of horror. Just what Rio said had been thrown around the line shack when they'd come for him before. And what had probably been used to set off the blaze that had finally destroyed it last night.

There was little doubt that the same thing had been planned for this building tonight. Mac took a breath, thinking what a near thing it had been. If the stallion hadn't awakened him… *Nothing's going to happen tonight,* he'd promised Jenny, and then he had nearly slept through it all. Nearly allowed the bastard to get away with it.

Finally he noticed that the stalls on either side of the aisle were empty. Jenny's three horses were gone. Docile as sheep, they must have been led quietly out of the barn, their passage not making enough noise to awaken Mac. Apparently the intruder had saved the black for last.

Because he'd known the stallion's reputation? Mac wondered. If that was so, then why hadn't he just left the black alone. Why risk detection in order to get the horse out?

For the exact same reason Mac hadn't be able to squeeze off a shot into the darkness. *Horseman,* Mac thought. Whoever had been in here was a horseman. He was more than willing to burn down the barn, but he had gotten the stock out first.

Stupid, maybe, but no more stupid than Mac's own reluctance to risk hitting the black by taking a wild shot at the intruder.

Mac took a breath, trying to remember anything about the shape he had half seen in the darkness. Not Rio, he realized. Rio would have been the one person who could probably have gotten the stallion out without any trouble and without the telltale noise that had given it all away.

Although Mac had never really believed his half brother was involved in this, it was a relief to find his gut reaction confirmed by some pretty solid evidence. Suddenly the rusted hinges on the double doors creaked again.

"What's wrong?"

It was Jenny's voice, coming from behind him. But Mac had already whirled, gun pointed at the opening a split second before he'd identified the speaker.

"Matt?" she said. Her eyes were wide and dark with shock.

He lowered the gun, feeling his accelerating heart rate begin to return to something approaching normal.

"What's going on?" Jenny asked.

"Somebody was out here," he said.

Her eyes surveyed the interior. They lingered for a moment on the gasoline can and then checked, as his had, along the row of stalls.

"They were going to burn the barn?" she breathed, her natural horror mingled with shock, despite all that had happened around here lately.

"They led the horses out first."

"Why?" she asked.

"Because they like horses," Mac said. "And around here that narrows the field of suspects, doesn't it?" He didn't hide the bitterness. He'd botched this chance as badly as he'd botched things the night he'd let them gun down his brother.

Jenny shook her head. She was shivering, whether from shock or because the thin nightgown she wore was providing little protection against the cold.

"Why would anybody want to burn the barn?" she whispered. She put her hands over their opposite shoulders and rubbed them up and down her arms. Mac fought the urge to gather her trembling body against the warmth of his.

He was moving past shock into anger. Whoever was behind this was a coward. Terrorism, Mac thought. Burning property and shooting out of the darkness. And of course, that was the answer to Jenny's question.

"They want you out of here," Mac said. Her eyes came back to his face, the pupils still dilated despite the time they had had to adjust to the light in the barn. "They just want you gone, Jenny. They want you off this ranch. You and Chase."

"Then Buck's right?" she questioned. "They want this land badly enough to do anything they believe will drive us out?"

"Anything," Mac agreed, his face tight set as he looked at the gasoline. Next time it could be the house. He fought the images of flames leaping upward in the room where Jenny was sleeping, her slender frame curled inward against the cold.

"They'll do anything," he whispered again. "Including murder."

Chapter Ten

"None of the three Matthew Dawsons fits."

"How do you mean?" Rio asked. He could hear the undisguised excitement in Trent Richardson's voice despite the distortion of the phone line.

"They're all too small, for one thing. One's retired, all right, but he's over sixty. Another's in his late twenties. The last one is maybe the right age, but at five-foot-eight, it's obvious he's not our man. Which means Dawson's link to Chase McCullar wasn't through the DEA. *Or* his name isn't really Matt Dawson."

There was something almost triumphant in his brother-in-law's statement, Rio realized. Something that Rio, despite his run-in with Dawson and his subsequent warning to Jenny, wasn't entirely comfortable with.

"I need his social-security number. Maybe just an address. Something like that, anyway, in order to get a handle on who this guy really is," Trent continued.

"I think that's carrying it too far," Rio suggested.

"To protect Jenny?" Richardson questioned. "There's not much I *wouldn't* do to protect Jenny from that bastard."

Rio wondered about the hostility. It hadn't been there at lunch yesterday. But then, there had been something strange about Richardson suddenly deciding to go back to San Antonio last night. Even Anne had commented on her brother's change of plans.

Was it possible, Rio wondered, that Richardson had been *asked* to go home? If Jenny had done that, then it probably meant Trent was right to be concerned about the direction her relationship with Dawson was taking.

"I don't know any way we could come by that information," Rio said reluctantly.

"You could look. You're staying in Chase's house. There may be an envelope, an address book somewhere. For Jenny's sake, Rio, just take a look around. I wouldn't ask you if I didn't believe it's important. There's something about that guy that doesn't ring true. My instincts cry out that something's wrong."

Rio had felt the same uneasy reaction to Matt Dawson. It had kept tugging at the back of his mind, occasionally brushing through his consciousness like an insect at a picnic. There was something about Matt Dawson that Rio knew he ought to have figured out by now, but he hadn't.

"Okay," Rio agreed, still reluctant. "I'm not promising anything, but I'll take a look around."

"Call me if you find something," Trent said. "Meanwhile, I'm going to keep checking at this end. I'll be in touch."

Rio put the receiver down and looked around Samantha's kitchen. Everything in it was neat and orderly, from the bills stacked in the letter file on the counter to the messages, block printed on the small refrigerator chalkboard. No skeletons in this sunny room. Not Matt Dawson's or anybody else's, he thought. And not much trace of Chase, either, he realized.

Of course, that wasn't surprising because Chase hadn't been living here very long. Not enough time, maybe, for his stuff to have filtered throughout the household. He would have moved his personal things from California, but maybe he hadn't even had time…

Suddenly in Rio's mind was an image of cardboard boxes, stacked one on top of the other. They were in the closet where

Anne had asked him to put the vacuum cleaner away this morning. And those boxes had been sealed with tape, as if in preparation for being moved, he realized.

"Always walked the straight and narrow?" Matt Dawson had asked him. Rio had read mockery into that question, but the truth of the matter was, he hadn't. Not always. His scrapes with the law had been relatively minor, and they had happened a long time ago, but it wasn't as if he'd never done anything that couldn't be construed as being beyond the boundaries.

As rummaging through Chase McCullar's personal papers would be. Except somebody had shot Chase and burned Jenny's bunkhouse. Justification enough, Rio thought, to venture into territory he had sworn never to enter again. He had made that unspoken promise to Mac McCullar a long time ago, but somehow he didn't think Mac's ghost would object to him trying to protect Jenny and Chase.

When Rio opened the first of those cardboard boxes, he didn't even have to look very hard to find what Richardson had asked him for. And a whole lot more, besides.

"I DON'T UNDERSTAND what you think this means," Jenny said.

Rio had phoned first, of course, before he'd come over here. He hadn't wanted to confront Jenny with what he'd found if Dawson was around. But Matt had driven in to the hospital to see Chase. He had left only about thirty minutes before Rio's call, which meant he wouldn't be back for at least a couple of hours.

"You tell *me* what it means," Rio suggested.

He watched Jenny's small fingers move again, hesitantly, over the canceled checks he'd spread out on her kitchen table. Half of them had been written to her and the other half... It was what was written on the other half of those checks that had sent him here.

"These are from the trust fund Chase set up with the insurance money," Jenny explained. "I guess they returned them to him because he was the executor of Mac's estate."

"Insurance money?" Rio questioned. It seemed she still didn't understand the implications.

"Mac's life-insurance policy with the county. The one we had was pretty small. I didn't even know about the one the county had taken out on Mac. But...if it hadn't existed, I probably wouldn't have been able to hold on to the ranch. It seemed like a godsend when Chase told me about it."

"A Chase-send, more likely," Rio said.

Her dark eyes came up to his face, questioning.

"There was no insurance money, Jenny. Every cent that was put into that 'trust fund' came from Chase McCullar. You can trace the deposits. Some pretty damn big ones. He put the money in, and the bank in California wrote you a check every month. No insurance money," Rio said again. "There never was."

"You're saying that Chase gave me that money?"

Her voice had been full of disbelief, but at whatever she saw in his eyes— —conviction, maybe—she looked down again at the papers he'd brought over. Her fingers turned the bank statements toward her, and Rio knew she would see what he had seen—a list of deposits made into the account and a list of withdrawals.

The checks written to Jenny McCullar's bank account had been monthly, regular as clockwork. Enough to allow her to hold on to her home and to live in it comfortably. But that wasn't true for the others. They were for irregular amounts and issued at irregular intervals. Some of the sums were enormous; others, much less. That list of withdrawals matched the rest of the canceled checks. Rio had verified that, carefully checking them against the withdrawals on the statements.

The checks not written to Jenny had been made out to a variety of different payees—all of them hospitals or rehabilitation centers, doctors or private therapists. The amounts had been huge at first and then they had dwindled in both size and number. But one thing had remained constant. At the bottom of each check someone had carefully printed, in a neat book-keeper's hand, "For Matt Dawson."

"I don't understand," Jenny said, her eyes again raised to his. Her voice had changed from shock to puzzlement, faced with the evidence of what Rio had discovered.

"Chase created that trust fund he told you about with his own money. Only two people benefited from it. You and Dawson."

"But why would Chase pay Matt's medical expenses?" Jenny asked. And then, running her fingers down the list of deposits, she whispered, "My God, where did Chase get this kind of money?"

"Look at the first deposit. Look at the date. Does that mean anything to you, Jenny?"

"That's... That must be the money that came from the ranch. That's approximately when he sold his half of the McCullar land."

"That sale provided the first deposit into this fund."

"And the rest of it?" she asked.

"I'm willing to bet those deposits would correspond to the trips Chase made into Mexico. Those are the payments for the recoveries he negotiated for kidnap victims, his percentage of the ransoms the corporations paid for their releases. Some of the others are probably payments from the companies he worked for as a security consultant. It looks like Chase McCullar did pretty well financially during the last four years."

"And all of what he made went into this account," Jenny said softly.

"If you look at those medical bills, you'll see that it all went out again. Damn near all of it, Jenny."

"But why? Why would Chase risk his life like that, time after time, and just give the money away? He was under no obligation to take care of me," she said, shaking her head.

Then her eyes lifted again to Rio's, troubled with that realization.

"Mac was his brother. *Those* payments I understand. It's the others I don't get. Why would Chase feel obligated to take care of Dawson's medical expenses?"

"Maybe they were partners," Jenny suggested hesitantly. "Maybe Chase felt responsible for whatever happened to Matt." She shrugged. "There are a hundred explanations, I guess. Maybe the DEA was funneling money into the account to take care—"

"Except Matt wasn't DEA," Rio interrupted. "Trent determined that without much doubt."

"Trent?" Jenny's voice was sharp again with disbelief, "What in the world does Trent have to do with this?"

"We were concerned about you. Even more so now, I guess."

"What does that mean?" she asked.

"It means I want to know just exactly who Matt Dawson really is and just exactly what he's doing here. And I promise you, Jenny, with your help or without it, I intend to find that out."

"CHASE'S ASLEEP," Samantha said. "He's been sleeping a lot. I was worried about that at first, but they say it's natural. That it's what his body needs to heal."

"Looks like you could use a little," Mac suggested gently.

There were smudged circles of exhaustion under the emerald eyes, and the strain of the last few days was evident in her face. Not that much could distract from Samantha Kincaid's looks. Hers was a rare, natural beauty that had been justifiably celebrated in south Texas since she'd turned fifteen. About the time Chase had first noticed her, Mac thought. Or she had first noticed Chase.

"I'm fine," she said, denying his concern, but she smiled at him.

"Why don't you at least get out of here for a couple of

hours? Go get something to eat or just walk around outside in the sunshine. I'll sit with Chase. I'd really like to do that. I guess there's not much else I *can* do for him right now.''

Nothing besides trying to take care of you, as Chase has taken care of Jenny, he thought. But Samantha had to think it. And why not? To her, he was virtually a stranger.

"I'm not going to let anything happen to Chase while you're gone," Mac added, finally returning her smile.

He didn't know if it was that or the other enticements he'd offered, but Samantha nodded. She gathered up her purse and put the book she'd been reading on the nightstand by Chase's bed.

They'd moved his brother into a room, which Mac knew represented an upgrade in his condition. Mac knew all about the rules that governed hospitals—far more than he had ever wanted to know.

"See you later, cowboy," Samantha said softly to her husband. She bent to press a light kiss on Chase's forehead. "Thanks," she said, turning back to Mac.

"You're more than welcome. Take as long as you need. I'll be right here when you get back."

Again, she nodded. Her eyes moved to the sleeping man and then away, and finally, reassured, she left them alone.

Mac walked over to his brother's bedside. Even asleep, Chase looked a hundred-percent better. Even with the bandages.

"We got lucky, little cowpoke," Mac said softly. "Damn lucky your head's still as hard as it's always been."

But Mac acknowledged that this good fortune probably meant the McCullars had used up their share of that commodity. If he managed to find whoever had shot Chase, Mac knew it would not be a result of luck, but of the other—sheer bulldog persistence. McCullar stubbornness.

Since they were alone, he touched Chase's cheek with his fingertips, feeling the slight stubble. He could even see his brother's whiskers, glinting gold in the light from the windows. For some reason he thought of Mandy, her blond hair flying around her small face as Jenny whirled her in an ever-decreasing circle. And that was another loss. Another destruction.

Mac took a breath, thinking about what he needed to do before he left. To find whoever had shot Chase and to find out about the heroin, about who was bringing it into this country across McCullar land. And he needed to do those two things before what was between him and Jenny—what had *always* been between him and Jenny—slipped out of his control. Then he needed to get the hell out of here. Just leave before he destroyed Jenny's life all over again.

And what about Richardson? Could he undo the damage he had done there? Maybe he should explain things to the senator, Mac thought bitterly. Just put all his cards on the table.

This is my wife, Jenny, whom I love better than I love my own life, for whom I would sell my soul and my body and whatever else the good Lord has ever given me. Would you take her, please, and keep her safe? Make love to her in the darkness. Feel her body move under yours...

With that image, Mac McCullar knew that was nothing he would ever be able to say to anyone, much less to Trent Richardson. No matter how much Mac loved Jenny, he wasn't man enough to do that, and therefore, not man enough to undo all the damage he had done by coming home.

"What the hell am I going to do, Chase?" he whispered, taking his brother's limp fingers in his. "What the hell can I do about that?"

There was no answer from the sleeping man, but it didn't really matter, Mac acknowledged, because there really *was* no answer to that particular question. Somewhere inside, he had already figured that out.

MAC WAS SITTING beside the bed, in the same chair where Samantha had been sitting earlier, when Sam Kincaid came into the hospital room. Mac stood automatically, easing upward slowly and carefully, his hip stiff because of last night.

Sam had gestured for him not to get up, and Mac found himself wishing he'd obeyed. Too damn old, he thought again. Or just too *impaired*. Again Jenny's word rankled, especially because he'd spent a lot of the last few hours thinking about Trent Richardson.

"Had to see him for yourself, I guess," Sam said. "Had to make sure he really is all right."

"Something like that," Mac agreed.

"I can't say that I blame you. My guess is you owe a hell of a lot to Chase McCullar."

Mac nodded, again wondering how much Sam had figured out.

"You were right, by the way," the old man said, his shrewd eyes not releasing Mac's. "That stuff's Colombian. Pure as the driven snow, they tell me. Much purer than anything they produce in Mexico."

"I was afraid of that," Mac said.

"Afraid?"

"New business, new people running it. It makes it harder to get a handle on who's involved."

"Or it might be the same old people just moving into new territory. You thinking this might be related to the other?"

"The other?" Mac repeated, but he knew what Kincaid was fishing for.

"I'm not as dumb as I look," Sam said softly. "Never have been. Five years ago somebody took out the best law officer south Texas ever had. Took him out of action deliberately. I always figured that was done to open up this county for the garbage that was already flowing into the others."

"You're talking about Mac McCullar's death," Mac said.

He was pleased with the lack of emotion in his own voice, the lack of inflection. Sam Kincaid might suspect, but he couldn't prove a damn thing. And thankfully the old man was wise enough to figure out that the only one who would be hurt if he tried was the one person who didn't deserve to be hurt anymore.

"Yep," the old man agreed, his eyes still holding Mac's. "I'm taking about Mac McCullar's death."

"This stuff from Colombia wasn't being produced five years ago. Not in any quantity."

"That don't mean somebody didn't have plans for this county. Plans to take advantage of *whatever* opportunities come along. They get rid of McCullar, and they think the sailing's gonna be smooth."

"The job doesn't die with the man," Mac reminded him. "There's still law in this county, and a good lawman providing its enforcement."

Sam nodded. "I've never heard anything to the contrary. But Buck Elkins ain't McCullar. He ain't smart enough, for one thing. That don't make him suspect. Just ineffective, maybe."

Kincaid might be right about that, Mac thought. *Ineffective.* He had heard that a lot since he'd come home. Mostly from Rio, of course, who had cause to dislike the sheriff.

"I'd be looking to discover who's showing signs of wealth around here," the old man advised. And then he grinned, belatedly realizing that he was by far the wealthiest person in the area. "New money," he clarified. "What's that they say? 'Show me the money.' You show me somebody that's all of a sudden *got* some money in *this* economy, and I'll show you somebody that's a hell of a lot smarter than the rest of us or somebody who's crooked. That's your two choices."

"You know somebody like that?" Mac asked.

"I know some ranches that two years ago couldn't pay their bills and all of a sudden they seem mighty prosperous to me."

"You want to give me some names, Mr. Kincaid?"

Mac knew that whatever the old man told him would be accurate. *If* Sam told him anything. Mac wasn't the law anymore. Not here and not anywhere else. He had no official capacity, and Kincaid owed him nothing. Not even cooperation.

Sam's eyes held Mac's for a moment longer and then they moved to contemplate the rugged features of his son-in-law. "I didn't pick that man for Samantha," he said. "He wouldn't 'a ever been my choice." Sam took a breath, and his lips pursed. "But he was hers. Always was, from the time she was old enough to know what it was all about. And I sure don't like somebody putting a bullet in him." The hazel eyes swung back to Mac. "You gonna find out who did that?"

"Yes, sir."

"Reckon you will at that," Sam said. And then he added, "Phil Warren, Cal Salinas, and Pirkle. Too much money too quick. I'm not saying it's drugs. I'm just saying that what they're showing don't add up with the hand they been dealt. You understand me?"

"Yes, sir."

"You go on, now," Sam suggested. "I can sit here awhile. Leastways until Samantha gets back."

Mac nodded. Two pieces of information he needed had just been handed to him on a silver platter. He didn't know that they would amount to anything, remembering his ninety-nine-percent equation, but it was a lot more than he'd had before.

"Thanks, Mr. Kincaid."

"My friends call me Sam," the old man said.

"Sam," Mac repeated obligingly. "I owe you."

"You don't owe me nothing. You get the bastard that shot that boy, and we'll be more than even."

Mac nodded. He turned and had begun walking out of the room when the old man's question stopped him.

"How's Mrs. McCullar?" he asked. There was nothing in Sam's tone beyond polite interest. "You're staying out there, I hear. Looking after things."

Mac turned, but the old man's face was as innocent of accusation as his voice had been.

"Jenny's fine," Mac said softly.

"That's good," Sam said. "I was real worried about her for a while. Didn't think, strong as she is, she was going to make it through all that. It'd be a shame if anything else happened to upset her."

"Like what?" Mac asked. He was still trying to read Kincaid's intention. Warning or simply conversation.

"Like this," Sam said, jerking his head toward the bed. "I heard somebody torched her bunkhouse. Looks like she needs somebody to watch out for things out there. Looks like she needs her a man. It's sure not like it used to be around here."

Kincaid was right about that. Mac's family had lived on that property since shortly after the Civil War, and it had been a damn long time since any of them had had to sleep with a rifle as Mac had done last night. Standing guard over Jenny.

"Somebody's watching," Mac said. He nodded again to Sam and then his eyes moved to his brother. He'd stay on the ranch until Chase was able to assume that role again. Despite what had almost happened between him and Jenny last night, it didn't really seem as if he had a choice.

MAC LITERALLY BUMPED into Buck Elkins on his way out of the hospital. He hadn't decided whether or not he was ready to share what Sam had told him with the sheriff, but when Buck point-blank asked what he'd found out, it seemed like fate was pushing him to.

"It was Colombian, all right," Mac admitted.

"Hell," Buck said. "I was hoping…" He shook his head, his lips closing over whatever else he wanted to say. "Guess our luck had to run out someday."

"Luck?"

"We've been damn lucky in this county. Especially when you consider what's happening everywhere else. Mac McCullar was responsible for that for a long time. Everybody knew Mac wasn't going to give. That nobody was going to buy his cooperation. And then… I guess this sounds strange, but I think the uproar when Mac was killed was some kind of protection in itself. The reaction of south Texans sort of scared the bad guys off. At least for a while. I guess they figured that the folks of this county wouldn't stand for any more. But now…'' Again Buck paused, shaking his head.

''I asked you the other day to think about who might be showing evidence of prosperity more than their neighbors. I just wondered if anybody's come to mind.''

Buck hesitated, maybe still remembering the edge of animosity that had colored their last conversation, but the knowledge of the Colombian connection had shaken him. Mac could tell that.

''A couple,'' he admitted. ''Ben Pirkle's adding on to his house. Bought him a few new cows. But I know for a fact his wife's daddy died over in Fort Davis about eight months ago. I figure he must have left them something, or they sold what the old man had and are investing the proceeds in their spread. And I have to tell you, it could stand the investment.''

''Anybody else?'' Mac asked.

''Phil Warren's making some noticeable improvements. But his daddy was a drunk. He had let the place go down so bad that it's hard to judge just how much of what Phil's spending is new money and how much is just no more wasting of what that ranch had always been capable of generating.''

''Is that it?''

Buck nodded. ''That's all that's come to mind since we talked.''

''Well, I appreciate the information.''

''Sharing,'' Buck said softly. ''I believe that's what you suggested.''

Mac knew Buck still had the impression that he was acting in some official capacity, and he decided it wouldn't do any harm to let him keep thinking that for a while.

''You let me know if you think of anything else, Sheriff Elkins. I'd appreciate it.''

''Same here,'' Buck said. ''How's he doing?''

"Chase? Chase is doing good, they say. He was sleeping the whole time I was there."

"I heard he was talking. I'd like to ask him about that night. About what preceded it."

"It's probably a little early for that."

"Then why don't you come on down to the office and let's go over what happened. You can do it at your convenience," Buck offered. "No real hurry, I guess. If it *is* what Jenny suspects, then, after five years, a couple of days won't make much difference."

"I thought you were convinced whoever shot Chase did it because of the drugs."

"I don't ever rule out any possibility," Buck said. "I learned that from Mac. Keep all your options open. Don't discount anything, no matter how unlikely it may seem, until you got proof positive of what really happened."

"Sounds like good advice," Mac said.

"Yeah," Buck agreed, grinning. "I always thought so. Course, Mac never gave me any bad advice. Except maybe to get into this line of work in the first place."

Mac laughed. He remembered the day he'd hired Buck. He remembered a lot about working with him. As Sam said, he might not be the brightest guy in the county, but he and Mac had been friends. Good friends.

Mac hadn't thought he'd like working with anybody else after Chase left, but Buck had been eager to learn and respectful of Mac's experience. They'd gotten along fine from the beginning.

"You take care now," Buck said. He touched his hat and then moved on down the corridor toward Chase's room.

Warren and Pirkle, Mac thought. Two of the same names Sam Kincaid had given him, and that meant, of course, that they needed to be checked out. He'd ask Jenny what she knew about those two situations when he got back to the ranch. She was bound to be as up on county gossip as anybody else around here. Besides, he remembered, she was out there all alone.

Mac didn't think anything was going to happen in broad daylight. He wouldn't be here if he did. But Sam was right. It wasn't the way it used to be down here. And it probably never would be again.

Chapter Eleven

Mac could smell the fried chicken as he climbed the back steps. And there were biscuits browning in the oven. That much was obvious, even standing on the back porch.

Those smells evoked memories. Nights he'd come home, later than he should have, totally exhausted, to find this house redolent with the odor of Jenny's cooking, aromas filtering out onto this porch, just as they were now.

Mac opened the kitchen door and saw Jenny standing at the stove, her back to him. She didn't turn around, even when he closed the door behind him, loudly enough that he knew she must have heard. He wondered suddenly if she was mad at him.

This was usually how Jenny's quiet, controlled anger was expressed. She never said much, but her back would get stiff, her small shoulders tight with righteous indignation over whatever stupid thing he'd done, just as they seemed to be now.

She hadn't been mad at him last night, Mac thought, trying to figure out what might be wrong. They had rounded up the other horses, but not the black, who was having nothing more to do with anybody, not even Jenny, whom he knew and trusted. By the time they'd decided it was no use, dawn was breaking.

Mac had tried to convince Jenny she needed to get some sleep, but she had refused to go back to bed. She had been understandably upset, disturbed over the attempt to burn the barn and frightened about the danger to the house and the animals, but she hadn't been angry with him. Not then, anyway. So something must have happened while he was at the hospital this morning.

"Chase is good," Mac offered into her silence, still studying his wife's back, trying to read her body language. He used to be pretty good at that.

Jenny took a deep breath, her shoulders moving against the thin knit of the pink T-shirt she wore, stretching the cloth across them, but still she didn't turn around. Mac glanced at the table. The violets he'd bought had disappeared from its surface, replaced by some scattered papers and what looked like a couple of stacks of canceled checks.

Maybe she'd been paying the bills. There had been months when that activity had been enough to set Mac's teeth on edge. But Chase had assured him that Jenny was making it. The ranch was free and clear, and Mac had put aside a nice little nest egg. Jenny was good at managing, and besides, Chase had kept telling him not to worry about anything. He was keeping an eye on things, his brother had said, and Jenny was doing just fine. If Chase said it, Mac knew he could count on it being true.

"That's good news," Jenny said. She forked the last piece of chicken out of the skillet and put it down carefully to drain on the paper towels she'd laid out over the platter. "I guess you wouldn't want anything to happen to Chase, would you? I guess you couldn't really *afford* that."

The words had been all right, but the tone of that comment had been wrong. And while Mac was still trying to figure out exactly what her tone had implied, Jenny turned around.

Dear sweet heaven, he thought, looking at her face. The olive skin was absolutely gray beneath its surface tan. Jenny hadn't had any sleep to speak of in the last three nights, and her eyes this morning had reflected that exhaustion, as he imagined his had. But this…

Whatever the hell had happened while he'd been at the hospital had hit Jenny hard. He had never seen her look like this before. Not even when he'd been hurt. Of course, he hadn't been able to see anything then. His eyes had been covered by bandages, along with pretty much every other inch of his burned and broken body.

Mac pulled himself out of the past, trying to concentrate on whatever was wrong now, on whatever had created the devastation that he could clearly read in her eyes. They were examining his face, he realized, tracing slowly over his features, lingering over every mark, on every centimeter of damaged skin. He waited, his lips tightening involuntarily, hating the prolonged examination she was making. Hating having her look at him, even after all this time.

Her scrutiny shifted, touching on the scarred throat, trailing down to examine the nearly useless hand, its thumb hooked again into the belt loop of his jeans, and then down the length of his legs to the worn boots. Jenny shook her head, slowly, before her eyes came back to his. To hold them. Trying to tell him something, Mac knew, but he couldn't figure out what.

"I guess you owe Chase McCullar a hell of a lot," she said.

It fit with what she had said before—about not being able to afford to have anything happen to Chase—and yet it didn't fit, somehow. It echoed in Mac's brain a split second before he realized it was almost the same thing Sam Kincaid had said to him at the hospital this morning. *"My guess is you owe a hell of a lot to Chase McCullar."* Except with Sam...

The realization hit Mac's stomach like a sledgehammer and then, like Jenny's gaze, it too traveled downward to his feet, a roiling, ice-cold wave of fear, weakening everything in its path. His heart thundered in his ears, so damn loud it blocked out everything around him.

She knew. Jenny knew who he was. That knowledge was burned into her face, seared into the delicate curve of her cheek and in the tight, uptilted angle of her chin, and it stared at him out of the dark, dilated pupils of her eyes.

"Hello, Mac," she said softly. "Long time no see."

He had never heard her voice like this. There wasn't a black place in Jenny McCullar's soul, but her voice was hard and so damn cold, it froze him to the bone. He shivered against the force of it. That was shock, he thought, trying to explain his trembling. Because he'd had no warning. No time to prepare.

"Jenny…" he began, but his throat closed over whatever useless words his brain was trying to feed it. And that was just as well. At the sound of her name on his lips, her mouth had clenched into a line, every muscle in her face stiffer somehow, and colder. Her eyes filled with moisture, but their blackness didn't warm, and she didn't let the tears escape. That was sheer determination not to let him see her cry, he knew.

Jenny McCullar wasn't a crying woman. He could count on the fingers of one hand the times he had seen her weep. When they'd gotten married. When her mother had died. And the night he had made Chase promise to do what he had asked.

Only, Mac hadn't seen those tears. He had listened to them instead, through the long, agony-filled hours of his nightmare darkness. A darkness he had believed would be forever. He had lain there—blind, paralyzed, so badly burned that no one had believed he *could* survive—and he had listened to Jenny cry.

"So why did you finally decide to come back, you lying son of a bitch?" she asked.

Mac had never in his life heard Jenny use language like that. Not to him. Not to anyone. He shook his head. There was no explanation he could give her. None he had any right to make.

Because I couldn't stand the thought of another man making love to you. That was the total reality of what he had done. But how the hell could he say that to her, when he knew it was unforgivable? He was destroying her life all over again.

"Because all those doctors Chase kept risking his life to pay for finally made you better?" she asked. "Because they got you put back together into something you think you can live with now? Is that it? Is that why you decided to show up again? Because you're all better now?''

"Jenny—''

"Humpty damn Dumpty,'' Jenny interrupted, each word cold and distinct and full of fury. "Is that what this is, Mac? Is that what this is all about?''

He didn't even try again. He stood there, bracing himself to take whatever she wanted to say to him. Knowing that he deserved it. And more. He should never have come back. *You can't go home again.* He couldn't remember who had said that, but it was true. He should never have tried, no matter what was happening down here.

"Well, life isn't eggs,'' Jenny said.

She still hadn't raised her voice, and he found himself wishing she would. Wishing that she'd shout at him. Throw things. Break something into a million pieces. Break him.

Maybe he could deal with that. It was how McCullars reacted. Not like this. Not this cold…hatred. He flinched against the word. No matter what he'd come to understand about the wrong he had done Jenny, he had never expected her to hate him for it.

"You *can't* put it back together again,'' she whispered. "And even you ought to know that.''

"I know,'' he said. At least he had finally figured that much out. He should never have come back. If he hadn't, Trent Richardson would still be around, and Jenny's eyes wouldn't look like they did now. Black and almost dead. Dead to emotion. Dead to him. "I know I can't,'' he repeated softly.

He made himself hold her gaze. She had a right to do this. A right to say whatever she wanted to say to him. He was acknowledging that. This time he wasn't running away.

"Why?'' she asked. "Just tell me why. Make me understand, Mac. Tell me what I ever did that made you think I deserved that.''

"I thought…'' Again, his voice faded. *I thought I was doing what was best for you.* That had been the justification for it all. From the beginning. There hadn't been much left of Mac McCullar. Jenny was right about that. Just about everything that could be broken or destroyed had been, and it had taken a long time to heal what was left.

And when he had made that decision, no one had given him hope that any of it *could* be healed. Even Chase had admitted that. It had been the one argument his brother couldn't get around. No one had given them any hope that anything would change about his condition—not for the better.

Jenny's head tilted, questioning.

"I thought it would be better just to disappear," Mac said.

"The word is *die,* Mac. That's what you did. You didn't disappear. You died. That's what Chase told me. No wonder he wouldn't let me see your *body,*" she said sarcastically. "I might have noticed that you were still breathing. Don't you think I might have noticed that?"

"This is not Chase's fault. Not any of it. I made him promise."

"Promise that he'd lie to me for five years? Is that what your brother promised you?"

Mac finally remembered to breathe, but he didn't answer. There was nothing else to explain. Nothing he could explain.

"I couldn't figure it out," Jenny said.

Her voice had changed, softening finally. Not the volume of it, which had never been raised, but the hardness. Mac didn't ask what she meant. He knew she would tell him. And he knew she needed to say it all, to get it all out in the open. The anger and the bitterness.

The smell of the chicken was sickening now, nausea pushing upward into his throat. But he held to the thought that Jenny had cooked his mother's chicken. Just like she used to. Cooked it for him? he wondered, almost daring to hope. It was the one positive note in this cruel symphony of disaster.

"I couldn't figure out why I reacted to you the way I did. Why I..." Jenny swallowed suddenly, the motion running down the slim line of her throat. "Why I wanted you so much. Or why I *knew* how your hands would feel on my body. I couldn't figure that out," she said again. "And then last night... If you had asked me last night..."

Her voice faltered, but it didn't matter. He knew what she meant. He had known it then. Had felt it. Her need. Her desire. Which had matched the nearly overpowering force of his.

"I guess it's a damn good thing you *didn't* ask, you bastard," she finished.

Gut shot. At least that was what those quiet words felt like. *"It's a damn good thing you didn't ask."* A good thing he hadn't made love to her.

Her eyes traced over his face again. "I'm not sure I *ever* would have figured it out," she said. "Even with what Chase said, I still didn't have a clue. 'Tell Mac to be careful.' I just thought..." She laughed—a small, bitter breath of sound. "I guess it doesn't really matter what I thought. But I never would have figured it out on my own," she said again.

"Who?" Mac asked. Who the hell *had* figured it out? he wondered. He still didn't believe Kincaid would tell her, and besides, Sam hadn't had time. Or did he tell Samantha, Jenny's best friend?

"Rio," Jenny said. "Rio found those."

Her dark head gestured toward the table, and Mac's gaze followed the movement. Checks? he thought, wondering what they could have to do with this.

"He didn't know what they meant," Jenny said. "Neither did I, at first. But then I realized the dates were the same."

"The dates?" Mac asked. He still didn't have any idea what she was talking about.

"Chase sold his half of the ranch and used the money to pay Matt Dawson's hospital bills. The first of hundreds of medical bills he's paid for Dawson during the last five years. But I had always believed Chase sold out because of Mac's death, because he couldn't stand living here without Mac."

She paused for a second, perhaps realizing that she was still speaking about him in the third person, and then she went on. "And the more I wondered about that, about which one was the real reason, the stranger that coincidence got—Chase selling his ranch just in time to pay for medical treatment for someone who'd been terribly hurt. And then, when I realized it wasn't a coincidence at all, *everything* made sense, even what Chase was trying to tell me at the hospital. 'Tell Mac,' he said, but I didn't think I could ever tell Mac anything. Not ever again."

The last words were whispered. Her voice as she said them was so full of pain it broke Mac's heart. He knew he was hearing a fraction of what he'd put Jenny through, an unwilling expression of some small part of the agony he had caused her during these last five years.

"When were you going to tell me, Mac? Maybe when we finally made love? Is that when you were planning on telling me the truth? Or is the truth that you weren't *ever* going to tell me?"

The truth, he thought. He wasn't sure he knew what the truth was anymore. Not the truth of why he had come back here. Or the truth about what he had intended to do. Truth had gotten all mixed up with need and want and the endless memories. Loving Jenny. All his memories of loving Jenny.

"I don't know," he said. That *was* true. Maybe all the truth he understood. And he knew he could never lie to her again.

Jenny nodded. "Okay," she said. Very softly. As softly as she had whispered that same word last night.

They said nothing else for a long, long time. Standing together in the house where they had lived as man and wife for five years. Where they had made love to each other through the warm, still hours of darkness. Where they had made plans and shared hopes and dreams and so much laughter.

And where there was nothing now. Nothing left between them but a cold and empty silence.

"Do you want me to go?" Mac asked finally, and he waited, his heart again like thunder in his ears.

After an eternity Jenny nodded, her dark eyes never leaving his. "I *do* want you to go," she said. "I just want you to go away and leave me alone. Just get the hell away from me," she whispered.

When Mac closed the door behind him, he didn't look back.

AFTER HE WAS GONE, Jenny took a deep, shuddering breath, still fighting tears. She shouldn't be crying. She had cried over Mac McCullar for five years, she thought.

And then he walks back onto this ranch and begins to court me all over again. Just as if nothing had happened. Just as if kissing me would make all the misery he's caused go away.

She knew it didn't make any sense to make him leave. She had loved Mac McCullar all her adult life, and she loved him still. But no one had the right to do what he had done. No matter what the circumstances. *No matter what,* she thought fiercely, and felt the tears threaten again.

She finally became aware of the smell. Angry at its intrusion into her justifiable fury, she turned around to cut off the oven, and using a dish towel, she took the baking sheet out of it. Black smoke rose from the bottom of the biscuits, the scent of it vile and nauseating.

Or maybe that was something else. Maybe that was the smell of all the lies they had told her. Chase and Mac. Always united against the rest of the world. She had known that, of course, but she had never thought the rest of the world included her.

Using its foot pedal, she opened the lid of the garbage can and dumped the biscuits into it. She had to pry a couple of them off the sheet, burning her fingers in the process. That small physical pain felt good somehow, and it was a legitimate excuse for giving in to the sting at the back of her eyes.

She walked to the stove and threw the empty baking sheet down on top of it, right next to the chicken. She didn't understand why she'd cooked all this. Was she so warped that her only reaction to finding out her dead husband was alive was to cook his favorite meal?

Maybe she was, because that was exactly what she had done, just as soon as she'd figured it all out. Angry now with her reaction, she picked up the platter of chicken, and the golden-brown pieces followed the biscuits into the trash.

She could occupy maybe ten minutes cleaning up the kitchen. It would give her hands something to do. But eventually, of course, she would have to think about what had happened this morning. And about what she intended to do about it.

Mac wouldn't leave. She knew that. She knew him so well, she thought. She understood exactly the way his mind worked. She even understood why he had "died" five years ago. Maybe she couldn't forgive him, but she knew why he had done it. Just as she knew he wouldn't leave her and Samantha out here alone. Not with Chase injured. Not with the drugs and the violence.

Despite what he had said, Mac McCullar wasn't going anywhere. And that would at least give her time to think.

"Get in," Rio ordered.

Mac hadn't even heard the approach of the car. He hadn't heard anything since Jenny had told him to get out of their house. Her house, he amended. But when he had, there had been nowhere to go, no means of transportation except the pickup, which also belonged to Jenny, of course.

He stopped walking and bent reluctantly to look through the open passenger-side window at his half brother. The same knowledge that had been in Jenny's eyes was in Rio's. After all, Rio had been the one who had helped Jenny figure it out.

"You didn't have to tell her," Mac said. "I wasn't planning on staying."

"I didn't tell her," Rio denied. "I didn't have any idea what was going on. Other than the fact that you weren't who you said you were. Jenny figured out the rest by herself. Look, just get in the car. I'll take you wherever you want to go. You're in no condition—''

The suggestion was cut off, maybe in reaction to the sudden coldness in Mac's eyes. "I'm fine," he said distinctly.

He had taken another couple of steps before he realized that wasn't exactly true. After last night, he probably wasn't up to hiking off a McCullar "mad." Until he'd stopped walking, however, he hadn't realized how badly his hip was objecting to the pace he'd set.

"Get in," Rio said again. He was holding the car to a speed that matched Mac's limping stride. "I just want to talk to you. And I swear I didn't tell Jenny who you are. But whatever happened between you and Jenny, you and I still need to talk.''

Mac finally stopped walking. "About what?" he asked. He didn't bother to bend down to window level to say it.

"About what's been going on down here. About last night. Jenny told me what happened. We need to make some plans.'' Rio's voice was sincere, but strangely disembodied, coming from inside the car, which had now stopped beside Mac.

As good an excuse as any to stop this mindless journey to nowhere, Mac thought. And certainly the best offer he was likely to get out here. Hell, even as well as he knew this county, he wasn't real sure where he was. He had just started walking. Just doing what Jenny had told him to do.

He opened the car door and crawled inside. He supposed it felt better to sit down, to get off his feet, but he knew the getting up would be hell. Rio began to turn the car around on the narrow dirt road. Mac didn't attempt to figure out exactly where they were. It didn't really matter as long as Rio knew.

"Jenny said somebody tried to burn the barn last night and you stopped them," Rio said.

"They took time to get the horses out. I heard the black having hysterics. *He* stopped them. Not me," Mac said.

"They'll try again," Rio said. "That or something else.''

Mac nodded. His breathing had begun to ease, and he realized that he felt better talking about it. And for some reason he felt less hopeless just knowing that Rio was here. That he was going to be here.

"So what do we do now?" Rio asked.

Mac turned his head. His half brother's classic profile was silhouetted against the window. Its lines were as pure and as finely shaped as Trent Richardson's, Mac thought. He took another breath, trying not to think about that. Trying to concentrate on the other. *What do we do?*

"The stuff was Colombian," Mac offered.

Rio nodded. "I was pretty certain of that, just from looking at it."

"You know anything about the distribution? And before you go off half-cocked, that's not an accusation. It's a request for information." He watched one corner of Rio's mouth lift.

"McCullar temper," his half brother said. "I apologize for losing it that day." His dark eyes, filled with amused self-mockery, flicked off their focus on the dirt road to meet Mac's and then went back to his driving again.

Suddenly, despite all that had happened today, despite the way he had felt when Jenny threw him out of his own house, Mac found himself smiling, too. *McCullar temper.*

Rio was his brother, his flesh and blood. Another McCullar. Until this moment Mac hadn't realized how much he had missed Chase, missed having someone he could trust, someone to talk to about whatever the hell was happening out here. Someone willing and more than able to help him fight against it. Now he knew he had someone beside him who would. *What do we do?*

"Maybe we need to shake the trees a little more," Mac suggested. "But first we have to get the women and children out of here."

"That's pretty old-fashioned," Rio said. "And if you're serious, I don't think you should let Jenny hear you say that. Anne either, for that matter. They're both pretty handy at defending themselves."

"Then I guess it's up to you to convince them this isn't the time or the place for them to try." Mac knew he couldn't tell Jenny to leave the ranch. She wouldn't listen to him. That was another right he had forfeited.

"You have any idea how I'm going to accomplish that?" Rio asked, that quiet amusement back in his voice.

"Lie to them if you have to, but convince them to go somewhere that's safe. Just for a few days. Maybe to your brother-in-law's house in San Antonio."

Mac had made himself say the words, had forced them past lips that were reluctant to form them. It hurt just to think about Jenny being with Richardson. He had believed his voice was controlled, but again his brother's black eyes left the road to study his face.

"You really want me to send Jenny to Trent's?"

"And Anne and Mandy," Mac agreed. "It's the safest place, it seems to me. He'll look after them, won't he?"

It was too long before Rio answered, obviously thinking about that question. Or maybe about what had prompted Mac McCullar to make the suggestion, and about its implications.

"With his life," Rio agreed finally.

"That's what we want," Mac said. "Somebody who won't let anything happen to them while we finish up down here."

"Are you absolutely sure that's what you want to do, Mac?" Rio asked. This time he didn't look at his half brother.

"I'm sure," Mac said quietly. "That's just about the only thing in this entire fiasco that I *am* sure of."

"ALL WE'RE ASKING IS that you help us finish what Chase started before he got shot," Mac said.

Buck Elkins's eyes didn't react, but his lips pursed slightly, so Mac knew he was thinking about it.

"What he *started* got Chase shot. Did you think about that?"

"I guess that's the point. Somebody reacted. Only we don't know exactly who he talked to."

Buck's eyes shifted to Rio, who hadn't said a word so far. He and Mac had decided it would be better that way. There was no love lost between the sheriff and Rio Delgado. No respect, either. After a moment, Elkins's gaze left Rio's expressionless face to come back to Mac.

"I don't know who Chase talked to, either," Buck said. "Except for me. He came in here and told me what you all were planning to do. I told him he was a fool. You don't deliberately stir up a nest of rattlers. Not if you're smart. I'll tell you two the same thing."

"Maybe you do if that's the only way you can get 'em to come out of their holes," Mac said. "Apparently, it worked. They're running scared. They shot Chase, burned the line shack where I was supposed to be sleeping, and last night they tried to burn Jenny McCullar's barn. It seems to me all the stirring that's been done so far's been on their part. And I have to tell you, Sheriff, I'm pretty tired of the McCullars being their target."

Elkins drew in a breath and then expelled it. Noisily. "So what do you want me to do about it?" he asked.

Not agreement, Mac thought, not yet. But at least he was still listening. "You and Sam Kincaid gave me identical names of folks in this county who all of a sudden have more money than they should have. You both mentioned Ben Pirkle and Phillip Warren. Sam added Cal Salinas."

"Cal?" Buck asked. "Hell, Cal is no more running drugs than I am. Is that what Sam told you? That old bastard doesn't—"

"Mr. Kincaid just said Salinas has more money showing than the hand he'd been dealt justifies."

"Cal had two kids in college at the same time. They graduate, he gets himself a raise. It's as simple as that."

And if it were, Mac thought, then Sam Kincaid would probably have known about it. "And you think Pirkle's windfall is an inheritance of some kind?"

"That's what I hear," Buck agreed.

"Which leaves Warren," Rio said. "A matter of simple subtraction."

Elkins's eyes again shifted focus. "And just exactly what do you want me to do with the result of your math?" he asked.

Sarcasm and dislike had colored the question. Apparently the animosity was mutual between those two, Mac realized. *But you shouldn't ever let your personal feelings influence an investigation, Buck. I taught you better than that.*

"I just want you to squeeze him a little," Mac said aloud. "Just to see if he jumps."

"I got no cause to hassle Warren."

"But you got cause enough to get in that county-paid-for car and ride on out to his place and ask a few questions," Mac suggested quietly. "You've had an attempted murder and a case of arson in your jurisdiction during the last week, Sheriff. I think you got ample cause to be asking *somebody* some questions."

"Is that a fact?" Buck said. The reddish stain was again under the skin that stretched over his cheekbones.

"That *is* a fact," Mac agreed softly.

Maybe Buck didn't like hearing his criticism, but Mac hadn't seen much evidence that the sheriff was pursuing what had happened to Chase or trying to solve the fire at Jenny's ranch. He hadn't seen much evidence at all of Elkins nosing around the county since he'd been home.

"You know, things were pretty quiet around here until *you* showed up," Buck said to Mac, his hazel eyes cold.

"That's not how I remember it," Rio said.

The telltale flush deepened. "And the first wave of trouble rode into town when you did," Buck countered, looking at Rio again.

"This is getting us nowhere," Mac interrupted before his half brother could retaliate. "All I'm asking you to do, is to ride out and question Phillip Warren. Just mention the things that have happened lately. Just see what happens."

"You're hoping if I do that, he'll react in some way?"

"That's what we're hoping."

"And if he jumps?" Buck asked.

"We'll be ready for him."

"You're going to stake out the McCullar ranches?"

"We're already doing that. But there's just so many nights you can sit up with a rifle for company. We just want a little pressure applied to certain people to see if they react."

"I don't like vigilante justice," Buck said.

"Neither did I," Rio said.

Out of the corner of his eye Mac could see Rio's lips tilt again, his slow smile mocking the sheriff's statement. Elkins hadn't prevented the kind of justice he claimed to despise when somebody in this county had come out to the ranch to beat Delgado up.

"If you're doing a stakeout," Buck said, "then you're gonna have to do it the right way. The official way. I'll be out there with you."

"You're more than welcome," Mac agreed. "But first talk to Warren. Put some pressure on him. Make him think things may be coming unraveled, that we know more than we really do. If he is the one, give him some reason to try again."

"And if he's not?"

"Then I would imagine nothing's going to happen tonight," Mac suggested. "Except we're all going to lose a few more hours of sleep."

Chapter Twelve

If anything, Mac thought, looking at the sky, it was even darker than it had been last night. Darker and colder, but then the nights were cold this late in the year.

He shifted his weight, straightening his shoulders against the rock behind him. They were still stiff, but he felt a hell of a lot better than he had last night, probably because he had slept most of the afternoon, stretched out on Mandy's bed.

And while he slept, he hadn't had to think about anything. Not about what had been in Jenny's face this morning or what she had said about Chase risking his life to pay his medical bills or even about what had happened here last night.

So at least he wasn't in danger of drifting off as he had been then, he thought. Besides, he now had all those things to think about, and a whole lot of darkness to do it in.

He hadn't seen Jenny after the scene in the kitchen this morning. She had agreed to Rio's suggestion that she'd be wise not to spend the night out here alone. Rio had somehow managed to convince the two women to take Mandy to San Antonio. They had left at twilight, with Anne driving, and they were going to stay there for a few days.

Mac didn't know how much Rio had had to tell Jenny about what they planned to do. Not much, Mac guessed, or she'd still be here. Jenny wasn't the kind to cut and run. Not from danger. Not from anything, he thought, a smile touching the still-mobile corner of his mouth.

And soon she would be with Trent Richardson, he thought, the smile fading. Although he knew that was for the best, his gut ached every time he thought about her there, every time he pictured that handsome bastard's face or thought about his hands touching Jenny.

Again, Mac was determined *not* to think about Jenny and Richardson. Tonight was about something else. Remembering Jenny's eyes and the coldness in her voice this morning wouldn't do him any good in getting ready for what might happen here in this other cold darkness.

True to his word, Buck Elkins had arrived a few minutes ago, about an hour after nightfall, driving in with his lights off so that anybody watching from the bluff or from anywhere else around here wouldn't know what was going on. Like the McCullars, Buck knew this land well enough to navigate it in the dark. After all, it wasn't as if there would be any traffic to avoid on these dirt roads, Mac thought.

Not unless they got real lucky.

THEY HADN'T TALKED MUCH as the miles sped by in the growing darkness. Jenny had seen the same unspoken anxiety in Anne's face that was probably reflected in her own. Despite Rio's assurance that this hurried trip was only a precaution, all of Jenny's well-developed instincts had been screaming warnings since she'd gotten off the phone with him.

She had been a lawman's wife for too many years not to have those instincts. And too many years not to listen to them. Mac always said he heeded them, that they had saved his life on more than one occasion.

Mac, she thought, regret tightening her throat and threatening the fragile control she had managed to impose in the hours since he'd walked out her back door. After five years of endless, gnawing loneliness, she had been within ten feet of Mac, and all she could do was curse at him and then throw him out of his own house. It was as bizarre a reaction, she now knew, as cooking lunch had been. As bizarre as everything she'd done since she had found out he was alive.

And all that anger was because he had tried to protect her. That was the bottom line of what Mac had done. She had realized that as soon as she had worked past her fury and her bitterness, past all the hurt. There had been no reason for the lie Mac had created other than to protect her, just as he had always protected her. This time, from what he thought he had become—a man too badly injured to ever recover. To ever be a man again.

That was something else she had done after she drove Mac away. She had sat down with that stack of checks and tried to imagine what the last five years had been like for him. How many hours of suffering were represented by this one or by that? The sheer number of those checks moving through her trembling fingers told their own story.

And how great had been *his* loneliness? she had finally thought to wonder. Mac McCullar had been isolated from everything and everyone he had known in his entire life while he fought a battle whose victories would be measured in millimeters of movement and counted in blessed minutes that were sometimes free from pain. *Sometimes* free, she thought, remembering all the changes. Remembering Mac, as she had all afternoon. So many things to remember.

"There's something wrong about this," she said softly.

"Wrong?" Anne asked.

"About our leaving. Something wrong about running away."

"But Rio said—"

"Rio was lying," Jenny interrupted. "Couldn't you tell he was lying? And I'm willing to bet Mac put him up to it."

"But why?"

"I don't know, but something's…" Jenny paused, shaking her head in frustration because she really didn't know. "I have to go back," she said finally.

"Rio said—"

"Whatever's happening back there, Rio's in it up to his neck. You take Mandy on to Trent's, but... I'm sorry, Anne, but I have to go back."

"If something *is* going on, then the ranch is the last place you need to be. You know that, Jenny."

"He wanted to get us out of the way," Jenny said softly. "Out of the way of whatever's going to happen. Damn him. Damn them all," she said fiercely.

The McCullars and their overdeveloped sense of duty, she thought. If he were able, Chase would be right there with them, in on whatever they had planned. Right there sticking his head into another noose, as Mac and Rio were. Putting themselves in harm's way because it was the right thing to do. Because... Because they were McCullars, she thought. Because they were lawmen. And that's what lawmen did.

"I'm going back," Jenny said again.

"Not without me, you're not," Anne said, and then her voice softened, filled with tenderness. "Remember, that's my hardheaded husband we left back there."

Jenny smiled, thinking about those words, about having the right again to say them. "Believe me," she said softly, "I understand exactly how you feel about that."

"I'm sorry, Jenny. I didn't mean to remind you of Mac," Anne said.

"You didn't remind me. Someone else did that. And about a lot of other things I had forgotten. That's part of why I have to go back."

"What about Mandy?" Anne asked.

"I know where we can take Mandy," Jenny assured her. "And maybe...maybe get them some help at the same time."

"Help?" Anne repeated.

"I know just the place and the person who can arrange for both," Jenny said.

So FAR IT HAD BEEN as silent as a tomb out here, Mac thought, if he discounted the noises that were so familiar he almost didn't hear them. Even after five years away from this desert where he'd been born, its night sounds were still as familiar as his own heartbeat.

He glanced to his right, toward the house. He knew Buck was hidden somewhere in the shadows there, but he couldn't see him. He couldn't see anything but the shape of the McCullar homestead looming out of the darkness. But he knew the sheriff would be right where he was supposed to be. As would his brother.

They had decided they couldn't risk leaving either ranch unprotected, even if it meant splitting their forces, so Rio was at Chase's, keeping watch there. Their prearranged signal, two shots fired into the air, would bring Rio here in a matter of minutes. Or send Mac and Buck over there.

Mac glanced back toward the barn. It was as ghostly as the house. Nothing moving. Nothing out of the ordinary. Mac sighed in frustration. He had never thought Ben had anything to do with drugs. Or Cal Salinas, for that matter. What he remembered about Warren, however, had seemed to make him a more likely candidate to be involved in something like this.

"The apples don't fall far from the tree," his grandmother used to say. That wasn't always true, of course. You just had to look at Drew McCullar's sons, he thought, and it was obvious—

Mac's head came up, his eye straining to see into the darkness. It hadn't been a sound tonight that had caught his attention. It was a shape, a more solid darkness, moving across the empty space between the shadow of the barn and the back of the house.

The house? Mac thought with a frisson of fear. There was nobody inside, of course, but the adrenaline had starting pumping at the thought. His great-grandfather had built that homestead, hauling the lumber in by wagon. And Mac wasn't about to sit here and watch somebody set it on fire.

He eased up, trying to make as little noise as possible, fighting the aching stiffness of his body. Too old? he wondered again. Or maybe just too beat-up, he amended. Then he banished the thought. Neither Rio nor Buck had suggested that he wasn't up to this, so he wasn't going to start doubting himself.

But in thinking that, he wondered suddenly if Buck was aware that they had company. He looked again to his right, but he still couldn't see anything of the sheriff. Was it possible that it had been Buck he'd seen moving between the barn and the back porch? Had Buck heard something that had caused him to risk changing his position?

That was the danger in this kind of thing. Not knowing where everyone was. Somebody could get hurt playing games in the darkness. He wouldn't have agreed to this if he hadn't been sure Buck understood how this was done, sure he could count on him not to start shooting at the first sound, the first movement. They had worked this kind of stakeout before. A long time ago, of course, but its rules were something you never forgot.

Mac began easing toward the barn. He intended to skirt along the far side of the building and then come around the back to follow whoever he had seen moving toward the house. Suddenly, there was that old familiar prickling along his spine—that cold breath fluttering along the sensitive nerve endings there. *Lawman's instinct.*

The shadows were deeper behind the barn, and he could already smell the gasoline, the fumes drifting toward him from the direction of the house. There were noises, too. Possibly too soft to awaken someone sleeping inside, but he wasn't sure about that, and he wondered how the arsonist could be.

It was almost as if whoever was over there didn't care if he made some noise. As if…he *knew,* Mac realized. As if whoever was throwing gasoline around the McCullar homestead *knew* there was no one inside.

And it even made sense. Would someone who had taken the time to get the horses out of a barn before they burned it be willing to set fire to a building where he thought people were sleeping? Only, the question that followed that line of reasoning was, *how the hell could he know the house was empty?*

"That's about enough. You can put the can down now."

Buck Elkins's voice was commanding and full of authority. Full of confidence. That was something else Mac had taught him. To sound like you were in charge, that you were totally in control, whether you believed you really were or not.

The beam of Buck's flashlight had stabbed out of the darkness to catch a bending figure holding a jerrican, just like the one that had been left in the barn last night. Mac wasn't near enough to see the man's features, but whoever their terrorist was, he wasn't moving.

"Put it down," Buck ordered, "and get your hands up."

The figure hesitated, still caught in the slender shaft of light that pinned him against the surrounding night. Slowly, he set the can on the ground and straightened.

"Dawson, you there?" Buck asked, pitching his voice a little louder, probably in the mistaken belief that Mac was still at his original post.

"I'm right here," Mac said.

The figure that had been frozen by the light moved, a half turn toward the shadows behind the barn where Mac was standing. Surprise that there was a second man? Mac wondered. Or surprise that he was this close?

"What the hell's going on?" a voice questioned.

Not Buck's voice, Mac realized. The man with the can. And instead of sounding frightened that he'd been caught, there had been some other emotion in his tone, something Mac couldn't quite identify.

"It's over," Mac said. "It's all over."

"Who the hell are you?"

If that question had been addressed to him, Mac thought, it wasn't one he was ready to answer. Not yet, anyway. Not until he understood what this was all about—drugs or a long-ago "murder," or maybe even both.

"What the hell's going on, Buck?" the speaker asked again. "You—"

The last few words were hidden by Elkins's voice, which had been raised over them. "You just keep your mouth shut and your hands in the air. You'll have plenty of time to talk when we get down to the sheriff's office."

There was silence after that. Apparently the man with the gasoline was taking Buck's injunction to heart. As Mac watched, the sheriff moved out of the darkness behind the house. The flashlight pinpointed his location, its beam projecting waveringly from the black emptiness behind it as he walked.

"Come on out here, Matt, and take a look at what I've found," Buck said. "You aren't going to believe this."

Which meant it wasn't Phil Warren, Mac guessed. Or any of the others they'd suspected. But somebody he knew, somebody Buck thought he'd recognize. Except…why would Buck Elkins believe he'd recognize anyone from this county? As far as Buck knew, he was a stranger to them all. Unless…

Mac had already begun walking forward as he reasoned, nearer to the two men. He was still holding the heavy Colt, but his fingers were relaxed around it. It was over, the capture made, and the adrenaline rush was beginning to subside, his heart rate to slow, although for some reason the primitive warning still danced along his spine.

That instinct had failed him only once, Mac thought. That night he had climbed into his truck and turned the key in the ignition. He hadn't had any inkling of what was about to happen. Not like now. Not like this growing unease. He had a premonition deep in his gut that something was wrong, except he had no concrete reason to think that. He hadn't heard or seen anyone else moving in the darkness, and Buck seemed to have this guy under control. Why, then, Mac wondered, did he feel so vulnerable? So damned exposed?

He was close enough now that he could see the face of the man revealed by Buck's flashlight. The man who had held the gasoline can was Phillip Warren. He looked enough like his dead father that Mac knew he wasn't mistaken, even though it had been a long time since he'd seen Warren. So what Buck had said made no sense.

"What the hell is this, Buck?" Warren said again. "Who's he?" This time the emotion in his voice was recognizable. It was fear. Sheer, undiluted terror.

"The McCullars say they're tired of being targets," Buck said softly. Then the beam of the flashlight went out, suddenly plunging the three of them back into the moonless darkness.

Acting on that nagging instinct alone, Mac threw himself to the ground, landing hard, just as two shots rang out. His left arm had automatically been extended to break his fall, and the big Colt he'd been holding, too damn loosely, he realized, skittered away into the darkness as he hit. Buck's words echoed in his head, along with the report of the gun and the sounds that followed it. Something or someone falling. And then movement.

"The McCullars say they're tired of being targets."

He thought for a split second that Warren had shot Buck. But then he knew that was wrong. The flashlight had gone out before those shots were fired. It had been deliberately cut off so Elkins couldn't be pinpointed by its light.

Buck had called Mac to come out here, out of the shadows, supposedly to identify Warren, and then he had given it all away by what he had said. He just couldn't resist letting Mac know, making him understand before he shot him that he knew who he was.

"The McCullars say they're tired of being targets." Only it had been *Mac* who had said that, in Buck's office this afternoon, and it hadn't been phrased exactly that way.

Those realizations came lightning fast, and Mac acted on them. He rolled, just as the third bullet struck the earth, too near to where he had been. Maybe Buck's night vision was better than his, Mac thought, scrambling away, trying desperately to reach the shadows of the barn. Not the other way, because Elkins had been between him and the house. *Had* been. Now Mac had no idea where Buck was.

There was another shot before he reached the enfolding darkness beside the barn, but it wasn't close. Apparently Buck hadn't seen or heard enough to figure out where he was. But Buck still had a gun, and through his own stupidity he no longer did. Somebody could get hurt in the darkness, Mac had thought before, and now he knew that someone was probably going to be him.

Mac got to his feet, moving carefully, noiselessly, despite the fact that his knees were trembling. He leaned against the wall, trying to force his body to blend into it. Trying to become invisible. Trying to control the sound of his breathing. Again, he strained to see, to hear, to find Elkins, but the night was as silent as it had been before all this had started.

He knew now what Buck had intended. Everybody was supposed to end up dead. Buck had planned to kill all of them. Phillip Warren, whom Elkins had somehow gotten to show up out here with that can of gasoline, his fingerprints all over it, would be blamed for Mac's and Rio's deaths, for the arson, and for shooting Chase.

Chase, Mac thought suddenly. Who wouldn't know what the hell had gone on out here. Who would believe that the threat was over. Who would no longer be on his guard.

Eventually, he realized, Elkins would get Chase, too, and then the sheriff could keep on doing what he'd been doing for the last five years. Allowing the drugs to come in. Cooperating with the cartels. Doing whatever else would make him a profit.

They hadn't been able to buy Mac when this was his county, but apparently Buck Elkins had succumbed to the lure. It was a hell of a temptation and a damned profitable business. All a lawman really had to do was to look the other way, just leave the bastards alone. That was all they wanted.

Mac put his head against the roughness of the wooden planks behind him, listening for Rio's arrival. Sound traveled a hell of a long way through this cold, clear air, which was why they'd arranged that signal. When he heard those shots, his half brother would come. And Mac realized there was no way to warn him without revealing himself to Elkins.

The noise he heard, however, wasn't Rio. It was near at hand. Too close for comfort. Mac edged along the wall of the barn, toward the front and away from the sound. He thought about going inside. He knew the barn far better than Buck, but he also remembered the stallion and what had happened last night.

If that had even been Buck last night, he realized. There was always the possibility that Warren had been the one sent to the ranch with the gasoline last night, just as he had been tonight. That would explain Warren's surprise when Buck had stopped him from throwing the gas around. And why he hadn't been worried about making noise. Buck had *told* him that everybody was gone. That way Warren would make enough noise for Mac to hear. He'd be killed in the act, and it would be made to appear that he'd killed the McCullars. That was Buck's plan. Everybody had to end up dead. So Buck wasn't going to leave now. Not with him or Rio still alive. He couldn't afford to.

Maybe he could get the black to react as he had last night, Mac thought suddenly. Make enough noise to lure Buck inside the barn to try to find him, just as that noise had lured Mac last night. And Mac would be waiting for him in the darkness of a building he knew far better than his assailant. It wasn't a very good plan, but it beat the hell out of doing nothing and letting his unsuspecting brother meet up with Elkins in the dark.

Mac lifted the wooden latch that barred the double doors and opened the left-hand side. Not the door with the squealing hinges, but the other, which moved smoothly and silently. It wasn't the time for noise. Not yet.

He slipped inside. The animals were quiet, unalarmed by his presence. Mac felt his way along the stalls. In the darkness his hand brushed against an inquiring nose thrust out over a half door, but the horse, probably Jenny's gelding, made no sound.

Mac reached the stall in which the stallion was kept and began unfastening the gate. The black reacted, all right, just as he had last night, making exactly what Mac had been hoping for—maybe enough noise to get Elkins to come in here to find Mac. He kept the stallion inside long enough for him to get pretty upset and then, just in case Buck hadn't figured out where he was...

"Get," Mac said softly. He stepped away from the opening, finally allowing the black to go past him. It didn't take a slap on the rump to get him started tonight. The stallion was out the barn door Mac had left open in a matter of seconds.

As Mac listened, he held his breath, trying to find any noise other than the sound of the stallion's hoofbeats. For a long time there was nothing. And then there was. A telltale whisper of noise. Someone had entered the barn. Mac flattened his body against the wall, deeper into the shadows.

Come on, Buck, he urged. *You got no choice. If you don't take me down, it's all over. All finished. All the rot you've brought into my county will be ended.*

Elkins was moving now along the line of stalls. Mac could hear him. An occasional sound. Coming closer to the deepest darkness where he was hiding. *Near enough,* Mac prayed. *Just come near enough.*

And then the door creaked. It couldn't be Buck, Mac had time to realize, before the finger of flame from Elkins's gun answered that noise and was answered by an outcry. But in taking that shot, the sheriff had pinpointed his position.

Mac launched himself toward it, and his arms closed around Buck's upper body before he could get off another one. But the right elbow Elkins slammed backward and the outward pressure from his left arm loosened the hold of Mac's good hand on his own right wrist.

Then Buck twisted his body, breaking Mac's grip entirely. Elkins staggered backward, carried by the momentum of his unexpected success, and Mac lunged for him again, knowing that he had to keep him off-balance, had to keep the muzzle of that gun pointed away from his body.

Thank God Buck was right-handed, Mac had time to think, before the reaching fingers of his good left hand found and fastened around the revolver. He held on for dear life, but Elkins was flailing at him with his other fist, most of the blows glancing off his arm or his ribs.

Mac used his weaker right arm like a shield, trying to deflect the punches. At the same time he fought to keep the gun pointed upward, using his weight to push Elkins toward the door. Someone had been out there—Rio, Mac believed. And if Buck's shot hadn't brought his brother down, then it was possible that between the two of them...

Elkins was rabbit-punching now, getting the rhythm of it. Short, hard jabs, some of which were landing solidly against Mac's ribs and solar plexus. And they were having an effect.

The air was beginning to thin around Mac's head as it had last night when the black had thrown him to the ground. He was literally attempting to wrestle Buck out through the open doors, but he knew he was running out of strength.

The revolver was slippery in his grasp, the metal wet with his own sweat, making it damn hard to hold. And then he wasn't holding it anymore. Buck stumbled out the double doors, falling backward, and as he fell the gun was pulled from Mac's fingers. Off-balance, Mac went down on top of the sheriff.

There was a second when neither of them moved, stunned by the force of the landing, and then Elkins's body arched upward, attempting to roll Mac off. Instead, Mac used the last of his strength to try to throw himself over the gun, to pin Buck's arm to the ground. But he misjudged where it was and hit only dirt instead.

He managed to get to his knees before Buck swung the revolver in a whistling arc, slamming the butt into Mac's left temple. It slid across his eyebrow, cutting the flesh to the bone.

Mac fought to stay conscious, fought to protect himself now, as the revolver came at him again.

Mac hadn't even been aware that he had gotten his hands up, but he must have. The gun butt struck the knuckles of his good hand, and the next blow ricocheted off his wrist. He could hear that one, could feel the numbing force of it, but the pain was delayed. Shock maybe, or adrenaline, but he knew it would come, knew that he'd feel it eventually. *If* he survived long enough.

His left wrist was probably broken, he thought. His mind seemed to be working far better than anything else right now. His thought processes were for some reason crystal clear. Even the thought that it might be better this way. Better for Jenny.

With the effect of those three rapid blows slowing his opponent, Buck had gotten to his knees. Mac took a roundhouse swing at the sheriff with his right arm, using the hand he couldn't even fold into a fist. It struck Buck's shoulder and glanced upward to impact harmlessly against his cheek. There was not enough force behind it to rock him.

All those crystal-clear thoughts that had been skipping through Mac's head seconds before had disappeared behind the mist of pain and fatigue. All that guided him now was instinct—a primitive desire for survival that overrode anything else.

Mac had gotten halfway up, one leg under him, when Buck drove his shoulder into his chest. The momentum of it lifted Mac and shoved him backward. The ground came up to meet the back of his head as it had last night. Came up fast and hard.

When he looked up through the veil of blood from the cut over his good eye, Buck was standing over him in the darkness. The sheriff's legs in their khaki uniform pants were spread wide to maintain his balance, and his body swayed slightly. Fatigue, maybe, but Elkins wasn't the one who was down. And he wasn't the one who looking up into the muzzle of a .45.

"You son of a bitch," Buck said softly. "You just don't know how to give up, do you. You McCullar bastards won't even stay in your damn graves."

"How did you know?" Mac asked. *Just keep him talking. Try to think of something.*

"All those things you used to preach to me about. Cooperating with other agencies. Getting out of the office in our 'county-paid-for cars.' You ain't really changed, Mac. Still preaching those same old sermons. Only this is my county now, and I don't need you to tell me how to run it."

"You were the one," Mac said. "It was you five years ago."

"I knew you weren't ever gonna take their money. Too stupid, I guess. And if you didn't, then I knew I couldn't."

"You set me up?"

He couldn't see Buck's face, couldn't see much of anything anymore, truth be told. Jenny had asked him that. *What is the truth?* But *that* truth was something else he didn't understand, and he guessed now he never would.

"I always liked you, Mac, but you were just too damn bull-headed to listen to reason. And I knew you never would."

"The money meant that much? Enough to kill me for?"

"The money," Buck agreed. "Being in charge. I *ran* this county when you were gone. Opportunities you never saw. Things that could have made us both rich. But I always knew you wouldn't listen. So I put that bomb in your truck. And I'd do it again. You aren't going to come back here and screw up what I got. What I worked for. This time, you son of a bitch," Buck added softly, "this time you're damn well gonna stay dead."

The gun was directed toward his heart, and Buck was probably right about it all. This time he *was* going to stay dead.

Suddenly the black stallion exploded out of the darkness, his big body aimed directly at the man holding the gun. Buck had time enough to turn and fire, but the bullet was wild. The

black careened by him, close enough to force Elkins away
from Mac.

As soon as he had heard the stallion's approach, Mac had
curled into a ball, pulling his legs up into his chest, but he
hadn't entirely escaped the horse's hooves. And he also wasn't
dead, he thought, which seemed like more than a fair
exchange.

Mac rolled once and then crab-crawled out of the black's
way. He could hear the stallion behind him, the thunder of his
passage on the hard-packed earth of the yard. He could hear
the movement of his big body, could even hear his breathing.
The black cut the sheriff off again and then reversed immediately, coming at Buck from the other direction now, pushing
Elkins farther away from Mac. Mac finally realized what was
going on.

Rio was using the quarter horse to cut Buck Elkins like he'd
cut a cow, keeping the sheriff off-balance and having to dodge
the massive weight of the animal, which came dangerously
close with every short, quick pass. Keeping Buck from having
time enough to aim and fire. Keeping him dodging to prevent
being knocked down under those ironclad hooves.

And it was working. He could hear that, too. The sounds
of breathing. Both man's and beast's. Elkins's was growing
louder the longer it went on. And if he fell...

Then there was something else. A growing thrump that
wasn't part of that battle. And the yard was suddenly both too
loud and too bright, the ground around Mac dissolving upward
into a whirlwind, pulled by the rotor of the helicopter that
hovered, searchlights flaring downward on the scene below.

And the voice, amplified by a bullhorn, was unmistakably
the voice of authority. The voice Buck Elkins had finally
achieved. ''Throw the gun down and back away from it. Back
off, both of you.''

That was when Buck Elkins made his fatal mistake. Instead
of obeying that voice, he tried to run from it. Gun in hand,

apparently forgotten, the sheriff took off toward the county-paid-for car he'd driven out here. The amplified voice tried a couple more times to stop him, but it didn't do any good. Elkins never even slowed until they shot him.

Chapter Thirteen

And when it was finally all over, there were only the two of them left.

Anne had gone to the hospital with Rio to get Buck Elkins's bullet taken out of his forearm. Mac now knew that his half brother had ridden his black stallion left-handed and bareback in that incredible display of horsemanship. And they had saved Mac's life.

He probably should have been on his way to the hospital with them, but Mac hadn't mentioned his wrist to anybody. He could still move his fingers, so he guessed that meant the arm wasn't broken. Right now he didn't care much if it was. He was almost too tired to think. Too tired to deal with getting a professional assessment of the injury. Just too damn tired to do anything.

The authorities that Sam Kincaid had brought in had finished up out here. The two bodies had been carted away, and the questions Mac had answers for had all been answered. Slowly, gradually, the yard cleared of choppers and vehicles and people.

Mac had already started moving, unthinkingly, toward the house, toward the McCullar homestead, when he realized he was the only person out of the mob that had been here tonight who didn't have some place to go.

No home. No wife. And still no name.

The last had been his decision, he supposed. Despite the look Sam Kincaid had shot at him from under those bristling white brows, Mac had introduced himself to the officer asking the questions as Matt Dawson.

It was as good a name as any. He was getting used to it, anyway. Mac turned away from the house, away from the false welcome of the porch light someone had switched on. When he looked up, he saw Jenny standing alone in the middle of the yard. Watching him.

Just as it had been in their bedroom, her face was illuminated by the soft light coming from behind him. Mac knew his would be hidden in the shadows it cast. That was pretty much where his face belonged now, he supposed.

"You okay?" Jenny asked.

He nodded, but he didn't take another step, frozen in place by hope. By memories of other times when her voice had sounded like that. Soft with concern. Concern for him.

Hell, he reminded his suddenly racing heart, Jenny was always concerned. About everybody. Taking care of the world. There was nothing personal about her question. Nothing he should read into it beyond the obvious.

"Thanks for bringing us some help," he said. "For thinking about going to Mr. Kincaid. I still don't understand how you knew what was going on out here or knew we were in trouble. Even we didn't know for sure if anything would happen tonight."

"Just...lawman's instinct, I guess," Jenny said.

She smiled at him, obviously remembering that that was Mac's phrase. Maybe remembering those days when he had been the sheriff of this county and they had lived in this house together.

Maybe remembering it all, he thought, just as he was. When he didn't return her smile, those memories still too painful, she looked down at her hands, twisting together in front of her slender body, before she glanced up again. And her smile was gone, her voice almost impersonal.

"We had to have *some* place to take Mandy," she said. "I sure wasn't going to drive all the way into San Antonio and back while you and Rio played lawman out here. Sam's ranch was closer."

And Trent Richardson wasn't there. Mac had done the right thing—had tried to, at least, but he couldn't find any regret in his heart that Jenny was standing here with him instead of being in San Antonio. He had no regrets at all about that, but he did still have some questions. And Jenny seemed to be willing to answer them. At least they kept her talking to him.

"You and Sam convinced the state to come in here on the *chance* that something might be going on?"

"Sam didn't want to interfere with whatever you had set up. He alerted the authorities, and then he made us wait. When we heard the first shots, he put in the call for the state to get out here. But…" Her voice faded, and she shook her head. "It took them so long to get here. An eternity."

"It's over, Jenny," Mac said, comforting as he had always comforted. "It's all over."

Now, finally, after five long years, it seemed it really was. And there was only this left. Only the two of them again.

"Are you hungry?" Jenny asked.

Suddenly his vision blurred. "Are you by any chance offering to feed me, Jenny-Wren?" Mac asked softly.

His throat was so tight it hurt from pushing those words past the constriction. He wondered if she could possibly know how much that had meant to him, and yet he still wasn't sure that she ought to.

"I'm offering to feed you," she agreed. "But first you'll have to come inside. First—" She stopped suddenly, her voice breaking, and it was a couple of seconds before she went on. "First you'll have to come home," she said.

Mac nodded, knowing he couldn't risk trying to make a verbal response.

"Come home to *me,* Mac," Jenny added softly. "Really come home. And don't ever go away again."

The shadowed silence stretched between them for a long time. Jenny's eyes were still waiting, focused on his face.

"You sure you want me, Jenny-Wren?" he asked finally. "There are some things—"

"Don't," Jenny whispered. "There's nothing you can tell me that would make me *not* want you here. So don't try. And stop trying to give me to Trent. I'm not yours to give away." She took a breath, her small shoulders lifting in the darkness. "But I *am* yours in every other way. I always have been. I even seem to remember taking a vow to that effect. I just wish..." She hesitated again. "I just wish you had remembered it."

Till death us do part. Maybe he *had* been wrong to do what he'd done. Wrong about it all, but Jenny didn't know what those years that lay between them had been. He was the only one who really knew it all, and he also knew that he'd never tell her—not all of it, anyway.

"Are you sure, Jenny?" he asked. *One more chance, Jenny-Wren. One more opportunity to walk away from what I am. Because if I touch you...*

"I have never been as sure of anything," she said. "Except the first time I said those words to you, Mac McCullar. And just in case you've forgotten them, I'll say them again. 'Till death us do part,' Mac. And even when it does..."

Her voice broke again. He could see the glint of tears streaming down her face. She tried to wipe them off her cheeks with the heels of her hands. Because, of course, Jenny McCullar wasn't a crying woman.

"And even when it does," she repeated doggedly, "I'll still want you. Still love you. Still need you beside me. God, Mac, I've needed you so much."

She was crying openly now. So Mac was the one who took the steps. Mac was the one who closed the distance between them. All the distances. And when his arms enclosed her, he knew *this* time that it really would be forever. He'd never let

Jenny go again.
   Till death us do part.

THE DARKNESS WOULD have been kinder, Jenny supposed, but she had deliberately turned on the bedside light. She wasn't having any more deception. No more pretending.

And besides, she wanted Mac to understand that she didn't care. Not about any of it. Not now and not ever. She had meant what she'd said in the yard. There was nothing that could make any difference to the way she felt about him.

She had once trained to be a nurse. She had married Mac McCullar instead of completing that training, but she probably knew a little more than most laymen about the kinds of injuries Mac had had. She had understood the implications of them even five years ago.

There had been some spinal-cord damage, they had told her, although at the time of Mac's "death," the full extent of that hadn't been determined. Or how permanent its effects would be.

She guessed that was what was wrong with his hand and probably the cause of the limp that grew more pronounced when he was tired. And she knew about all the other complications that could result from that kind of injury. Knew and had accepted the reality of them.

There were dreams, she thought, and then there was reality. And the center of Jenny McCullar's reality, the center of her entire world, had always been Mac.

Chase and Samantha would have other children. As, in time, would Rio and Anne. And Jenny knew she would love those children as much as she loved Mandy. It would be enough. It really would be. Just as long as Mac was beside her, always beside her through the rest of the years they would share.

When she looked up, Mac was standing in the doorway that led to the bathroom, watching her. He had insisted on taking a shower, although she hadn't cared about that, either. His hair was still damp and slightly curling. The gray at the temples was less obvious in the low lighting, as were the scars. So damn many scars.

He looks so tired, she thought, her heart turning over with how much she loved him. She could take care of him, now that he was home. *Home,* she thought again, savoring the sound of it, the feel of the word in her head. Mac was home.

"You look exhausted," she said.

The corner of his mouth moved, almost a smile. The single eye was focused on her face. And it was blue again, she realized. McCullar blue.

"What I probably look right now is scared," he said.

She laughed, relieved and reassured somehow by that comment. By the fact that they could still laugh. Even here. Maybe *especially* here.

"Scared of *me,* Mac?" she asked.

"Scared of disappointing you, I guess."

His mouth had tightened, and she watched him swallow— swallow hard—before she realized that he really was.

"You've never disappointed me in your life, Mac McCullar. You aren't going to now. No matter what," she added, just to make sure he understood that she knew what he was worried about.

"The doctors said..."

His voice faded, and he took a breath, deep and slow, the muscles in his broad, bare chest lifting. She didn't prod, waiting instead through the silence. He'd tell her what he needed to tell her in time. That was something they had plenty of, now. Lots of time.

"They said there wasn't any reason to worry about...sexual function."

Jenny fought her smile and nodded instead.

"And there have been times," he continued, "since I've been home that you've sure given me cause to believe they were right."

She laughed again, feeling better by the minute. He was still Mac.

"I remember those times," she said softly. "I kept wondering how long it was going to take you to get around to a demonstration."

"It wasn't that I didn't want to, Jenny-Wren. Don't you ever be in doubt about that."

"You just hadn't decided that you were going to stick around," she said.

"I guess I hadn't decided whether I was up to being a replacement for Richardson."

"A replacement for Trent?" she asked disbelievingly.

"He's…younger than I am, for one thing," Mac offered.

"Yes, he is," Jenny agreed, watching his face.

"A damn sight richer."

Her lips lifted, but she didn't give in to the urge to laugh.

"A hell of a lot better looking," Mac said softly.

She allowed her eyes to move over his face, to examine again every mark and scar. They fastened finally on his mouth.

"I don't know," she said. "You've got a really nice smile."

She was rewarded by his laughter, the sound of it deep and rich, and it curled through her veins like a living flame. She had always loved to hear Mac laugh. And when the echo of it faded from the room, he was still watching her. Still holding her eyes.

"And he can give you a baby, Jenny-Wren. Lots of them, if you want. He can give you all the babies you've ever wanted. And…maybe I can't."

She had known this was the heart of what he had wanted to tell her out in the yard. And being Mac, he *had* told her. Because it was his duty to say this. He still believed it was his duty, despite what she had said.

She felt the tears begin again because he thought it mattered. Because he still believed that *anything* mattered to her besides having him back.

"Make love to me, Mac," she said simply. "Make love to me before I die of wanting you. Of needing you. Because…"

She hesitated, wanting to be very sure before she said it, so she could make him believe. "Because you are all I have ever *really* needed," she said. "And you are all I ever will."

SHE HAD TOLD HIM he could never disappoint her. And he didn't. He never had.

"Bad hand," he said softly as his lips closed around the small, pearled nipple. It had been teased and tautened to a hard, aching peak by the slow caress of his tongue. By the gentle tension of his teeth. And by the warmth of his breath feathering over the moisture his mouth had left.

"I know," she whispered, finding it hard to respond. Hard to force her mind to think of the necessary words.

"Not that one," Mac said, his lips still fully occupied so that the words were indistinct. She could feel them on her skin. Dear God, could she feel them. "*Two* bad hands tonight," he whispered.

Two bad hands? She tried to think about that, to think about anything besides what he was doing to her, anything besides how his mouth felt against her breast. But thinking was something that was almost impossible. "I don't understand," she breathed into the darkness.

"It doesn't matter. Just makes this more challenging."

"What?" Jenny whispered. Her hips arched, seeking. So many years. So much loneliness.

"Making love to you. A whole hell of a lot more challenging." His mouth deserted the demanding ache he had created and brushed across to her breastbone. His tongue made slow, wet contact, trailing over her skin, tantalizing, all the way down to her belly button.

There it stopped, as he shifted his upper body downward. Her hand fastened in his hair. Holding on as he buried his tongue in the small depression, licking it as a cat would clean a kitten. Long, slow, incredibly thorough strokes.

Jenny felt the heat building, and she pushed upward, lifting again against his caress.

"You in a hurry, Jenny-Wren?" Mac asked softly. The words slipped past the wetness his mouth had left, touching it so that it became a small coldness in the center of the heat.

Not the center, she thought, as his mouth continued to move. To trace lower across her shivering skin. Over her belly. And then lower. Finally centering her need. All the needs that had gone unanswered for so many years. Needs that had only been waiting. Waiting for Mac to come home.

Her hips twisted against the damp, tangled sheets. Her legs drifted apart and her mind drifted away. Away from the loneliness. The regret. The anger and the bitterness. All of them floated away, as she did. No longer attached to the earth. Held by nothing but the reality of Mac's mouth moving against her. Lips and tongue. Teeth. Torturing and fulfilling.

The gasping ecstasy found her unprepared. Unprotected from expressing her needs. It screamed in her head until she wondered if he could hear it. Until it was too late to wonder anything. Other than whether or not she would survive. Whether she could rebuild the practical, controlled Jenny McCullar everyone believed her to be.

Only Mac had ever known *this* Jenny. This mindless, wanton creature who begged in the darkness for his touch. Whose essence melted into his, under his. Whose body responded to his voice, to the simple touch of his hand. Responded with need. With desire. With the hot moisture of passion. It flooded between them, becoming the sweetest nectar of what they were together.

She was never this Jenny, never this woman, anywhere but here. With Mac. With Mac within her. The taste and feel of him on her tongue. The secret scent of him in her nostrils. So that she became one with him. One in him. Him.

Finally, slowly, her body fell from the place where he had taken her. Her fingers combed slowly through the silken hair she had grasped. Down his cheek. Feeling under their trembling tips the slick moisture of his skin. His tongue touched again, teasing.

Aftershocks exploded, shook her still-too-sensitive body with new eruptions. And she cried out with the incredible wonder of it, shimmering through exposed nerves that had not had time to still yet from the first.

She felt him move, his damp chest sliding over her body. His mouth finding the open, gasping outcry of hers. His breath mingling with hers, whispering her name. His need.

Again her thighs opened. Unspoken permission to be one with her. Invitation that needed no words. No expression other than this. Her body lifting into his. Accepting the hard, downward thrust of his hips. His arousal as strong and powerful as any she ever remembered. As anything she had ever wanted. Enough and more than enough.

And she knew again, as she had promised him, that this was all she would ever need.

"I love you, Jenny-Wren," Mac McCullar whispered into the darkness of her hair, which clung to the sweat-dewed temple his lips had found. Then, as her legs wrapped around his narrow hips, holding him to her, his body released, his hot seed rushing into the waiting emptiness of her body. Filled now with Mac.

Till death us do part, Jenny thought again. Only that would ever be able to separate them. That was another promise. Made to Mac or to herself? She wasn't sure, and it didn't matter. Again, they were one. And it *was* enough. Far more than enough.

"SO ELKINS WAS BEHIND it all?" Chase asked.

"That's what the feds think," Mac agreed. "We know he was in charge of the heroin, at least. Buck had gotten in on the ground floor. He'd been biding his time, making sure no one suspected he had anything to do with putting that bomb in my truck. Apparently no one ever did."

"Five years is a long time to wait for a payoff," Chase suggested. "I never would have thought Buck had that kind of patience."

"He had some other things going," Rio put in. "The illegal immigration that he blamed on Morales was almost certainly Buck's operation."

"And he shot Ray to keep his own role from coming out?" Chase said.

"Warren knew that," Mac said. "That's why he was so afraid last night. He realized Buck was planning to do it again."

"It worked with Morales," Rio said. "We all thought Buck was a hero for killing Ray. And the same thing would have worked tonight, except you figured it out in time."

"Morales was guilty—of Doc's murder and probably a lot of other things—but the authorities think Elkins was the mastermind," Mac said. "Of that and of almost everything else that's gone on in this county during the last five years. The heroin was fairly new, but already becoming highly profitable."

"The authorities are still untangling things, including the money he laundered," Sam Kincaid said. "But everything they've found tracks back to Elkins."

"That's enough," Samantha said, smiling at her father. "You can talk about all this later. Chase needs to rest. And frankly, judging by the way you look, so do the three of you."

She was probably right, Mac thought. They did appear to be the worse for wear. Rio's injured arm was protected by a sling, and Kincaid's eyes were red-rimmed and rheumy from lack of sleep. The old man was showing his age, but still, he had been there when it had mattered.

He and Rio probably owed Sam Kincaid their lives. Mac McCullar was a man who believed in paying his debts. All of them. And that reminded him of some unfinished business between him and Chase. Something he intended to take up with his brother before he let Samantha run him off.

"Thanks for the help last night, Mr. Kincaid," Mac said. "I don't think I've told you how grateful we are."

"I told you my friends call me Sam," Kincaid said, dismissing the gratitude. "You decided yet who you're gonna be?"

The eyes of the others joined the old man's in their focus on Mac's face.

"I've decided," Mac said.

"I'm betting from that look on your face it ain't somebody named Dawson," Sam said, grinning suddenly.

"No," Mac agreed, thinking about what that meant. "It's somebody named McCullar. Again."

"Mrs. McCullar put her seal of approval on that?" Sam continued.

Mac didn't control his urge to answer Sam's widening grin. He guessed he could phrase what happened last night as Jenny's seal of approval. "Yes, sir," he said.

"Well, you remember that this county's suddenly got an opening for a sheriff. We need us a good one. Used to have one. A man people could trust to look out for them."

"I don't think—" Mac began, but the old man cut him off.

"You just think about it. I'll back you if you'll consider taking the job. You got my guarantee on that, and, old or not, my say-so still carries some weight around here. You talk it over with your pretty wife. Maybe with that one there," Sam said. He jerked his chin toward his son-in-law. "This county used to have a *couple* of good lawmen, both of 'em named McCullar."

"Sam," Samantha objected. "Chase has got more to do than he can handle. You know better than anybody how much work a breeding operation requires."

"I know you can hire good people to do most of that," the old man said. "People who really understand horses."

Kincaid's gaze moved to Rio Delgado, who was leaning against the wall. The black eyes Rio had inherited from his Mexican mother met the old man's unflinchingly.

Horsemen, Mac thought. They were two of a kind. Sam Kincaid, who had the finest horses in this state, and this McCullar half-breed bastard, who literally had nothing. Nothing but a crazy black stallion and a wife who loved him enough to marry him despite that fact. And a brother whose life he had saved last night. They owed Rio another debt, Mac realized. A McCullar debt that needed to be paid; one that was long overdue.

"You all can go on," Mac suggested. "But I need to talk to Chase a minute. In private," he added, just in case they didn't understand.

He watched Samantha study her husband's face, looking for signs of fatigue, he supposed, but when Chase smiled at her, she took her father's arm and led him outside. Rio pushed away from the wall. In his eyes was what Mac suspected had always been there—the knowledge that he was an outsider, always excluded from the bond of the McCullar family.

"Not you," Mac said. "You're in on this, too."

Whatever had been in the depths of those remarkable eyes disappeared, replaced briefly by surprise, before Rio leaned back against the white wall again.

Mac turned to Chase. "Jenny said you risked your life to pay my medical bills. You told me the sale of the ranch covered those. I want to hear the truth from you. I don't intend to be lied to again. And I'm still man enough to beat the hell out of you if you try. Especially in your present condition."

Blue McCullar eyes met and held. There was a long silence before Chase asked softly, "Was it worth it, Mac? Last night, I mean. With Jenny. Was that worth a little risk?"

Not exactly a fair question, Mac thought, his stomach lurching. And not easy to answer. "Last night would have been worth anything to me," Mac said finally. "Except your life."

"Which is mine to risk," Chase said. "I've got no regrets, Mac. Not one. Not a damn one. And I don't ever want to hear about it again. You would have done the same for me. We both know that, so it's not worth talking about. Not between the two of us."

He was right, of course. Mac *would* have done the same. And would never have counted the cost. So he nodded, letting that debt, which could never really be paid, go. It was time, he knew, to move on to the other.

"We have to do something about Rio," Mac said.

Out of the corner of his eye Mac saw his half brother straighten away from the wall again.

"What do you have in mind?" Chase asked, his gaze moving to Rio's face.

"To give him his share of the McCullar land. Help him build a house, maybe. *If* he wants to live there." Mac turned to look at his half brother's dark, beautiful features. Rio's black eyes moved from one strong McCullar face to the other.

"He will," Chase said softly. "He always has. When it comes to that land, Rio's all McCullar."

"If you two are going to talk about me like I'm not here—" Rio began.

"As good with horses as Sam suggested?"

"The best I've ever seen," Chase said honestly. "Samantha says he's the best she's ever seen, and that's saying a lot."

"Good enough to help her run the stables?" Mac asked.

"A hell of a lot better than I can."

Mac nodded again, holding his half brother's black eyes.

"Are you thinking what I think you're thinking?" Chase asked, and Mac looked back at the man in the hospital bed.

"I'd have to talk it over with Jenny, but Sam's right. This county needs a couple of lawmen. You take the sheriff's job, and I'll be your deputy," Mac said.

Chase laughed. "And have to listen to you tell me how to do that job every day? How to run *your* county? Not on your life, big brother."

"Nobody's gonna let me be sheriff," Mac said, but he realized Chase was right about part of that. He still felt as if it was his county.

"Hell, if Sam Kincaid backs you, you can be governor. Take the job, Mac. I got your back," Chase said, smiling. "You tell Jenny I'll be right there beside you no matter what

happens. Besides, nobody's going to tangle with the Mc-
Cullars. Especially since there's three of us now.''

Chase looked again toward the bastard brother he had sent
to prison. A man who had been born an outcast and robbed
by his own father of his birthright. There was no reason for
Rio to forgive all that the McCullars had done to him.

"You game to run what's going to become the finest breeding stables in south Texas while Mac and I play lawman?''
Chase asked.

"You don't owe me anything," Rio said quietly.

"This isn't about owing. It's about family," Chase said.
"You want to be a part of it or you don't. Nobody can make
you, but a third of that land is yours. You got the same blood
in your veins as runs in ours. All you have to do, baby brother,
is say yes.''

Blood's thicker than water. Mac remembered telling Rio
that. It had been a long time ago, but it was still true. He just
hoped his half brother remembered.

"Yes," Rio said softly. "I want to be a part."

Epilogue

Almost two years later

Baked beans, coleslaw, blackberry cobbler, and the makings of homemade ice cream in the refrigerator. Jenny McCullar looked at the food lined up on her kitchen counter, mentally enumerating the dishes.

Anne was bringing the bread and chips. With a seven-month-old and morning sickness from an unexpected second pregnancy, Anne hadn't needed to be responsible for anything complicated. Not in this heat. Jenny and Samantha had decided they could handle the rest, and as promised, Chase had arrived early to cook the ribs.

Now if only Mac would get back from Austin in time for supper, Jenny thought, hugging that possibility to her as she had all afternoon. He had been there three days, testifying before a state committee about the threat of drug running for isolated border ranches such as theirs. Those powerful men would listen to him, she knew, respect what he told them because they would know there was no one better qualified to tell that story.

The back door opened, and her heart skipped a couple of beats before she realized it was Rio, his arms laden with a sack filled with bread and bags of chips and a diaper bag. Anne followed with the baby, fat and healthy and almost as beautiful as her father. Dark-haired and dark-eyed, Annemarie Delgado had enchanted them from her anxiously awaited birth. The waiting room had looked like a McCullar family gathering. Just like the one today.

Jenny wiped her hands on her jeans and reached for her niece. The baby responded by leaning toward her aunt, begging to be taken. She tangled her fingers, wet from their recent immersion in her mouth, in Jenny's short hair as she and Anne made the transfer.

"She's teething," Anne said. "At least I think that's what's making her fussy. I hope it's that and nothing catching. Samantha would probably want to kill me."

Samantha's two were outside, Mandy being little mama to her towheaded year-old brother. Jenny smiled, putting her forehead against Annemarie's and then kissing her nose.

"I don't think she's got anything the other two haven't already had," Jenny said practically. "Or will have," she added under her breath as she turned to plop the baby into the waiting high chair.

"New teeth," Rio said decisively. "Anne worries too much."

Jenny's eyes met Anne's, and they smiled at each other. Rio had proved to be an incredibly competent father, who was also his daughter's favorite person in the entire world. But then Annemarie had made it obvious from the first that she really preferred men, and she certainly had the three McCullar males wrapped around her fat little fingers.

"What can I do to help?" Anne offered.

"I think everything's ready. I hoped Mac would get back in time to eat, but the little ones are hungry, and it's late...so maybe just help me take things out to the picnic tables."

"We can wait," Anne said. "It would be a shame to eat without him."

"No, Mac won't mind if we start without him. And he may not—" Jenny's voice stopped, her heart fluttering again, as the door opened.

This time it was Mac's big frame that filled it, his gaze automatically seeking Jenny. The corner of his mouth tilted when he found her. Jenny felt the impact of that crooked smile within her body, jolting through all the secret places that ached for Mac's touch.

That sense of unease, which was always with her when Mac was away, suddenly disappeared. Mac was home. Despite the fact that he had been "home" now for almost two years, she still acknowledged his presence here with a sense of wonder. And with endless gratitude.

"About time you showed up," Rio said. "Jenny was getting worried." He had picked up the sack with the bread and chips, balancing the big bowl of coleslaw on his other palm as he disappeared through the open door.

"Worried?" Mac repeated, his eyes studying Jenny's face.

She could feel the slight flush along her cheeks, but maybe he would put that down to the heat of the kitchen.

"Not worried," she said, smiling at him. "Just…hoping you'd get back in time to eat with us."

Mac nodded, his gaze still holding hers.

"Why don't I take the rest of this outside," Anne said. She picked up the baked beans and walked past Mac, who was still standing beside the door. "Welcome home," she said, smiling at him before she followed her husband outside, leaving a somehow awkward silence behind.

Suddenly, Annemarie pounded both palms up and down on the metal tray of the high chair. That noise was accompanied by a burst of singsong nonsense.

"They were in such a hurry to get out of here that they forgot their baby," Mac said. "Or maybe that was deliberate. Maybe they were just making their escape."

"Or maybe they thought we'd want some privacy to say hello," Jenny suggested.

"I guess they forgot how long we've been married," Mac said, smiling at her again.

"But I *would* like to say hello to you. And I would like to do it in private."

"Just what did you have in mind, Jenny-Wren?" Mac asked, his voice suddenly low and seductive, his grin almost lecherous. "Chase says the ribs are almost done. Much as I'd like to oblige you, sweetheart, unless you're thinking about the kitchen table again, I doubt we'll have enough time—"

"Behave yourself," Jenny interrupted, laughing. "There are children present."

"One child," Mac corrected. "Who is certainly not listening to me." He put his Stetson on the hook by the door and walked across to the high chair. The baby reached out to take a swat at his leg, leaving a smear of dampness on the khaki pants before she stuffed her entire hand back into her mouth.

"And I'm willing to bet this one's seen a kiss or two in her time," Mac said. He bent to put his lips against the top of the baby's head.

"Kissing?" Jenny said, her dark eyes smiling. "You were talking about *kissing?*"

"At this stage of the game I'm talking about any kind of welcome home. Which I haven't gotten yet. You mad at me, Jenny-Wren?" Mac asked, straightening and turning around to look at her.

Before Jenny could answer, the baby began to whimper. "Anne thinks she's teething," she explained, walking toward the high chair. But by the time she got there, Mac had already lifted the little girl out and had her propped comfortably on his left hip. The baby's fingers found the star pinned to his uniform shirt. When Mac looked down to see what she was doing, his head was right next to the dark, glossy curls of the baby.

"You look good doing that," Jenny said, her voice very soft. "Holding a baby. But then I always knew you would."

Mac's head lifted slowly, and there was something in the blue eye fastened on her face that Jenny hadn't seen there in a long time. Something that she recognized, and something that didn't belong. So she smiled at him. After a moment, the tightness in Mac's face relaxed, and he returned her smile.

"I guess that's a good thing, too," Jenny said.

"As many of these as we're gonna have around here," Mac agreed easily. "A McCullar population explosion."

The baby had lost interest in the familiar star, so she leaned back in Mac's arm, trying to see his face. Her fingers found the black patch that covered his right eye, and she patted it. Then, apparently questioning the difference, she poked an exploring finger at his good eye. Mac shifted his head, dodging the reaching finger.

"Look out, angel," he said, laughing. "I didn't know babies could be dangerous."

He looked up at Jenny again, inviting her to join his laughter. At what he saw, however, the joy faded from that lean, scarred face.

So Jenny smiled at him through her tears. She knew she needed to explain, but her throat had closed, hard and tight over the words she had practiced saying to him for three months. Words she had believed she might never have a chance to say to him.

She had waited, wanting to be very sure that this second miracle was going to be granted. A miracle she had never even prayed for, because, as she had promised Mac, what they already had was really enough. More than enough. Most people didn't have one miracle in their lives. And she...

"Jenny," Mac said softly. All the pain of the night Buck Elkins had been killed was back in his deep voice. The night Mac had told her what he feared. Told her because he believed it was his duty.

Jenny shook her head, still fighting tears. She was making such a mess of this. And she was probably scaring Mac to death.

"It's a good thing you like babies," she managed finally. "A really wonderful thing, because..." she added softly, before her throat closed again.

It took him a minute to figure it out. To move past disbelief. A minute to verify that incredible suggestion by reading the glow in Jenny's dark eyes. But then Mac McCullar had always been good at reading Jenny.

And so lucky, he thought. They were so damned, incredibly lucky. Or maybe, he amended, as Jenny walked into his arms and he crushed her to him, the fascinated little girl between them, maybe this miracle wasn't attributable to luck. Maybe this was the result of the other. Of sheer, dogged McCullar persistence. In loving Jenny.

▼™ SILHOUETTE
INTRIGUE™

COMING NEXT MONTH

MARRIED IN HASTE Dani Sinclair

McKella Patterson had barely said 'I do' before her groom disappeared and a stranger swept her off her feet—and out of the way of a speeding truck. He told her his name was Greg Wyman—and that her marriage was a fake. But could she accept this stranger's protection?

FIRST-CLASS FATHER Charlotte Douglas

Heather Taylor had never told cop Dylan Wade that she'd had his baby. But now her son had been kidnapped, and Dylan was the only one who could help her find him... Dylan had said he still loved her—but that could change when he found out that the missing boy was his son...

NO ORDINARY MAN Suzanne Brockmann

Jess Baxter's new tenant Rob Carpenter was definitely the sexiest man she'd ever met! But no matter how hard she tried, he wouldn't let her get to know him. Then the murders started—all women who looked like her. And the profile of the killer matched Rob... Was he being set-up—or was he a murderer?

SEND ME A HERO Rita Herron

Detective Nathan Dawson had been warned about Veronica Miller's 'false alarms' but instinct told him she wasn't imagining things. Someone *was* stalking her. And he was going to risk his job—and his heart—to keep her safe. Only first they had to uncover the truth about a night she couldn't remember...

COMING NEXT MONTH FROM

SILHOUETTE®

Sensation

A thrilling mix of passion, adventure and drama

A MAN LIKE MORGAN KANE Beverly Barton
RANCHER'S CHOICE Kylie Brant
MAN OF THE HOUR Maura Seger
OWEN'S TOUCH Lee Magner

Special Edition

Compelling romances packed with emotion

SNOW BABY Cathy Gillen Thacker
WARRIOR'S WOMAN Laurie Paige
A MOTHER FOR JEFFREY Trisha Alexander
STRANDED ON THE RANCH Pat Warren
THE COWBOY TAKES A WIFE Lois Faye Dyer
PARTNERS IN MARRIAGE Allison Hayes

Desire

Provocative, sensual love stories

BELOVED Diana Palmer
THE BABY CONSULTANT Anne Marie Winston
THE LONE RIDER TAKES A BRIDE Leanne Banks
COWBOYS ARE FOR LOVING Marie Ferrarella
A SPARKLE IN THE COWBOY'S EYES Peggy Moreland
OVERNIGHT HEIRESS Modean Moon

MARIE FERRARELLA

invites you to meet

THE CUTLER FAMILY
*Five siblings who find love in the
most unexpected places!*

In July:
COWBOYS ARE FOR LOVING

In September:
WILL AND THE HEADSTRONG FEMALE

In November:
THE LAW AND GINNY MARLOW

And in January 2000:
A MATCH FOR MORGAN

▼™ SILHOUETTE
DESIRE®

FREE
2 BOOKS
AND A SURPRISE GIFT!

We would like to take this opportunity to thank you for reading this Silhouette® book by offering you the chance to take TWO more specially selected titles from the Intrigue™ series absolutely FREE! We're also making this offer to introduce you to the benefits of the Reader Service™ —

    ★ FREE home delivery   ★ FREE gifts and competitions
    ★ FREE monthly Newsletter   ★ Exclusive Reader Service discounts
          ★ Books available before they're in the shops

Accepting these FREE books and gift places you under no obligation to buy; you may cancel at any time, even after receiving your free shipment. Simply complete your details below and return the entire page to the address below. *You don't even need a stamp!*

YES! Please send me 2 free Intrigue books and a surprise gift. I understand that unless you hear from me, I will receive 4 superb new titles every month for just £2.70 each, postage and packing free. I am under no obligation to purchase any books and may cancel my subscription at any time. The free books and gift will be mine to keep in any case.

19EC

Ms/Mrs/Miss/Mr ....Initials ....
BLOCK CAPITALS PLEASE

Surname...

Address...

....

....Postcode ....

Send this whole page to:
THE READER SERVICE, FREEPOST CN81, CROYDON, CR9 3WZ
(Eire readers please send coupon to: P.O. BOX 4546, DUBLIN 24.)

Offer valid in UK and Eire only and not available to current Reader Service subscribers to this series. We reserve the right to refuse an application and applicants must be aged 18 years or over. Only one application per household. Terms and prices subject to change without notice. Offer expires 31st December 1999. As a result of this application, you may receive further offers from Harlequin Mills & Boon and other carefully selected companies. If you would prefer not to share in this opportunity please write to The Data Manager at the address above.

Silhouette is a registered trademark used under license.
Intrigue is being used as a trademark.

When winning is everything...
losing can be deadly.

HIGH STAKES

Rebecca Brandewyne

Angela Marlowe's parents were dead,
murdered by powerful, ruthless men.
Now Angela is starting to put the
shattered pieces of her past together
and finds herself entering a maze of
danger and corruption.
But she is not alone.

Available from July

MARIE FERRARELLA

invites you to meet

THE CUTLER FAMILY

Five siblings who find love in the most unexpected places!

In July:
COWBOYS ARE FOR LOVING

In September:
WILL AND THE HEADSTRONG FEMALE

In November:
THE LAW AND GINNY MARLOW

And in January 2000:
A MATCH FOR MORGAN

▼™ SILHOUETTE
DESIRE®

FREE
2 BOOKS
AND A SURPRISE GIFT!

We would like to take this opportunity to thank you for reading this Silhouette® book by offering you the chance to take TWO more specially selected titles from the Intrigue™ series absolutely FREE! We're also making this offer to introduce you to the benefits of the Reader Service™—

- ★ FREE home delivery
- ★ FREE monthly Newsletter
- ★ FREE gifts and competitions
- ★ Exclusive Reader Service discounts
- ★ Books available before they're in the shops

Accepting these FREE books and gift places you under no obligation to buy; you may cancel at any time, even after receiving your free shipment. Simply complete your details below and return the entire page to the address below. *You don't even need a stamp!*

YES! Please send me 2 free Intrigue books and a surprise gift. I understand that unless you hear from me, I will receive 4 superb new titles every month for just £2.70 each, postage and packing free. I am under no obligation to purchase any books and may cancel my subscription at any time. The free books and gift will be mine to keep in any case.

19EC

Ms/Mrs/Miss/Mr ....Initials ....
BLOCK CAPITALS PLEASE

Surname...

Address...

....

....Postcode ....

Send this whole page to:
THE READER SERVICE, FREEPOST CN81, CROYDON, CR9 3WZ
(Eire readers please send coupon to: P.O. Box 4546, DUBLIN 24.)

When winni everything...
losing be deadly.

HIGH STAKES

Rebecca Brandewyne

Angela Marlowe's parents were dead,
murdered by powerful, ruthless men.
Now Angela is starting to put the
shattered pieces of her past together
and finds herself entering a maze of
danger and corruption.
But she is not alone.

Available from July